ADMISSIBLE AFFAIR

ADRIAN J. SMITH

To all the woman who have made poor decisions, may we make better ones next time.

CHAPTER 1

"THAT'S NOT WHAT I MEANT, AND YOU KNOW IT," Bellamy attempted—trying to calm the conversation.

They had argued almost from the moment they had entered the restaurant, definitely from the moment they sat down. Bellamy had tried to keep her tones hushed and the argument confined to their table, but Kendra either didn't care or she wanted the attention. Sighing, Bellamy gnawed on her already raw lip as tension rose in her chest.

Kendra sent an icy glare her direction. "What I know is you need to stop stealing my clients."

Bellamy was about to retort when the waitress came over. She picked up an empty plate before asking, "Can I get either of you another drink?"

"Absolutely not," Kendra spoke sharply. "She's well over her limit."

Bellamy rolled her eyes and collapsed in the chair. Her one drink compared to Kendra's four was hardly over her limit, but when Kendra was mad, nothing was out of bounds. Glancing up at the waitress, Bellamy shook her head.

"I'd like to pay the bill now, if you would get that." Disdain and entitlement leached from Kendra's tone.

"Yes, ma'am," the waitress replied before scurrying off.

Clenching her fists and her jaw, Bellamy shot Kendra a dark look. "You didn't have to talk to her like that. She's only doing her job."

"And a piece of shit one at that. Constantly interrupting us, asking stupid questions."

Bellamy tuned her out until the black folder was brought back with the check. Kendra snatched it up before Bellamy could. It didn't take long for Kendra to pull out cash for the bill and toss it on the table.

"You can find your own way home."

"What?" Shaking her head in surprise, Bellamy asked again, "You're leaving me here?"

"Nothing you don't deserve."

"Kendra!"

But it was too late. Kendra had already pushed her chair out, threw a disgusted look over her shoulder and sauntered toward the door with her hips sliding side to side in a sashay Bellamy knew was meant for everyone in the room but her.

Making a sound of disgust, Bellamy grabbed the bill and rolled her eyes when she saw Kendra had left zero tip. She reached into her black purse and pulled out a twenty, tossing it in the folder before downing the rest of Kendra's froufrou drink. The waitress came over and took the bill.

"Are you sure there isn't anything else I can get you?"

Bellamy looked up at the waitress for the first time, noticing her soft and young features. Rubbing her eyes, Bellamy sighed. "No, I don't think so, thank you. And . . . I'm sorry for her. She's in some kind of mood today."

The waitress gave her a wry smile and looked side to side before she shrugged and slid into the chair across from Bellamy.

"Let's start right, then. I'm Payton." She held out her hand,

2

which Bellamy gladly accepted. "And you don't need to apologize for someone else being an asshole."

Chuckling, Bellamy nodded. "And a fine asshole she is. She's perfected it for years. I'm Bellamy, by the way."

"Sounds like it," Payton added wryly.

"Again, I'm sorry. No one deserves to be treated like that."

Payton went to stand. "Sure you couldn't use an extra drink?"

"Actually, a dry martini sounds perfect right about now."

Smiling, Payton nodded. "Coming right up."

It didn't take long for Payton to arrive with the drink. She slipped it onto the table before gathering the rest of the dirty plates and left over food. Bellamy watched her work and took a long sip of her drink, savoring the slight burn it had on the way down. It was exactly what she'd needed after fighting with Kendra.

Their fights were getting to the point where they were almost never ending, and for some reason, Kendra seemed to always have the last word. Sighing into her glass, Bellamy grimaced. Nothing she'd done had improved the situation, and she doubted anything would. Kendra simply refused to even see there was a problem.

She was into her second drink when Payton slipped into the chair across from her. Bellamy had been so lost in thought she hadn't even noticed what time it was. Payton gave her a sweet smile, her eyes crinkling in the corners as she ducked her chin.

"Did she leave you here?"

"She did," Bellamy whispered. "I'll call a cab in a few minutes. Thanks for the drinks."

"Just doing my job, ma'am. But I'm off in about ten minutes. If you want to wait around, I can just give you a ride home. I have a few errands to run anyway and don't mind."

Bellamy was about to shake her head no when she stopped. Something in her chest told her to accept the offer. It was pouring down rain outside, as was the norm in the Sound that time of year, and while it would have been smarter to just call for a cab, something about Payton's offer intrigued her.

"If you're sure you don't mind. I don't exactly live around here."

"I don't mind. I don't either, actually. This is just my day job while I'm in school. I graduate in a few weeks and can finally start looking for a 'big girl' job." Payton rolled her eyes when she put in the air quotes and laughed. "But really, any job with an income is a real job."

"Agreed. But only if you don't mind, really. It's no hassle for me to call a cab."

"I don't mind at all." Payton got out of the chair and put her hand on Bellamy's. "It's the least I can do. After the way she walked out of here? You deserve a bit of a comeback."

"Ain't that the truth," Bellamy replied, grinning.

"I'll bring your check over for the drinks."

"Thanks."

TEN MINUTES LATER, TRUE TO HER WORD, PAYTON arrived at the table with a smile and her apron slung over her shoulder. "Ready?"

"Absolutely."

Bellamy followed Payton outside to the far side of the parking lot where she shoved her key into the door of an old and rusting car. They got in and sat down but not before Bellamy noticed the car seat in the back.

Once they were settled, Bellamy nodded her head toward it. "Do you have a child?"

"It's for my nephew."

"Ah. How old is he?"

Payton turned to Bellamy with a proud smile on her lips. "He's six months and cute as a button."

"I can see you love him."

"I do."

Bellamy pulled out her phone and plugged her address into the directions app she had and handed it over. "This will take you to my house, but just get on I-5 going south to start."

"All right." Payton put the car into drive and pulled out of the parking lot. "So . . . was she your boss?"

Bellamy snorted. "She likes to think so. She's actually my wife and my business partner."

"Your wife left you with no way to get home?" Payton's tone was full of surprise, and Bellamy didn't blame her. Most people would think it unconscionable.

"It's not the first time. Doubt it'll be the last. When she's angry, she angry. She just needs some time to cool off, and she'll be better by tonight."

Payton shook her head. "I wouldn't put up with it. You must be one strong woman to manage that."

Bellamy hummed her agreement but secretly thought it was the opposite. She stiffened her shoulders before speaking again. "She's really not a bad person, most of the time. Lately, well a lot lately, we've been having a few problems. It's probably time for some therapy or some lawyers."

"Ah."

Bellamy continued, not sure why. "One thing I can honestly tell you if you ever get to the marrying stage, don't go into business with your spouse. It's a whole added level of stress and conflict."

Smirking, Payton nodded. "I can only imagine."

Making idle conversation for the next thirty minutes, Bellamy guided Payton to her house even though the phone clearly gave directions. Payton pulled up outside on the street and shoved the car into park. The windows in the house were all dark, and Bellamy let out a heavy sigh.

"I doubt she's even home."

Payton gripped her hand, and the warmth from her fingers seeped into Bellamy.

"Is it bad that I don't even want to go in right now?"

Shaking her head, Payton said, "Not at all. Not sure I'd want to either, but it always takes me hours and hours to calm down from a fight."

"Yeah, I don't take hours to calm down. She does."

Payton didn't say anything, and Bellamy didn't make a move to get out of the car. "I had all these dreams for us, you know? House, babies, careers . . . seems it didn't make a difference."

"Did she have the same dreams?"

Bellamy didn't answer right away, mulling through the question. Finally, she turned to Payton and shook her head. "Honestly, I don't know. How pathetic is that?"

"How long have you two been together?"

Snorting, Bellamy smirked and rubbed her thumb along Payton's fingers as she realized she was still holding her hand. "Probably too long. You know, you're being a very good friend to someone you barely know."

"Don't think anything of it. I'm always helping out damsels in distress." Payton squeezed her hand again. "Want to go park somewhere for a bit and talk? I feel like you need someone to talk to."

Bellamy smiled genuinely for the first time. "Yes, that would be lovely. I'm sorry to dump this on you, but I guess I don't have anyone else."

"It's not a problem."

Payton let go of her hand and drove down the road a few blocks. She went until she found a dark and empty parking lot where she pulled into the back, shoved the car in park, and took off her seatbelt. Bellamy followed suit and turned so she could face Payton full on. She truly was a beautiful and young woman. Bellamy hadn't taken the time to notice before, but her dark brown hair was cut short against her face, styled out of her pale baby blue eyes.

"Do you have anyone special in your life?"

Payton shook her head. "No, just my nephew. He's my light and life."

"You sound very close. Are you and your sister or brother close?"

"Not really."

The look on Payton's face changed. She went from being proud to hiding. Bellamy had seen that look too many times to count in many of her clients before. Deciding to avoid the topic, she changed to a new one. "No boyfriend?"

"No, no boyfriend or girlfriend, for that matter."

Bellamy's heart thudded. Her gaze slipped down from Payton's eyes to her lips, thin and painted a dark purply-red. Temptation called to her like it hadn't in years, and desire curled its way through her body. Cupping Payton's cheek, Bellamy brushed her thumb along the dark line of Payton's lower lip. She could do this. It wasn't for payback or revenge or to make a point. It was for herself. Purely for her own physical pleasure that she hadn't had in longer than she cared to count.

"Want to do something unexpected and perhaps a bit adventurous?"

Payton's lips curled upward slightly. "What did you have in mind?"

They moved together, their voices quieting in the dark as they inched closer. Payton opened her palm against the back of Bellamy's hand and threaded their fingers together. Bellamy grinned.

"Oh, you know, in here, one night, no strings?"

Payton nodded as she released a shuddering breath. "And your wife?"

Bellamy shook her head. "It's been long over."

Payton hummed while she dashed her tongue out to lick Bellamy's thumb. "I could certainly use a night of my own. It has been a while."

Wrapping her hand around the back of Payton's neck, Bellamy pulled her until their lips were close enough to brush with each word. Anticipation built in her chest, her heart beating rapidly. She was going to do this, and there was no way she would regret it. Years of living in an argument had worn her down, and she deserved some kind of relief. "What do you say? A night of fun or should we head back?"

"Is this something you've done before?"

"Never. I'm not typically a one-night kind of gal." She leaned back and couldn't tear her gaze away from Payton's lips, those lips that curled into a broad grin. God, she wanted this. To be free, to be wild, to take one risk she never would normally take.

"Me either."

Before Bellamy could say anything, Payton's mouth was against hers. Electricity shot through her from her lips down to her toes. Bellamy gasped and hesitated before she pushed into Payton, giving the same amount of pressure she received.

Payton's hair was as soft as she thought it might be. It slid through her fingers as she carded her hand through it before bringing her finger against Payton's cheek. Her heart jumped when Payton shifted to lean farther across the center console and press Bellamy into the door of the car.

Bellamy groaned and scraped her teeth along Payton's bottom lip. Her chest rose and fell rapidly, and heat pooled in her core. One-night stands were not her typical fashion, but Payton was gorgeous and far too sweet for her own good. Bellamy dropped her hands to her own chest and pulled the buttons on her blouse to open it for Payton's benefit.

True to what Bellamy thought, Payton brushed her rough fingers below he black lace of her bra without hesitation. She dipped below the fabric to find her nipple, which hardened on contact. Bellamy gripped Payton's cheek again to bring her into another bruising kiss.

Payton awkwardly propelled herself closer to Bellamy, who pressed even harder into the door, her back arching when the handle poked her sharply. She grunted, and Payton moved her lips to Bellamy's ear and whispered, "Sorry. Shift up so you're on the seat."

Following instructions, Bellamy turned her body so she was seated. Payton reached between her legs with a sly grin on her face and pulled the bar underneath, sliding the seat backward with a great force. Bellamy grinned. "Brilliant."

"Not my first time doing this."

"I gathered as much." Bellamy reached to her side and pulled the lever to lower the back of her seat.

Payton swung her leg around then shifted down so her knees were on the floor of the car. Curious, Bellamy watched her with a narrowed eye in the dim of the vehicle as she pressed both her palms to the tops of Bellamy's thighs.

"Good thing you wore a skirt today," Payton commented.

Bellamy swallowed. "I wear one just about every day. Have to look good for my clients, and professional."

"It's going to come in handy. Lift up."

Pressing her stilettos into the floor of the car, Bellamy lifted her hips. Payton didn't pull her skirt down like she thought she might. Instead, she shoved the fabric upward until it was above her hips. Bellamy lowered herself down as Payton dove right in, shoving aside her underwear. She gripped the center console with one hand and the pillar between the doors with her other as she bit her lip and stared down at the blue-eyed beauty in front of her.

"My God," Bellamy breathed. "Whatever you're doing, don't stop."

Payton hummed against her, pleasure wrapping through her

body like licks of fire. Bellamy lifted her foot up onto the edge of the seat while widening her hips to give Payton better access. Her knuckles were white as she closed her eyes, focusing solely on the sensations Payton caused with her talented and sure tongue. She had no doubt Payton had done this many times before.

Bellamy's hips rocked up and down as Payton's mouth continued to move against her. Pleasure coiled tightly, dragging from her limbs to her belly to her core. Bellamy bit her lip as sounds wanted to escape. She'd trained herself to make no noises over the years of being with Kendra. Shoving the thought from her mind, she focused on Payton and her sweet and confident mouth. Confidence got her every time, and Payton had it in spades.

Groaning, Bellamy gave herself over to her orgasm. She let it rip through her, float in and out of her brain, shocking her body. Payton didn't stop right away, and Bellamy reveled in the last dregs of pleasure Payton pulled from her. She was still breathing heavily when Payton shuffled up the seat and pressed their mouths together, her warm juices mingling on both their tongues.

Bellamy glided her hands from Payton's waist to her hips and around to the front of her standard and cheap black slacks. She slid the fastener undone and jerked down the zipper until she could plunge her hand between the fabric and Payton's skin. While keeping Payton's mouth occupied, Bellamy ran her fingers back and forth over her slick folds.

Payton's forehead pressed into Bellamy's shoulder as she grunted with each thrust of Bellamy's wrist. Sliding her thumb in a circle, Bellamy found a pattern that elicited the most moans and a few hisses from her counterpart. It wasn't long until Payton tensed sharply and bit into Bellamy's shoulder as her release took over her. She'd have to cover that with makeup for the next week, but it had been worth it.

Their mouths danced together again before Payton pushed up. Bellamy waited, watching Payton's deft fingers fix her pants. Payton crawled into the driver's seat and let out a huff. Sighing, Bellamy shimmied her skirt down her legs and sat up to button her blouse. She'd have to tuck it in somehow before she got into the house to face down Kendra, who would no doubt be home by the time she returned.

"That was worth it," Bellamy said into the quiet car, turning her head in the seat with a smile. "Thank you."

Payton cocked her head in a grin. "I'm not sure anyone has ever thanked me for sex before."

Laughing, Bellamy shook her head. "They should far more often. Quite talented."

"As are you."

Snorting, Bellamy rolled her eyes and shifted to attempt to shove her blouse into the waistband of her skirt. "I guess I have to face the music."

"I suppose we both do."

Bellamy's brows knit together. "What music do you have to face?"

Payton shrugged. "Nothing like what you're going into."

Bellamy eyed her carefully. "I suppose we all have demons."

With the car in drive, Payton headed to Bellamy's house. Sure enough, lights were on in the first floor and one upstairs where the master bedroom was. Bellamy's heart sank. It was likely to be a very long night of arguing. All they did was argue, but to be fair, it was their paid profession. With one last-ditch effort, Bellamy reached across the center console and dragged Payton in for a long embrace. When she pulled away, she let out a huff and put her hand on the door.

"Wish me luck," Bellamy whispered.

"Good luck."

With a broad grin, Bellamy turned to Payton. "And to you as well, in whatever your music and demons be."

Without another word, Bellamy stepped toward the giant house she and Kendra had bought years before that had never quite felt like home. It was cold, mostly empty, and had never held the family she'd wanted. Payton waited until she was inside the front door before driving off. Bellamy shuddered and shook off the rain before she double-checked her blouse and skirt, her lipstick, and the bite mark still burning on her shoulder. Kendra didn't need any more ammo than she already had.

CHAPTER 2

PAYTON'S NERVES WORKED TRIPLE TIME. HER HEART raced as she checked her makeup in the bathroom mirror. Her eye caught something as she glanced in the reflection past herself to her nephew—well, basically her son at that point. Her sister hadn't been around in months, and she finally had enough legal reasons to seek termination of rights, if she wanted.

Her heart ached at the thought. She wanted her nephew to grow up with his mom—he deserved to grow up with her, to know her, to be her son. But Maddy wasn't going to be that kind of mom, at least not any time soon, and Payton had to do what was best for Liam, and that meant keeping him with her as long as possible.

He giggled as he sat in his baby chair while she once again checked her makeup. She was a nervous wreck. There was nothing that could hide it. She'd been so tense and stressed that she hadn't managed to sleep at all that night. It was her first real job interview since she had graduated and gotten her certification. She needed it more than she could admit. Working at the restaurant was nice and all, especially when she got big tips on the weekends, but the hours sucked, and she needed to be able to spend more time with Liam when he wasn't in daycare.

She checked over her mascara in the mirror, making sure she hadn't blinked and smudged it somehow. Her mom, Denise, came into the room and clucked her tongue. "You look perfect."

"I'm so nervous."

"You'll nail it. You always do. I'm very proud of you, Payton. You've done so much in this past year."

Payton shrugged, but the feeling of pride built up in her chest to the point she felt a little more confident. Denise smiled at her and leaned against the doorframe. "You'll have to tell me all about it when you get back, but I'm pretty sure you'll land yourself the job."

"I have to. Someone's got to pay the rent, and the bills, and the student loans."

Denise shook her head. "Worry about that tomorrow. Today, focus on the interview and getting yourself a job with better hours. You'll make it work out in the long run no matter what you need. You always have."

Smiling, Payton left the bathroom and picked Liam up, popping him onto her hip and making faces at him. Denise came over and took him, much to Liam's protest. "Don't want to mess up your outfit. You should get going. It's going to be a long drive in traffic, and you don't want to be late for something this important."

"Right." Payton nodded, firmly. "Thanks, Mom. Really. I couldn't do this without you."

"Well, none of us could do it without you." Denise grabbed Liam's small hand and tried to do a mini and weird dance with him.

Payton chuckled and grabbed herself a glass of water. She set it on the counter before double and triple checking everything in her purse to make sure she had what she needed, including the proper IDs in case she was hired on the spot.

"I'm so nervous."

"Payton. Go. Now. Come on. You're not going to get the job by standing here talking to me."

Payton grabbed her purse and keys, heading for the door to the apartment she had managed to rent with her mom as a co-signer. It hadn't taken much convincing, but she still didn't like the idea that her mom was on the hook if she failed. She wanted to be independent and wanted to be able to do what she needed for Liam without help all the time.

She slipped into her ancient car and put it into drive. With one last glance at the apartment building, she drove out of the parking lot and toward downtown. When she got into the area where her interview was, she was amazed. Payton had rarely spent much time in downtown Tacoma, but every time she made it there, its beauty stunned her.

Parking in one of the garages, she let out a breath and put her head to the steering wheel. She could do this. If she didn't get it, then she'd just find another job to interview for. Her skills as a paralegal would give her opportunity anywhere she went. That was why she chose to work in that field, that and the pay was decent. If she was going to be Liam's parent, she needed that stability.

The building was a high rise. She took the elevator up to the tenth floor and let out a breath before she walked through the front door to the office. There was no one in sight. Swallowing, Payton stepped in farther, hoping someone would have heard the door and come out. When no one did, she took a risk.

"Uh . . . hello?"

Rustling of papers and rolling of wheels echoed from one of the offices in the back. Payton straightened her spine and tried to plaster a confident smile on her face, but she was pretty sure it looked more like she'd swallowed a rotten fish she could in no way stomach.

The woman rounded the corner, her tight maroon skirt

hugging her curves in every sense of the word. Payton's mouth went dry. Her eyes were a cold blue, and her blonde hair was curled perfectly against her scalp, the short strands not straying one bit as she moved.

She looked oddly familiar, like Payton had seen her before, but she couldn't place her at all. Usually when that happened, Payton was pretty sure it was because she had served them at the restaurant but that they were forgettable. She'd seen so many faces there was no way to remember them all.

"I'm Payton. I'm here for an interview?" Her voice came off like it was a question, which Payton hadn't meant to do. Her nerves were getting the best of her.

The woman came closer, extending her hand with a half-seductive and over-the-top confident smile. "I'm Kendra. This is my practice."

"It's good to meet you in person, finally." Payton took Kendra's hand, her fingers warm against Payton's skin. She let out a breath and relaxed as best as she could.

"We can meet in my office. Follow me."

Kendra led the way. Payton tried to focus her eyes on the four-inch black stilettos that probably cost more than she had earned in the last year, but her gaze kept straying straight up to Kendra's ass and the way it swished back and forth in the tighter than tight pencil skirt.

As they got to Kendra's large office, Payton sat down in the offered chair. Kendra stayed standing and leaned against her desk, both hands splayed on the solid wood next to her as she shifted forward.

Her blouse was white, tucked neatly into her skirt, but the front had been left open enough that when she moved forward, Payton had an excellent view down the material and to her lacy white bra that stood starkly against her tanned skin. Payton immediately moved her gaze to the floor, then chastised herself for looking when she shouldn't, then not using eye contact to her advantage during an interview. Gathering the courage, Payton looked back up at Kendra and focused her gaze solely on Kendra's face.

"You graduated this past semester, right?" Kendra's voice was smooth.

"I did," Payton answered.

"What experience do you have working in an office like this?"

"I don't have much. But I do have the education, and I have a strong ability to learn and learn rapidly. I'm used to fast-paced environments that are constantly changing."

"Well, that's good, because that is how it works in a lawyer's office. Things happen very quickly."

"I'm a quick study."

"Good. Good. We need someone to begin immediately as our last paralegal left rather unexpectedly. When would you be able to start?" Kendra's ruby red lips shone in the light of the room, the gloss of whatever she had painted on them distracting Payton for a moment before she was able to find the words to answer.

"I can start tomorrow."

"Perfect." Kendra clapped her hands together then leaned over her desk, the pale skin of her breast exposed as she moved. Payton had to stop thinking about her that way. She had to think about her as a boss, as an employer, not in any sexual manner. Still, there was something about her so eerily familiar, but she could not place it no matter how hard she tried.

"You're hired. I'll need you to fill out this paperwork. You can bring it back tomorrow morning, and your IDs. We're going to hit the ground running come morning."

"Okay. Thank you!" Payton stood up and took the paperwork. That had been seriously the easiest job interview ever. Kendra's fingers touched hers briefly as she handed the paperwork over. Payton didn't pay attention too much as she stared down at the forms. "Really, thank you."

"Don't worry about it. Show up at eight tomorrow morning and we'll get you started. My partner will still be in court, so I'll show you some of the ropes before she comes in to show you the rest. She's really a much better teacher than I am."

"All right." Payton grinned, still standing awkwardly in front of Kendra. It didn't take much longer for Kendra to escort Payton to the door.

Getting into her car, she started the engine then did a happy little dance in the driver's seat. *A job!* It was exactly what she had needed, and no matter how easily it came, she deserved it. Breathing out relief, Payton headed for the nearest Walmart. She had to go shopping, massively. She only had one nice outfit, and she had worn it for the interview.

In the department store, she tried on piece after piece of clothing, shoving them into her cart. She knew the total was going to be high, that she'd be throwing it onto her credit card, that if she really wanted she could ask her mom for help to pay for the clothes, but she didn't. She needed to do this on her own.

The last thing she added to her cart was a new car seat for Liam. He had almost outgrown his last one, even though he was only ten months old. The kid could put away so much formula and food that he would eat her out of house and home faster than she could keep up, that was for sure.

She headed for the register, separating out her purchases into those going on the credit card, those that were WIC for formula, and those she would pay for with the money she got from essentially fostering her own flesh and blood, which would help cover the cost of the car seat. She had wanted to hold off a bit longer on it, but at the same time, she wanted to celebrate. Her mom would be so excited.

~

THE DRIVE BACK FROM THE COURTHOUSE HAD Bellamy in a good mood. She had won the motion, her client was happy, she was happy. She spent the time in her car congratulating herself, glad everything she had planned worked out in her favor. As she pulled up outside of her building in downtown Tacoma, she tensed. Kendra had told her the new paralegal was supposed to start that day.

For some reason, they hadn't been able to keep someone in the office longer than two months, and usually it was closer to a month. It had been that norm for the better part of a year. So often, Bellamy had found herself doing a lot of the work she wouldn't normally do because they simply didn't have someone who could. They were a small law firm—literally it was her and Kendra. They had a good client base—well, she did. Kendra did what Kendra did. She complained about bills for managing the office, bills for hiring a paralegal and secretary, which somehow Kendra had convinced Bellamy to morph into one position, which she had known was a bad idea from the beginning.

She rubbed a hand over her brow and closed her eyes. She didn't really want to go up there. It was going to be the exact same thing it had been for months and months. "Hi, I'm Bellamy. I'm your other boss. If you have any questions, let me know." It wasn't just that. Kendra consistently left Bellamy to do all the training. It was as if once Kendra did the hiring she was done with the person.

Bellamy groaned again before she gathered her bag with her papers in it. She had a lot of work to do on this case now, one that would no doubt take their firm to the next level. She had been working endlessly for months on trying to build up her client base. It was the only way she was going to be able to take the firm out from under Kendra and build it the way she wanted, and of course, she had to do everything herself because if Kendra caught any inkling of what Bellamy was planning, that would be the end.

Shutting the door to her Lexus, Bellamy slipped inside the building's elevator and pressed the button for the tenth floor. She waited, shifting from one foot to the other as her feet pronounced their soreness incessantly. Five more minutes, she would be in her office, settled, able to slide her shoes off her feet and relax as she got down to more work. She had a few more days before she had to go back to court for another case.

It was exhausting being the only person bringing in income, the only one doing work, but if she wanted to meet the criteria of the legal documents in order to buy the firm from Kendra, she was going to have to suck it up for at least another six to twelve months.

Bellamy put her hand on the door to her office, the opaque glass something that had been Kendra's idea. Apparently, it looked sophisticated. Rolling her eyes, she opened the door and stopped short right in the doorway. Dark, edgy bangs sliced across her head, just above her eyes, those baby blue eyes that had haunted Bellamy's dreams for months. Her breath caught in her throat, her heart thudded wildly, and her mouth went dry. For the first time in a very long time, Bellamy was at a loss for words.

She knew she wasn't smiling, that she was staring, and it was probably quite unnerving. But she had no idea what to say. What the hell would Payton be doing in her office in the middle of the day? If she'd wanted some kind of hook-up again that was off the table. They had specifically not shared any information with each other. Cheating on her wife was not something Bellamy did on a regular basis, or ever, except that one time in the front seat of an old beat-up car after a huge fight in the middle of a restaurant.

Oh God. Bellamy cleared her throat, still not sure what to say. It didn't seem like Payton was going to be making any moves in that direction either. They both simply stared at each other. Bellamy wondered briefly what was going through Payton's mind, but she was interrupted when her bombshell of a wife came out of her office in the back and toward the front reception area.

Bellamy placed a mask on her face, shifting her gaze from Payton to Kendra. "Hey, I won the motion."

"Did you? That's wonderful. So what now?"

"We make a new motion to dismiss."

"Good. I see you've met our new paralegal."

Bellamy's lips thinned into a sharp line as she once again flicked her gaze over to Payton. Oh, she had met their new paralegal, just not that day, and it hadn't been so long for Kendra either, though she doubted Kendra had even paid a lick of attention to Payton that awful day months before. Kendra wouldn't have even known Payton was the same woman.

"Y-yes."

"Her name is Payton. She just graduated from the community college, and this is her first paralegal position."

Of course it is. Bellamy grimaced as she watched Kendra move closer to Payton and slide her hands along Payton's shoulders. Bellamy's stomach clenched, and she wanted to tell Kendra to get her hands off, to leave Payton alone, to let her find a new job, one she actually had a chance at surviving.

Kendra turned to Payton. "You'll get to know Bellamy very well in the next few weeks. She's very busy though, so you'll have to make sure to pay extra special attention to all her clients and her cases to make sure she has what she needs when she goes to court."

Bellamy wanted to roll her eyes. It was as though Kendra was talking to a five-year-old. Nothing could be more humiliating than that. Payton seemed to take the dismissive and demeaning tone like a champ though. Whether it was because she hadn't been around Kendra long enough to figure out

Kendra was being an asshole or because she had worked with many assholes before, Bellamy had no idea, and she really didn't want to get to know Payton well enough to find out.

"I uh . . . I have some paperwork to file with the courts, so I'll be in my office." Bellamy pointed toward her door then made a fast escape for her sanctuary.

Her office was brightly lit with the sunlight. She had managed to snag it over the other office, which had windows, but not as many. Bellamy loved sunlight. She shut her door, tossed her bag onto the corner of the desk, and sat heavily in her chair. Collapsing in on herself, Bellamy shook her head as tears nearly fell from her eyes. Payton could not be there. It had to be an illusion or something. Her one-night stand from months ago could not possibly be her new paralegal, the one woman who could very well ruin her ability to divorce her wife, take the law firm, and start her new life over in the way she wanted. Damn lawyers for always drawing up tight documents including prenups and business arrangements. She should have never married another lawyer.

The knock on her door was surprising. Kendra never knocked. She just barged in at her own discretion whether Bellamy was with a client or not. Straightening her back so she wasn't slouching, Bellamy stared at the door like she could see through it and who was on the other side. Except she knew who was there, and she did not want to talk to her.

"Come in," Bellamy called, her own voice betraying her. She had nowhere to hide. Payton knew she was in there. She had just wanted an hour to figure her own drama out, freak out, then come to some logical conclusion before dealing with Payton and trying to get her to quit or run or get herself fired in some way.

Payton came through the door and shut it behind her. She gnawed on her lip as she stood at least three feet away from Bellamy's desk. She looked so small in that moment. She was a small woman in general, but she looked defeated and scared. Bellamy wanted to wipe that feeling from her, wanted to make her feel safe and secure, but she knew she couldn't.

"I . . . I didn't know this was your law firm."

"How could you not? My name is on the door."

"Your last name is on the door. Your first initial is next to it. I didn't know your last name. I never knew Kendra's."

Bellamy let out a sigh and rubbed the bridge of her nose between her thumb and forefinger. She was going to have a headache over this one for sure. "Why did you even apply?"

"I needed a job. I just graduated, I need a job to pay bills, I went to school for this, you had an ad for an immediate opening. The restaurant is great, but it isn't this. This comes with benefits. It comes with a salary."

"One that Kendra will no doubt make you work extra for."

"What?"

"Never mind." Bellamy bit her tongue and shifted in her seat. "She can't know."

"I wasn't planning on saying anything, ever. I knew what that night was months ago. I never thought I would see you again. Seriously, I'm just as shocked as you are."

Letting out a breath, Bellamy closed her eyes and listened to Payton's uneven breathing. "I'd much prefer if you didn't work here."

"I can't quit. I need this job. I just quit the restaurant with no notice. I doubt they'll take me back now. I need the benefits. Liam needs to see a doctor for his check-ups, and I need the cash to pay for rent. I need this job."

Opening her eyes, Bellamy stared over at Payton. She looked just as she had in her dreams only dressed differently, dressed like it didn't quite fit her, but it did fit. The tan pants formed to her hips perfectly before they billowed out down to the ground. She had flats on instead of heels like Bellamy, which was rather smart. Perhaps Bellamy should keep a pair in her desk drawer for when they didn't have clients visiting. Her blouse was crisp and white, no doubt new, and the vest she wore over it was a smart black with a satiny finish.

"I understand," Bellamy whispered.

"I don't think you do. I have custody of my nephew. Full custody. His mom—well, she isn't in the picture. I need to be able to take care of Liam. I can't afford to lose this job."

Bellamy put both her hands up in front of her. "I'm not planning on firing you."

Except she had been, just moments before, trying to come up with every way to get rid of Payton. What she had failed to realize in that moment was she could just wait it out. No paralegal lasted longer than two months. She could wait two months, be on her best behavior, hope and pray Payton didn't say anything to Kendra in an angry fit at the end when she no doubt screamed out she was quitting effective immediately.

"Oh good." Relief washed over Payton's face, her baby blue eyes, the pixie nose. A blush rushed to her cheeks. "I was so worried you were just going to fire me for nothing."

"No." Bellamy stood up then, moving over to Payton. In heels, she stood nearly a head taller. Curling her fingers into her palm, Bellamy tried to make herself not reach out and touch. It would be inappropriate. Except everything about the situation was already bordering on that. Cupping Payton's cheek, she turned Payton's face up so she could stare into those eyes—eyes with wisdom and depth she had rarely seen in such a young woman. "I won't fire you, but you cannot tell Kendra about that night. It will ruin me."

"I promise."

Bellamy paused, swallowed, and then licked her lips, imagining Payton's against hers. "I believe you."

She wanted nothing more than to kiss her right then, but after making the demand Payton keep everything a secret, it would be awful of her to do that. Releasing Payton's cheek, Bellamy stepped away and let out a breath.

"And it won't happen again." Those words pained her to say. She wanted it to happen again. It was very near the last time she'd had sex, except that one angry bout of sex when Kendra had gotten drunk after a trip to Cabo San Lucas the month prior. And that had not been good sex in any fashion.

"I understand."

"Good. Now, if you'll excuse me, I have work to get done."

Payton hesitated only briefly before she turned and exited through the door she hadn't gone farther than a foot from. Alone, Bellamy collapsed into her chair and closed her eyes. It was going to be a hellaciously long couple of months until Payton quit like the rest of them.

CHAPTER 3

Payton had managed to make it through her first day without seeing Bellamy again. At least not since the fateful office incident she'd prefer to never remember. Coming in to her first day of work only to find out she'd already slept with the boss had not been what she'd expected. Ever. The next day when she came in, the tension had been back in her chest, but Bellamy had been all business, explaining what she needed, when she needed it by. She was gentle in her corrections and guidance to make Payton's work even better.

However, by day four and the end of her first workweek, Payton knew something was amiss. She hadn't done any work for Kendra yet. Either Kendra always did her own grunt work or she didn't have any. She couldn't quite figure it out. Payton sat at her desk out front in the wide lobby area. The offices were shaped like a "T." Her desk was out front with a double-monitor computer where she could run her secretarial work and her paralegal work simultaneously.

Behind her was Kendra on one side and Bellamy on her other. Bellamy came and went often, going from court to meetings with clients. Kendra mostly stayed in her office. Payton had no idea what she was doing in there on the daily. Only once had a client come to see her—a busty blonde who Payton suspected wasn't there for legal advice, especially since she showed up when Bellamy was out of the office.

Keeping that information to herself, she put her head down to get back to work. If she could make it through one week, then she knew she could make it through a month and up to a year. If she could make it through a year, she could find a new job if she didn't like this one because her legal case for permanent custody of Liam would be done and over with. She wouldn't have to worry about proving her ability to financially support him.

She hung up the phone after scheduling another client for Bellamy, who had told her at one point to schedule her any client who wanted to see her, and if they specifically requested her to send them her way no matter what. Payton had no idea why Bellamy was dead set on working herself into an early grave, but it wasn't her concern. At least, it shouldn't be.

Grabbing her keys, she knocked on Kendra's door. "Come in."

"I was just going to pick up the lunch order. Was there anything else you needed while I was out?"

"No. If you need office supplies, now would be the time to get them."

"Uh . . . sure. Is there a specific card for that?"

"Charge it to the credit card."

"Okay."

Letting out a breath, Payton shut Kendra's door and backed away quietly. She turned around and ran straight into Bellamy. Jumping, she shook her head and issued a profuse apology. "I'm so sorry! I didn't see you there."

"Don't worry about it. I just came in. You weren't at your desk."

"I was about to pick up the lunch order."

"You don't have to do that. I already grabbed it."

27

"Oh."

Bellamy held up her hand, which had a white plastic bag in it and no doubt some Styrofoam containers with food. Not once during the entire week had the lunch order involved food for her, not that she had been told it would, but she had hoped at some point it would, perhaps just once. She was interested in what they ordered, in what they would eat from every restaurant they sent her to.

"I put yours on the desk."

"Mine?"

"Yeah." Bellamy's brow furrowed. "Why do you say that like you're surprised?"

"No reason." Payton pressed her lips together. Every time she was this close to Bellamy her heart rate ramped up and her voice caught in her throat. She always felt like she said the stupidest things that made hardly any sense. If she'd been attracted to Bellamy in that restaurant months before, being in close proximity to her every day was not helping her wandering mind.

Bellamy cocked her head to the side, studying Payton with those deep chocolate eyes that seemed to have so much depth in them. Payton's palms sweated as her nerves kicked into overdrive. Bellamy was working through something, and that steady and silent stare could easily be her undoing if Bellamy didn't speak soon.

"You haven't had lunch all week, have you?"

Payton's chest rose sharply as she sucked in a breath. She didn't know if she should lie or not or if Bellamy had expected her to have lunch. Kendra had been the one to put in the orders and tell her where to go and when to pick it up. Bellamy had been far too busy to even think about when she needed to eat nonetheless what the rest of them were eating.

Bellamy closed her eyes on a long sigh. Reaching out, her fingers gripped Payton's wrist firmly. "Anytime she *forgets* to tag on an order for you, feel free to add in your own. Lunch is for everyone, not just the ones who have law degrees."

"Okay." Payton's voice was quiet. She wasn't sure if she would take Bellamy up on that offer or not but at least it was there.

With Bellamy's fingers still on her wrist, she couldn't very well leave, but she felt odd standing outside Kendra's door with Bellamy touching her. Twisting her hand slightly, she broke Bellamy's grasp then took a step to the side and around the small hallway toward her desk.

"I'm serious, Payton. And don't hesitate to just ask next time what's normal and what's not. Kendra is . . . well . . . Kendra is Kendra. If you need something, come talk to me."

"Okay," Payton repeated, at a loss for words.

She escaped to her desk, smiling as she saw the container right in the middle of it. As she lifted the lid, shouts echoed out to her. She glanced around the room to make sure there were no clients before settling down. Kendra and Bellamy arguing was not abnormal. Even in four days working there, she knew they argued just about every day, if not multiple times a day. Sometimes she could hear every word of it, especially if they left the door open, and other times all she heard were whispered mumblings.

This time it was closed doors. Payton took the fork that had been left to the side of her meal and took a large bite from the pasta dish inside. It was heavenly. Focusing on the food and the work, she ignored everything going on behind her. They could go on for hours if they wanted. It had been that way at the restaurant the first time she had met them.

Taking another call from a client, she wrote the message on a piece of paper. She headed into Bellamy's office, leaning over her desk to set the message right in the center so Bellamy would see it first thing. Once again as she was turning around, she stopped. Bellamy stood in the doorway, staring at her with a lost look on her face.

"I'm sorry. I was just leaving you a message."

"It's fine." Bellamy looked far more harried than she had a few minutes ago, and the food she had brought with her was nowhere in sight.

Payton bit her lip. Normally she was a fully confident woman who spoke her mind, but since starting at the law firm, she found herself second and triple guessing everything she did. It was so not like her. Taking a deep breath then going for it, Payton said, "Are you okay?"

Tears brimmed in Bellamy's eyes before she drew in a long breath, her gaze hardened, and nodded. "Yeah, I'm fine. Or I will be. This isn't anything abnormal as I'm sure you've noticed."

"Yeah, but in my four days here there are two things I've noticed. The first is you're working yourself to death, fast. The second is you two fight a lot, for whatever reason. It's not really my business. But you, Bellamy, need a break. You deserve one."

Bellamy let out a sigh. "You may be right, but I don't have the time for it. Or the energy to figure it out."

"I can do that. If you really want me to schedule you something, I can. I run your calendar, remember?"

A light chuckle left Bellamy's beautiful pink-beige lips. "Thanks, but no. I think I'll let Kendra stick to the beach vacations."

"She take them often?"

"Yes." Bellamy moved from the door to her desk. She glanced over the note, nodded to herself, then set it aside. "I'll have to schedule in another meeting with Mrs. Klodski. She's a very needy client, and if I don't meet with her in person, she gets antsy."

"I'll call her back in a minute and set that up for you."

"Thank you."

Payton moved toward the door, sensing the conversation was

over. She didn't want to overstep her boundaries any more than she already had, and she knew she had. They had managed four days of purely professional conversation, but Payton had broken down and gave Bellamy a piece of her mind and word of advice when she hadn't meant to. She was just at the door when Bellamy's voice reached her and made her stop.

"And Payton, thank you, really. You may just be right."

"Doesn't mean you'll listen though."

"It doesn't, no."

Payton gave Bellamy one nod before slipping out of the door. Within seconds she went back into the office with the lunch Bellamy had left on her desk. She set it in front of her boss, smiled, and walked to the door. "I brought my lunch today."

With no other comment, Payton walked to her desk to call Mrs. Klodski for that meeting and to double-check Kendra's schedule. There had to be a way Bellamy could have at least a half-day off in order to take some time for herself. She was determined to find a way to do that while maintaining the status quo in the office. It was going to take a huge feat and probably a few weeks to shuffle everything, but Payton knew she could do it. She had to. Bellamy needed it, and for some reason, she wanted to give Bellamy everything she needed and more.

TWO WEEKS INTO PAYTON'S TIME WORKING AT THE office and Bellamy's head was officially spinning. She had done her best to avoid her, but when there were only three people working in the office, it was impossible. She needed to use Payton's skills every day in order to keep her own workflow going, and Payton had picked everything up very quickly.

Sighing, Bellamy glanced at her schedule, noticed she wasn't going to be in court again until the end of the week with one of her new cases and clients. She had managed to snag them from

31

a competitor when the competition didn't work fast enough. Bellamy, however, was determined to increase her client base, so overtime was something she was very used to working. In fact, she was pretty sure Kendra didn't even know what it felt like to have her sleep in the same bed anymore. It had felt like months since she'd last been in her bed for more than four hours.

She tidied up her office and her desk for a few minutes before a new potential client was going to arrive. She'd set up the meeting herself, asked Payton to find the time for it by rearranging some things. This client was huge. They could even just set her over the edge of what she needed in order to take the firm from Kendra officially, assuming they brought her in enough business in the long run. She would have to wait and see.

With a breath, she smoothed her hands down her skirt as she glanced in her mirror and checked her make up. As much as she hated to admit it, looking good did help her land clients. It was a woman's curse and blessing, the male-dominated society that was impossible to escape most days and dreams of escaping were always persistent. She touched up her lipstick and checked her hair. It was perfect.

Wincing, Bellamy leaned in. The streak of gray, which she had been so insistent on keeping because she thought it looked regal and added to her image of being wise was certainly bigger than the last time she had taken a serious look at it. Perhaps Payton was right and she did need a break. Scoffing at the idea, Bellamy brushed her fingers over the course graying hair. She wasn't a spring chicken anymore—there was no doubt of that. She wasn't going to fool herself in any way.

Unlike Payton, Bellamy didn't have the whole world in front of her. She had already lived over half her life. She had had the struggles of paying bills, of finding a new job right after law school, of working three jobs while in law school to pay for it, and of starting her own firm. She did not want to lose all that hard work because of a few stupid and poorly made decisions when she thought she was in love.

Slipping into her heels, Bellamy moved to her desk. She heard the front door to the office open then close, the loud booming voice of the client she had been waiting for, and Payton's sweet and soft voice as she asked him to wait. Sure enough, not five seconds later, there was a knock on her door.

"Mr. Bildridge is here for his appointment."

"Send him in."

Bellamy stood up one more time smoothing her palms over her skirt. When she glanced up, Kendra stood in the opposite doorway with a glare on her face and a flush in her cheeks. Bellamy knew that look. *Jealously.* If she had thought about it instead of rushing into trying to secure a new client, she could have guessed Kendra would be jealous. Kendra's family knew the Bildridges from something or another, and Kendra had been trying to get him as a client for years but had never managed to close the deal. Bellamy, however, stood a chance.

"Mr. Bildridge," Bellamy stated as he rounded the corner. She shoved her hand out in front of her to shake his. "It's so good to see you again."

Kendra's glare as Mr. Bildridge entered Bellamy's office was too telling. This was going to result in one of their worst arguments yet, no doubt of it.

About an hour after Mr. Bildridge left with a newly signed contract on her desk, Bellamy closed her eyes when she heard Kendra coming for her office. It was about to begin. She bolstered herself as much as she could for it, but honestly, every time they argued, the fights got worse and dirtier, and it got harder to maintain as much dignity as she could. She had no doubt Payton thought of her as some weak woman who took a bunch of crap from her wife, but also as someone who didn't have the balls to stand up during an argument. Not to mention that she was an awful person.

Whatever had been between them months prior when they'd hooked up was gone. Certainly Payton's view of her had changed so much in the past few weeks that she would never think of Bellamy like that woman again. When the click of her door signified it was shut, Bellamy wasn't prepared.

"What the hell do you think you're doing?"

Drawing in a deep breath through her nose, Bellamy let it out slowly, vowing to stay seated and remain calm the entire time. Well, at least for the first five minutes that she might be able to manage. "Securing us a new client." She wanted to add *something you have yet to manage to do in months*, but she bit her tongue hard to keep the comment to herself. They both knew Bellamy brought in the majority of their income, that without her, Kendra would be screwed.

"Bildridge is my account. You can't steal it."

Bellamy narrowed her eyes confused. Shaking her head, she tried to start over. "Bildridge is your account?"

"Yes! Their family has known my family for years. We are very well connected."

"Then why haven't you gotten a signed contract from him in the ten years we've had this law firm, hmm?" Bellamy raised an eyebrow and steepled her fingers. She knew she had Kendra caught and right where she wanted her. Kendra was speaking purely out of anger, which was actually rare for her, but Bellamy would be able to use that to her advantage in the fastest way possible. "I mean, if he's your client, then why was he in my office? Not to mention, Kendra, but I thought we were a team in this law firm. Wasn't that what we talked about for years when we were in school, dreaming up this business where two women were in charge with no men in sight? So tell me again how he is *your* client."

"You can't steal my accounts."

"I *stole* nothing." Bellamy relaxed into her chair, knowing the conversation was done. At least it was for her—apparently Kendra had other ideas.

"Don't you dare do that to me."

"Do what?" Confused, Bellamy waited for an explanation.

Kendra slapped her palm onto the table, a loud crack echoing around the room. Bellamy could only hope that the only other person in the office was Payton, although even then, she knew it sounded similar to something else. This time Bellamy did stand. She wasn't going to take threats, however simplistic in nature, sitting down.

"What did I do to you, Kendra? Come on, spell it out for me."

"Bildridge is my account."

"Then you should have closed the deal! Instead, he signed the papers with me, so Bildridge is my account. There is no way around that."

Snorting her anger, Kendra turned on her heel and stormed out of the room. Bellamy's anger finally surged, and she was quite annoyed Kendra had already left. She really could use someone to toss under the bus even more. Kendra knew how wrong she was, and that was why Bellamy had won that argument so readily.

Bellamy crossed her arms and strode to her window. She stared out at downtown Tacoma, watching people walk across the street in the early summer heat, the cars pass along. It was the few months of non-rain they had, but soon they'd be cast into the shadow of rain and winter.

"I'm sorry to interrupt."

At Payton's soft voice, Bellamy turned, all her anger fleeing. She loved how Payton could do that for her, could change her from being an old, bitter woman into someone who was happy or at least mostly satisfied with life. "You're not. I was avoiding."

"Right. I couldn't help but overhear, but . . . she didn't . . . there was a loud noise."

Bellamy choked. She put both her hands up and shook her head. "She didn't hit me. I swear. She hit the desk."

"Oh, okay. I just . . . I wanted to check. I'm sorry. I'll go now." Payton retreated out of the door before Bellamy even had a chance to say anything else.

Cocking her head to the side, she stared at where Payton had stood instead of turning back to her window. Whatever Payton had done was nothing she could ever imagine Kendra doing. Kendra was beyond self-absorbed. While it had been cute when they were dating, thirteen years later was a bit much. Bellamy tightened her shoulders and shook her head. "Huh."

The feelings swimming through her chest were nearly overwhelming, but she had felt them before. It had been a very long time since she had, but the fact that Payton cared enough to ask her, to look after her—it was sweet. With a skip in her heart, Bellamy moved to the window to stare out it again. She could afford five more minutes before she'd have to get to work. She could manage that. Perhaps it would even give her the elusive so-called break Payton kept reminding her to take every time a new client—or an old one with a new case—walked through the door.

Sighing, Bellamy wasted her five minutes thinking about Payton and whether or not she would make it another week or two, or if perhaps she would even beat out their longest standing employee in the last year. Bellamy had her hopes because the office would certainly be a whole lot lonelier without her there.

CHAPTER 4

A NEW WEEK AND A NEW DAY, PAYTON WAS READY. SHE actually enjoyed her job, for the most part. She liked the routine, the work and the quick pace. The environment—well, that left a lot to be desired, but if she thought only about the paperwork she created and filed, the keeping track of schedules and systems, she enjoyed that. It was such a different pace and refreshing change from the restaurant.

Both jobs included times where she would be working in rushes, although she felt and she knew her job with the law firm was far more impactful than delivering food to hungry customers. Here she could make it or break it with a mistake, and Bellamy and Kendra relied on her to do the best they could for their clients. Without her they couldn't function well as lawyers.

Proud, Payton dropped Liam off at the new daycare, one that had extended hours. Her mom picked him up from there often though when Payton had to work late. That was the part she didn't enjoy about her job. Because she was the only paralegal and because Bellamy easily overloaded her schedule by four or five times what Payton considered normal, she had to stay late many times to get her work done.

While she enjoyed it, she did miss her nephew, and she knew she'd have to take some time off soon to deal with some of the legal aspects of his being in her care. Unfortunately, she wasn't given options for dates from social workers or lawyers. They told her when to show up and where to be, usually not with a whole lot of warning. If anything, though, at least the office should understand being at the court's mercy.

When she got to the office, Kendra was waiting for her with a white coffee cup highlighting her bright red painted fake nails she had done every two weeks. Payton had to schedule it in for her several times already. Kendra had a sourpuss look on her face, her eyes narrowed and crinkled in the corners as she stared Payton up and down like she was some weird tasting dessert Kendra wasn't sure she wanted to try.

"We need to talk."

"Okay." Payton's heart picked up pace. It usually did any time Kendra told her to go to her office or talked to her in general. Something about Kendra's personality put Payton on edge every single time. Could be because she'd slept with Kendra's wife, once—knowingly sleeping with a married woman in the front seat of her car, but whatever.

Kendra turned and moved to her office. Payton took the silent command and followed after setting her purse and her shoulder bag on the floor next to her desk. It was eight in the morning, and the phone started going off the hook immediately like it always did. She ignored it, knowing she could call them back if they left a message, which would be her first task as soon as she sat down to get to some actual work done.

Once they were in Kendra's office, Kendra shut and locked the door. Payton's heart clenched. She had never been in a locked room with Kendra—or Bellamy, for that matter—but something about it seemed so final. She had no idea where the conversation was going or what Kendra was doing, but Payton had an inkling—no, she knew full out—she was not going to like whatever it was.

"Do you like working here?" Kendra started.

Payton stood in the center of the office, wringing her hands together and trying to figure out if she was going to be fired on the spot for something. She thought it had been going so well. "I do."

Kendra tilted her chin down and looked up at Payton through her lashes, eyeing her like candy, like a prize she had just won. She sat on the edge of her desk, splaying her hands to the side. The almost inappropriately-short skirt she wore riding up on her thighs and exposing even more skin. Payton couldn't help her gaze as it followed the line of the cloth as it moved. When she made eye contact with Kendra again, she could see Kendra was pleased with Payton's line of sight.

"Good, that will make this easier then."

"Make what easier?" Payton asked before she could bite her tongue. Her mother had always told her sometimes it was better to wait for people to share information than to try and drag it out of them.

"I need your help on a special project." Kendra shifted, a button coming loose on her blouse. Payton wasn't about to tell her as it was clear Kendra always wore the more risqué clothes compared to Bellamy. She didn't mind. To each woman their own, but it certainly could be distracting on occasion.

Payton let out a breath, her hands wringing together. "What project?"

"I know Bellamy has been bringing in new clients." Kendra's face went dark, eclipsed by some weird emotion.

"She's had a few new clients, but mostly returning clients." Payton wasn't sure why she felt this overwhelming need to defend Bellamy, but she did. She knew the ins and outs of both their schedules, and Kendra was the least busy of everyone in the office.

"Right. I need you, however, to do something for me."

"This special project."

"Yes." Kendra was back to her smiling and bubbly self.

Payton knew if she was on the receiving end of a seduction with Kendra that she would very likely lose whatever battle she tried to put up. Kendra knew how to use her body, her tone, and her mannerisms to get exactly what she wanted. She'd seen her do it time and time again with Bellamy, with clients who would come in for her, with Payton herself. She was glad that sexual energy wasn't turned on her, but at the same time, she worried whatever energy Kendra did turn on her would result in putting her in a compromising position.

"I need you to tell me when Bellamy is having a new client come in. Tell them to come in ten minutes before the meeting to fill out some paperwork."

"What paperwork?"

"Never mind that." Kendra waved her hand then crossed her arms, pushing her breasts up so they were more obvious than before. "Just tell them to come in ten minutes early."

"Why?"

"So I can meet with them."

Payton's stomach dropped. It didn't take a genius to figure out exactly what Kendra was planning. She wanted to steal clients from her own partner. Bile twisted in Payton's stomach, and she really wished Bellamy wasn't at court that morning and would be walking in on them at any time to put a stop to the conversation. But without that, Payton was left on her own. The phone shrilled at her desk. She wanted to try and use it as an excuse to get out of Kendra's office, but the door was locked and it wouldn't be an easy escape.

"Do you think you can do that for me?" Kendra's smooth

voice filtered through Payton's panic and rapidly-building distrust.

If she said no, she was sure it would be her job. And she needed the job. Her benefits were set to kick in within two months, and the paycheck had been nice. For the first time since she'd graduated high school and moved out of her mom's house, she had been able to pay bills without too much worry, though at the end of each weekly paycheck, she had wondered where it had all gone.

"Yes." Payton's voice was small, and she was not confident in her answer. She was going to have to find a way to work around what Kendra was asking. She couldn't be that person to throw Bellamy under the bus, to put her own job and client list at risk because her wife wanted something—whatever it was. Vengeance, payback, to win a pissing match—who knew.

"Good." Kendra clapped her hands and stood up from her desk. Her five-inch heels made Kendra taller than Payton, but Payton knew that Kendra would stand just shorter than her without them. Kendra walked over and put a hand on the small of Payton's back, turning Payton so they were face to face. Suddenly, that seductive grin was back, and Payton's chest constricted. "Then it's settled."

"Sure. I need to go answer that."

Once again the office phone was blaring through the closed door. Payton moved to the door, swiftly unlocking it and pulling it open, but Kendra's voice stopped her.

"Remember, Payton, not a word of this to Bellamy. We don't want her getting jealous of us."

If she could have snorted without fearing her job was on the line, she would have. Instead, Payton glared at Kendra as she looked her up and down, her good witch to evil witch personality flipping increasing drastically. She didn't want to verbally confirm Kendra's request because then it would make her liable, so she tried to slip away but Kendra gripped her wrist to keep her in place.

"Let me hear you say it."

Payton halted, frozen in place. That had been the one thing she had been avoiding, but Kendra was a thorough woman. "I won't tell Bellamy."

"Good." Kendra reached up and patted her smooth fingers against Payton's cheek like she was dog.

Filing away her humiliation and anger, Payton left Kendra's office and went to her desk. She did not want to think about what had just happened. The phone rang again as she settled into her chair and started unloading all the work she had brought home with her from her bag.

"Harringer and Ilam Law Firm, this is Payton. How can I help you?"

"Payton, I have been trying to reach you all morning. This is Faith."

"I'm sorry, Faith. I was in a meeting." Payton's heart rate ramped up again. Normally her social worker would just leave a message if she couldn't answer the phone right away. She knew she wasn't supposed to take personal calls on the office line, but she had given it in case of a last ditch emergency. "What can I do to help you?"

"Your sister wants to explore reunification again."

Payton's heart sank. They had tried this road several times already. Every few months Maddy would show up and try to regain custody of Liam. Payton would have to give in, let her have supervised visitation either with her or without her and would have to wait to see if Maddy would attempt to actually follow through with the plan Child Protective Services set out or not. The only blessing was Liam wasn't quite a year old yet, though he was getting very close to it, and he had very little idea what was going on.

It broke her heart though every time Maddy would show up

because Liam didn't know her, didn't recognize her. He would scream and cry for a lot of the visit and shy away from Maddy. It hurt her to watch him not know his mother, but it also hurt her to know Maddy felt the same pain.

"What does that mean?"

"It means we go back to square one. She has met the minimum requirements. She has been sober for thirty days. We will set up a supervised visit this week with Liam and her at our offices so they can be observed."

"How many times do we have to go through this before I can petition for permanent custody?"

Faith sighed. "She's supposed to go six months without contacting him or being involved. That, or she has to not make considerable effort to follow through with the reunification plan. That hasn't been happening. Liam isn't even a year old."

"He's a year next month."

"Right, but he's not a year. It hasn't been very much time. You know the entire purpose of foster care is reunification with the biological parents."

Payton clenched her jaw. She did know that. She also had very little hope in Maddy ever changing. Five years into drugs— she wasn't going to change anytime soon. "I understand that, but she's not making an effort."

"She is thirty days sober."

"For now," Payton muttered. "Just tell me when I need to have him there for the visitation. I really need to get back to work."

"I will call you with the details as soon as I can arrange them."

"Thank you." Hanging up, Payton let out a loud breath and closed her eyes.

Tears threatened to slip over her cheeks, but she shook her head and tried to rid herself of them. She would not cry in the office. As soon as she was home with Liam and no one else, then she would cry, but for now, she would focus on work and what she could accomplish.

She worked for five hours before Bellamy came back from court. She looked defeated. Payton tried to push her own worries to the side as she had a list of things for Bellamy to respond to, some of them immediately. But the look on Bellamy's face, the broken down and beaten expression wasn't giving her any chance of handing that list over. Bellamy shut the front door and let out a loud sigh and moan.

"Bad day in court?" Payton asked.

"The worst."

"What happened?"

Bellamy rolled her eyes. "You know, when clients don't tell you everything that is relevant to a case it makes it very difficult for you to do your job. I was blindsided by a piece of evidence I was not aware of that it was very clear Mrs. Jenkins *was* aware of."

"What was it?"

"Oh, just something stupid. Kendra still in?"

"Yeah."

"She had any clients in today?"

"No." Payton shifted her gaze from Bellamy, not quite sure where to go with the conversation but not happy to suddenly be thrust in between the two of them, again, in a way she most definitely didn't want to be.

"Figures," Bellamy muttered. "Any messages?"

"A lot." Payton lifted a stack of pink slips of paper she had been collecting for when Bellamy returned. Handing them over, she gave a wan smile. "The ones on top need to be answered immediately before the end of the day. The ones on the bottom are suspect."

"Suspect?" Bellamy smirked. "What does that mean?"

Payton shrugged. "I think Mr. Conan is trying to get something else from you other than a lawyer for a case."

"Ah. Yes." Bellamy blushed, her cheeks lighting up with a faint flush.

Thinking it was cute, Payton shifted in her spot behind her desk, trying to hide her own amusement.

"He most definitely is after something different. I'll deal with it."

"I mean, you could always send him to Kendra if you don't want to deal with him."

Bellamy laughed, her voice ringing through the office with a beautiful trill. Her lips were curved up a way Payton rarely saw. She liked it, and it sent a thrill up her spine then back down. Swallowing harder than she intended, Payton smiled when Bellamy's gaze turned to her.

"I could, but he's also a good client."

Payton shrugged. "I tried."

Bellamy shifted her bag over her shoulder and turned to move around the desk toward her office. Payton put a hand on her wrist to stop her as soon as she was close enough. Bellamy stared down at Payton's fingers before roving her gaze from her arm to her chest to her lips to her eyes. Payton shivered under the intense stare.

"Did you need something?" Bellamy asked.

"Uh, yeah." Payton's voice cracked. "I'm going to need some time off soon. I'm not sure when, but my sister . . . I need to take care of some personal things. I won't need more than a half day."

"I think we can survive without you for that long."

Payton still hadn't moved her hand from Bellamy's arm. As much as she wanted to, she didn't. She liked the warmth of Bellamy's skin under her fingers. Bellamy didn't pull away either. Instead, she continued to stare directly at Payton.

"Was there something else?"

"No." Feeling chastised, Payton removed her hand. She didn't step away like she wanted because she was locked in at her desk. Bellamy also didn't move, and Payton's heart rate ramped up as she tried to figure out what was happening.

"Let me know when you need off and we'll accommodate. Just don't make it on a day when I'm in court if you can."

"I don't have much of a choice as to when I'll need off."

Curious, Bellamy jerked her head slightly before cocking it at Payton. "I feel you're being cryptic for a reason, so I'll let it slide, but if you want to tell me, my door is always open. You know that."

"I do." Payton near whispered her last sentence. She had used the open door policy several times already and had planned on using it again when and if she needed it, which she figured she would.

"Good." Bellamy gave her another sweet smile, one that was genuine, before she stepped away from the desk and toward her office.

Payton watched her go and let out a breath. With a sigh, she plopped down into her chair to work on some filings and answer some emails coming in with questions. She had spent nearly an hour hunched over her desk when her cellphone rang. Glancing at the number, she knew who it was.

She almost didn't answer, but she knew what would happen if she didn't. Maddy would call her endlessly, leaving her voice-mails and text messages that would get angrier and angrier and more accusatory as she went. Biting the bullet, Payton slipped her phone to her ear, prayed no one would call the office while she was on her call and answered.

"Hello?"

"Hey Payton! How's my baby doing?"

"He's good. He's starting to walk and is getting really chunky."

"Don't you be overfeeding him now."

Payton bit her tongue. She had to keep her mouth shut and not antagonize her sister any. With a deep breath, she let it out slowly. "He's doing great, Maddy. The doctors say so every time he has a visit."

"Oh good! I just got off the phone with Faith. We're going to meet tomorrow afternoon! I can't wait to see my baby."

Payton's stomach dropped. Tomorrow. That gave her zero time to figure a way out of work, and Tuesdays were literally the one day a week her mother couldn't take the time to help and do transport. Closing her eyes, Payton flipped open the schedule on her computer to see if Bellamy would be in court. Sure enough, she was scheduled in at ten in the morning, which meant Payton had to have all the filings and paperwork ready to go that morning. Cursing under her breath, Payton wanted to cry. Nothing Maddy did was ever to her benefit or in Liam's. It was always about Maddy. Every time. That's what drugs did to someone, she supposed.

"Have you heard from Luis?" Maddy asked.

Payton stiffened. They never talked about Luis in a way that turned out well. He was the entire reason Liam had ended up in her care when he did. It wasn't because Maddy was a drug addict. It was because Luis had hit and beat a six-week-old baby so badly he ended up in the hospital. With a dry mouth, Payton answered, "No, and I don't expect to."

"His hearing is coming up."

Payton really didn't care. She did on some level, wanting to know Luis would be nowhere near Liam or another child if possible at any point in the future, but in terms of her personal life and raising her nephew, she wanted nothing to do with him. He wouldn't show up and claim custody, and he wouldn't try to fight for Liam. Luis had willingly given up his rights when he was faced with the fact he would never have his son back in his custody, and he could reduce his sentencing if he allowed someone else to raise his child.

"Oh," Payton answered, not knowing what to say.

"He says he's going to get out."

Doubting that, Payton let out a breath. "And then what?"

"Get a job. He's going to come stay with me."

"You're kidding me. Maddy. He can't stay with you if you're trying to get visitation with Liam. That's just stupid."

"I love him."

"You'll have to choose between him and your kid then because I know for a fact they're not going to let Liam back with you while you're with Luis."

The phone rang, thankfully giving her an out.

"Look. I have to go. I'll see you whenever."

"Payton—"

She didn't wait. Hanging up the cell phone, she answered the office phone with fear in her voice. The line was direct from Bellamy's office. When her voice left her throat, she knew she couldn't hide it.

"Do you have the paperwork for Mr. Bildridge?"

"Uh . . . I'll have it in ten."

"Payton."

"I know. I just . . . give me ten."

She hung up, took a deep breath and let it out. She had to get her shit together. Pulling up the file she was almost finished with, Payton concentrated on every word before she sent it over to Bellamy. It wasn't much longer before she heard her name called. Turning around, she saw Bellamy leaning against the wall with her shoulder, a pair of glasses between her fingers, her ankle crossed over her foot, and a sad look on her face.

"Payton, remember, the door is always open."

"I know." Payton's voice nearly broke. "I know."

CHAPTER 5

SOMEHOW, WHEN SATURDAY CAME AROUND, BELLAMY had no work to do for the day. Well, no meetings. She could always find work. She'd managed to sleep in, Kendra keeping fairly quiet that morning, which was odd in and of itself. Sighing, Bellamy brushed her fingers over her eyes and removed the sleep from them. Stretching, she groaned as her muscles moved in ways they hadn't in ages. Seven hours of sleep had done her wonders. Her mind moved rapidly, her brain picking up where she left off the night before.

She'd walked Payton to her car the night before, telling her to go home even though she knew work wasn't done. It was late —after eight—when she'd finally told Payton she needed to leave. As much as she loved the company, she knew it wasn't fair to keep her that long, especially when she had a kid at home. Surprisingly, Payton had made it a month. A whole month. She'd requested one half day off the following week, which Bellamy had granted happily. Still, she worried there was something going on she didn't know about—well, she knew she didn't know about it—but that it would eventually affect Payton's ability to work.

Sighing, she turned on her side and stared out of the window as it shone light down on her. It was a beautiful day, one in the middle of summer, but she knew it wasn't going to last. Storms were forecasted for the next week every evening. Finally pushing herself from the bed, Bellamy sat on the edge of the mattress and let out a breath. She would go in to the office later that day, finish out some paperwork for the morning then be home for dinner. Perhaps Kendra would even be interested in a dinner with her.

After dressing in a tight pair of old jeans she loved and a loose T-shirt, Bellamy threw her hair up into a messy bun on the back of her head and avoided any make up. With no meetings, she could dress down for once. Sighing, she moved through the halls and down to the kitchen. Kendra was nowhere to be seen, and a glance out at the driveway told Bellamy that Kendra wasn't at home.

Making herself coffee and a light breakfast, she gathered her supplies and headed in to the office. It didn't take her long to get there, but when she parked in the lot across from their building, she pressed her lips together. She recognized that car, had some very fond memories in that car—one memory to be exact. Curious, she grabbed her bag and her travel mug of coffee and headed inside.

Opening the door this time, Bellamy expected Payton to be there. Payton was hunched over her desk, her eyes locked on the screen until she heard the door click shut. Bellamy raised an eyebrow at her, daring Payton to come up with some excuse as to why she was there. When Payton said nothing, Bellamy stepped forward, setting her coffee mug on the desktop and leaning over it, her palm flat against the smooth blond wood.

"What are you doing here?" Bellamy asked.

"Uh . . . I left my phone here yesterday, so I came to grab it, but then . . . well, I got sucked into emails."

"Stop checking emails." Bellamy laughed. "You're as bad as me."

Bellamy was about to say something else when she heard a noise. Stopping, she straightened her back and stared at Payton again with a curious look.

"Did you bring your nephew with you?"

"Uh . . . yes . . . ? I hope that's okay. I really didn't think I'd be here this long."

Bellamy walked around the desk, and sure enough, right behind Payton and just out of her previous line of sight, sat a beautiful olive-skinned baby boy with bright dark eyes and dark hair. He grinned at her, and she melted.

"Oh my God, he's adorable!" Bellamy bent down, dropped her bag on the floor, and she grinned at the baby in front of her. "Hey there!"

"His name is Liam."

"Hi Liam. What are you doing?" Bellamy reached out to touch one of the toys he was playing with. "You got a ball?"

He grinned at her and made a babbling noise, and she melted even more. "Oh my God. Why didn't you ever tell me how adorable he is?"

"I didn't think you liked kids."

Twisting around, Bellamy glared at Payton. "Why would you think that?"

"You don't have any?" Payton said it like a question.

Bellamy tsked and turned back to Liam. She held her hands out to see if he wanted her to pick him up. When he reached out and mimicked her move, she grabbed under his armpits and lifted him onto her hip as she stood. Tickling his belly, she laughed and grinned at him.

"I love babies. Just because I don't have any doesn't mean I don't like them."

Payton shrugged. "Just didn't peg you for babies."

Bellamy rolled her eyes. "He's so cute, seriously. You got yourself a winner here."

"Thanks. I try."

Turning back to Payton, Bellamy stared at the screen only to realize Payton had not just been picking up her cellphone and checking emails, she had been doing work. "What did I tell you last night?"

"The work day was over."

"Exactly, and today is Saturday, which is a non-work day. Stop working."

Payton smirked. "So why are you here?"

"I'm the boss. It's my prerogative."

Narrowing her eyes, Payton shook her head, her short brown hair falling to block her view until she brushed her fingers across her forehead. "And do you know how hard I had to work to make it so you had no meetings this entire weekend? Pretty damn hard. And you're ruining all that work by coming in here on a Saturday."

Bellamy's lips parted as her mouth dropped. Her chest clenched, and she stared at Liam, who smiled at her. "Your auntie is pretty sneaky. How did I not notice you did that?"

Payton shrugged. "You've been a little preoccupied with, you know, work."

Bellamy rolled her eyes and turned toward her office. "I came to finish out some paperwork for next week."

"It can wait."

"So can whatever you're doing."

"Truce?" Payton put her hand out.

Chuckling, Bellamy took it and shook, but she didn't want to let go. Every time they touched, she wanted to let it linger, wanted to keep the contact. Kendra hardly ever touched her any more, except when she wanted something, not that Bellamy made much effort in that direction.

Payton moved, stepped back, and held her hands out for

Liam, who gladly slipped toward Payton. They stood facing each other, Bellamy's heart pounding so hard she thought Payton might be able to hear it. "We'll leave since we've been caught."

"All right, I'll see you Monday." But she wanted to see her sooner, wanted to invite her to hang out in her office and chat, wanted to spend that time with Payton and get to know her better, and definitely play with the baby a bit more.

Reaching down, Payton grabbed the diaper bag and slung it over her shoulder. She let out a breath before she walked toward the front door and called over her shoulder, "Take the day off, Bellamy, you deserve it."

Without another word, Payton left. Her scent lingered in the room, and Bellamy's stomach clenched. She would go home, as Payton had worked so hard to give her the day off. She'd be back in the morning, but Payton was right, a day would do her well.

When she got home, Kendra's car was in the driveway. Bellamy pulled into the garage and headed into the kitchen. As soon as she walked inside, she stopped. The noises she heard were familiar, the groaning and grunting a sure sign someone was having sex, and if she stood there long enough, she knew she would hear Kendra's high-pitched whine as she came.

It took her a minute to decide whether she wanted to follow the sounds or not, whether she wanted to catch Kendra once again cheating on her or if she wanted to walk back out of the door and hide away. The last time, and the time before that, and really any time she had been caught, Kendra had begged and pleaded and swore it would never happen again. Each time Bellamy took her back, for some stupid unknown and ridiculous reason, but she never thought Kendra would actually stop. It wasn't like they were having regular sex.

Walking to their liquor cabinet, she opened a bottle of Johnnie Walker Blue Label whiskey and twisted the lid off. She didn't even bother with a glass as she downed three large swigs of it. Setting it down on the table, she regretted it instantly and took another long chug. Bolstered enough, Bellamy headed up the stairs to where she heard the noises.

The master bedroom. Figured. Sighing, she walked through the open door and stood in the doorway with her arms over her chest and waited. They writhed, they touched, they licked. Kendra was wild. It wasn't the first time Bellamy had walked in on her wife like this, but she definitely wanted it to be the last. If anything, she knew her plans for divorce needed to happen as soon as possible.

"So you just think that I may be working all day and you bring someone home for this? What the hell, Kendra?"

They scattered. They covered themselves. They looked embarrassed and flushed—well, the other woman did. Bellamy didn't even pay attention to her. She would no doubt be name-less, faceless. She had no reason to be mad at her.

"You promised last time would be the last." Bellamy's voice broke. Her heart broke. It shattered into a thousand pieces. This happened every time she'd caught Kendra.

Kendra said nothing. The other woman gathered up her clothes and scampered out of the room, having to walk right in front of Bellamy who glared at her the entire time. When she was out of sight, she was out of mind. Bellamy focused in on her wife.

"What do you have to say?"

"Nothing," Kendra answered.

"You promised!" Bellamy's voice squeaked, she begged, she wanted this to not be happening. It was only a fluke she had even walked in on it. They would have no doubt been gone by the time she finished work if Payton hadn't been at the office.

"Like you promised?" Kendra asked, her voice low and dangerous. Her own anger grew, and Bellamy knew their fight was going to escalate.

Bellamy shook her head. "Do not dare use my one singular time of cheating in thirteen years to justify all the times you have done it. My once does not equate to all of yours. We have both made mistakes. The difference is I atoned for mine. I changed myself. You continue to make the same damn mistake every time."

Kendra stood up, letting the blanket fall around her as she left the bed and walked cockily and confidently toward Bellamy. "What am I supposed to do if you are never around? Hmm? I need to feel loved."

"I love you, Kendra. I always have. It's the only reason I'm still in this marriage. What I don't understand is if you love me. You always pull this crap, you're always doing stuff to break us apart not bring us together. You're always—"

She stopped when Kendra pressed fingers to her lips. Bellamy stared down at her, Kendra's much shorter form pressing against her. Bellamy tried to speak, but Kendra shushed her. Kendra leaned up on her tiptoes, her eyes had that daring and devilish look to them that Bellamy tried to avoid as best as she could, but she knew she was doomed.

"Let's stop fighting, please. I'm so tired of the arguments."

Kendra's words spoke right to her heart. She was equally tired of arguing, but she was pretty sure Kendra was only tired of it because she wasn't getting what she wanted. Kendra slid the hand that had been against Bellamy's lips to her cheek and dragged her down. Their mouths brushed gently, then firmly, Kendra's tongue dashing out against Bellamy's lips.

"You know you like to watch," Kendra whispered. "You can't tell me you didn't find that hot."

Bellamy whimpered. She would long some days for Kendra to touch her like she had been touching that woman, any woman. They were so distant from each other that even when they did have sex it felt like strangers in bed. Perhaps that was the only kind of sex Kendra enjoyed. Giving in, because Kendra was right, Bellamy grabbed the back of Kendra's head by her hair and walked her backward toward the bed she had just vacated. She had no desire to listen to another excuse fall from Kendra's lips, no desire to watch her try to spin circles to get out of her own mistakes. They could deal with that later.

She shoved Kendra onto the bed then stripped rapidly. She would take what she could of her marriage while it lasted. There was no reason not to at that point. They were both vibrantly aware of just how over their relationship was.

∿

MONDAY MORNING CAME AROUND QUICKLY, AND Payton had expected to see Bellamy already in the office when she arrived, trying to make up for taking the day off over the weekend. Instead, Bellamy was gone, some emergency hearing according to Kendra, who had actually come out of her office to talk to her.

Payton sat at her desk, booted up her computer and got to work. For the first time ever, she was shocked to see a client coming in to talk to Kendra. She was even more shocked to realize that the client had once been Bellamy's. She made a note to try and find some way to let Bellamy figure that out, but it was too late to do anything because the door to the offices opened and in walked the client.

Payton didn't even have a chance to stand up and greet him before Kendra was all over him. She led him to her office and suddenly Payton found herself alone with only the quiet mumbling from the closed off office behind her.

She had her second visitation with Maddy and Liam the next day, and she had to figure out how to work the schedule so she would be least missed in the office for a few hours. She rearranged some things, put some new things into the works then she got started on her paperwork.

Losing track of time, she was surprised when Kendra's office door shut and the client left. Kendra, however, came toward

Payton's desk and slipped a manila folder of paperwork over the Payton. "Would you file this?"

"Sure." Payton grabbed it but didn't flip through it as much as she wanted to. She wanted to be able to read it when Kendra wasn't watching over her.

"I need to speak with you, in private. It's about tomorrow."

"Okay." They were in private, but Payton knew that Kendra meant in her office.

Once again, Payton found herself in Kendra's office with the door closed and locked. She wasn't sure to where to stand, and Kendra hadn't offered her to sit in any of the chairs. Kendra took up her preferred spot and leaned against the back of her desk, her short skirt riding up. Payton swallowed.

"Bellamy said you are requesting half a day tomorrow."

"I am." Fear ran through Payton's chest, suddenly afraid Kendra was about to rescind her ability to take the time off to bring Liam to his visitation, and it was of course a Tuesday, so her mother was out. She was already working through her third and fourth back up plans when Kendra stopped her.

"I have some concerns about your work."

"I'm sorry?" Payton was lost. She had not been expecting this conversation. She thought everything was going well. Bellamy always praised her for her thoroughness and her ability to get work done quickly. Kendra hadn't made so much as a comment about her work. She'd just taken the papers and gone on with her day.

Kendra sighed and stretched her shoulders. "I asked you a few weeks ago to do me a favor, and you haven't done it."

Payton fell into her defensive mode. "Bellamy hasn't had any new clients."

"I asked you to schedule them in ten minutes before the meeting for Bellamy. You are not doing that."

Her lips opened and closed several times. She wasn't sure what to do. She had done it, she just hadn't told Kendra she had done it, and often times, Bellamy was so prepared that she was ready to go early and when she heard her clients come in, she would go find them. Payton couldn't control Bellamy, neither could Kendra for that matter, but Payton was pretty sure Kendra wanted to.

"I did—"

"Don't lie to me, Payton. I've seen the schedule. I know what you have done and haven't done, and frankly, I'm a little concerned about you losing your job if you can't meet our standards."

Payton was lost. Bellamy had said nothing on Saturday when she'd seen her, or Friday when they had both stayed late to work. But Kendra had access to Bellamy in ways Payton didn't, so they could have talked about it and she wouldn't have known.

"I can't lose this job," Payton answered, her voice wavering. "I need this job. I like this job."

"Well, we can do something about that."

"What can I do? I'll do anything."

The look on Kendra's face did not bode well for Payton's future. She'd gone from closed off to devilish. Kendra's eyes widened, but her lips thinned and turned upward into a half-sneer half-smile. Payton felt as though she was being stalked like prey. Her heart raced, her hands were sweaty, she had no idea what to do or what Kendra wanted, but she had a strong feeling she wasn't going to like it at all.

"I have seen the way you look at me."

"I . . . what?" Payton swallowed, trying to wet her suddenly dry mouth.

Kendra let out a breath and put her foot up on the seat of the chair next to the edge of the desk. Payton couldn't tear her gaze away. She knew what was happening, but she couldn't believe it. Nothing like this had ever happened to her. She couldn't force her legs to move—she couldn't make her voice work.

Kendra slipped a hand to her knee, never moving her gaze from Payton's face. "I think you need to show me how much you want this job."

"I . . ." Payton had no idea what to say. Her mind screamed no, but her voice wouldn't work. This woman held everything in her hands, all the power to fire Payton, to cut off her benefits which hadn't even kicked in yet, the power to ruin her ability to find another job in another law firm. She couldn't go back to school for something else. She didn't have the time or the money.

"Payton. I'm waiting."

"F-for what?"

"On your knees."

Payton's body moved of its own accord. She stepped forward, glancing once toward the door when she heard Bellamy return from a meeting. Kendra must have heard it too because the gleam in her eye deepened. Payton's chest rose and fell as she got onto her knees in front of Kendra, who pulled up her skirt and exposed herself, no underwear in sight. She gave a definitive look to Payton, ordering her to begin.

Payton drew in a deep breath and closed her eyes. Maybe if she closed them and didn't look then she wouldn't have to think about it. As soon as she started, Kendra's voice echoed. Kendra leaned back on the desk with a hand behind her and rutted her hips. Payton tried to work as quickly as possible to end the moment, to end the awkwardness, to end the tension.

Kendra reached down and gripped Payton's hair, tugging hard until Payton felt individual hairs rip from her head. Payton grunted at the pain and doubled her efforts. The fastest way out of the situation now was to get Kendra off. Then she could escape and leave. Her mind whirred with the possibilities of what might happen if she were to just get up and leave, but none of the scenarios were good, none of them came out the right way.

The knock on the door made Payton stop, but Kendra shoved her back down. Her voice called over, "Give me a minute, I'm in the middle of something."

"Okay," Bellamy's sweet voice called back.

Payton wished she would open the door so she would see what was happening, but then she didn't. She didn't want to be part of that hurt for Bellamy, didn't want to be the cause of it. Cast into silence, Payton focused on what Kendra wanted, gave it to her, then sat back, wiping her fingers over her mouth. She didn't dare look Kendra in the eye until Kendra reached down and lifted her chin up.

"That was good. I think you'll last. Now go on, don't want to keep clients waiting."

Payton stood up and headed for the door while Kendra shifted and pulled her skirt down like nothing had ever happened. With her heart still in her throat, Payton went to her desk. She struggled to concentrate on anything that day. Any time one of the office doors opened or closed, she would jump. Any time Kendra came into the main room, she would tense.

She kept waiting for it all to fall apart, for Bellamy to figure it out, for Bellamy to—in essence—rescue her, but she knew it wouldn't happen. Fairy tales weren't made for women like her. Women like Bellamy maybe, but not for ones like Payton. When the hour was up for the end of the day, Payton made a fast exit. She needed a shower, and she needed distance. She had no idea what she was going to do tomorrow.

CHAPTER 6

THE PAST WEEK HAD BEEN ODD. SINCE SATURDAY, Bellamy had had a strange feeling in the pit of her stomach, and she couldn't shake it.

Her marriage had no doubt been over for years. She couldn't take any more of the cheating, the lying, the pulling all the weight. But something about Kendra had been odd that week, too. She'd seemed happier than she had in a long time. Whether it was because Bellamy had finally broken down and had sex with her for the first time in months or if it was for some other reason, Bellamy had no idea. Just everything about Kendra had been weird. She tried to avoid her as best she could.

However, she had also noticed Payton's tension, which had been above and beyond anything she had seen in the past month. She knew there was something going on, something Payton hadn't shared. She'd deduced it had to do with Liam because anyone could look at that situation and realize it wasn't over and done with. Payton was protective of him, and she clearly loved him deeply.

There was hardly any resemblance between the two except the way they smiled. In that case, their cheeks moved the same way, and their eyes crinkled the same. Liam had made Bellamy's heart melt. She had enjoyed seeing him even for a brief few minutes. She glanced at her watch and noted that it was after five. Kendra had already left for the day, no doubt, but Bellamy still had a motion to file and a client to contact.

When she headed out to the front office to get some papers, she stopped. Payton sat at her desk, but she was completely still. Taking a risk, Bellamy stepped over to Payton and slipped a hand on her shoulder. Payton jumped, almost to a standing position as she spun around with wide eyes.

Bellamy stepped back with her hands up in the air, trying to make Payton understand she didn't want to hurt her. When Payton recognized it was Bellamy, she visibly relaxed and leaned into the back of her chair.

"I'm sorry," Payton muttered. "It's been a long week."

"What's going on? You haven't been yourself all week."

Payton's lips tightened into a thin line, and she refused to look Bellamy in the eye. Had Bellamy not been avoiding her and trying to keep distance from her and had they been in an entirely different situation, she may have reached down and tugged Payton's chin up to force her to look directly in her eye.

"Payton, talk to me. This isn't you."

"It's nothing."

"Come on, tell me what's going on. I can't have you freaking out on a client, but I really can't have you hurting and in so much turmoil. Please, let me help."

Tears welled in Payton's eyes, but she shook her head. "I'm fine."

"You're clearly not." Bellamy gripped Payton's hand and pulled her to stand. Then she dragged her into her office and shut the door. She thought about locking it, hesitated with her hand over it but opted to leave it open. She wanted Payton to feel like she could leave any time she wanted, but she also knew they needed the privacy and safety of the room. Payton looked so worn, so tired, so lost. Itching to encompass her small form in her arms and give her a hug of reassurance, Bellamy resisted the idea. Touching Payton hadn't done either of them well in the past, and touching her in the front office just now—that was weird.

Bellamy stared at Payton, hoping she would start the conversation, but when there was nothing, she let out a breath. She wracked her mind for what could be wrong, anything, because if she truly thought about it, she didn't know that much about Payton's home life. She knew she had custody of her nephew and she was fiercely protective over him, so she figured there was still some type of legal battle going on there, but beyond that, she knew very little. She hadn't pushed it either. She didn't want to seem overly friendly, to give Kendra any ammo. Kendra knew she'd cheated, that she'd had a one-night stand months before, but Kendra had no idea Payton was the other woman.

Going with the first question that came to mind, particularly with how Payton had reacted to the touch on her shoulder, Bellamy asked, "Is someone at home hitting you?"

"What? No." Payton shook her head, her eyes wide. "It's just me and Liam."

Bellamy wanted to walk closer, but she stopped herself. "Then please, tell me what's going on. I want you to thrive here, and you're distracted. Something is bothering you."

"It's nothing."

"Payton, don't lie to me. Please. We've built a good rapport here. Let's not ruin it because you think I'm stupid. I can clearly see something is bothering you."

"Nothing more than what is bothering you." Payton's baby blue eyes were sharp as an edge when they lifted to lock with Bellamy's.

"Excuse me?"

Payton drew in a sharp breath. "You told me months ago it was done between you and Kendra. I can see why. All you two do is argue and fight and shout and yell. The tension in this office is through the roof. Anyone can feel it walking in when the two of you are here."

"I don't see how this is relevant."

Snorting, Payton shook her head. "Don't try to fix my problems when you have your own to fix."

"Payton."

"No! Just stop. This isn't your problem."

"I can help."

"You don't even know what it is. Stop while you're ahead." Payton moved around Bellamy and headed straight for the door.

Surprised, Bellamy turned to follow Payton but stopped. Payton was right. That wasn't her battle. She wanted to be there for her, to support her, but she was Payton's boss first, and she was also still married to Kendra. Nothing she had done in the past six months had given her the ability to divorce her wife and get what she wanted from it. Letting out a breath, Bellamy closed her eyes when she heard the door shut as Payton left for the day.

With a heavy heart, she packed up her bag, vowing to work the rest of the night from home, but she wanted to talk to Kendra and get her thoughts on it. Kendra, while obnoxious most times, was very good at reading people in ways Bellamy was not. If there was something wrong with Payton, Kendra would know and would likely have some sort of solution.

As soon as she got home, she headed into the den and found Kendra at the table with papers strewn out. Files after files were there. Confused, Bellamy leaned over Kendra's shoulder and skimmed some of the words. "That's the Holt's file."

"It is," Kendra answered. "They have a trial coming up."

"That's my account."

"Not anymore."

"What?" Bellamy sidestepped so she could look Kendra full on. "What do you mean it's not my account?"

"They thought you were too busy, so they asked me to handle this one."

"When did they even come in to see me?"

"The fact you have to ask that means you are too busy." Kendra leaned over the desk and pushed one of her blonde curls behind her ear.

Sighing and giving up, Bellamy dropped into the chair next to Kendra and closed her eyes. "Have you noticed anything weird with Payton this week?"

"Nope."

"Are you sure? She's been . . . I don't know . . . weird."

Kendra shifted a glance to Bellamy before moving back down to look at her papers. "Maybe you should talk to her."

"I tried. She wouldn't tell me anything. Kept telling me to deal with my own problems."

"No doubt she is wise beyond her years."

"True." Bellamy picked up some of the almonds Kendra had in a bowl and popped one between her lips. "Are you sure, though? It's been all week."

Kendra let out a long sigh and shifted so her focus was on Bellamy. "Why do you want to know so badly? Interested in a quick tryst with her?"

Bellamy paled, the heat rushing from her face only to be replaced with a cold, clammy sweat. "I'm sorry, what?"

"Don't think I haven't noticed you two getting close. I know how you work, Bellamy. You do not make fast moves."

"I'm not—"

"Didn't say you were." Kendra shifted back to her paperwork.

Bellamy cocked her head to the side, trying to figure out what Kendra was not saying because there was definitely an undercurrent to the conversation she was missing. Biding her time and waiting in the silence, she eventually gave up.

"What are you talking about?"

"It's clear you don't want to be in this marriage." Kendra set her pen down on her papers and folded her hands. "It's clear what happened last weekend was pure pity and purely for your personal gain. And I know you have been stealing and shoring up clients. Here's the deal, Bellamy. You may divorce me, you can end this marriage that we have built for ten years, this relationship we have built for thirteen years, but you will never get *my* law firm."

Shocked didn't even cover what Bellamy felt. The entire plan she had built up shattered in front of her, but she knew she was still on the right track. Just because Kendra knew about her plans didn't mean she still couldn't put them into place. It meant she would have to work harder and faster. Keeping her cool as she had trained herself for years, Bellamy remained in a relaxed position as she popped another almond between her lips.

"I will divorce you, Kendra. This marriage has been over for years. There's nothing here for either one of us anymore. I will divorce you, and I will take our law firm out from under you so fast you won't even know how it happened."

With another almond in her mouth, Bellamy stood up and stalked out of the den and up to her office. Shutting and locking the door behind her, she let out a breath. They didn't even have it in them to argue anymore, and that said something. When Kendra fully gave up their dream, there was nothing left.

The pounding on the door surprised her. Bellamy jumped and stared at it as Kendra slammed her fist again against the wood. "Don't you dare walk away from me!"

Perhaps Bellamy had been wrong about how much fight Kendra had left.

"I know you slept with her."

Bellamy wanted to deny it, wanted to but couldn't. She had slept with Payton, one rainy night after she had truly given in to what she'd known for years. Kendra would never understand though, but that night of indulgence had been the best sex she'd had in over a decade.

"You're delusional," Bellamy answered.

"We'll see about that."

Bellamy didn't respond, but the assault on the door started in again. Kendra was pissed, and she was going to throw her fit until she got tired of it. Bellamy let out a breath and sat down in her chair, waiting it out. If she didn't react, it wouldn't last very long. If she didn't feed into the tantrum, it would end. She just had to keep telling herself that and hope it was true.

PAYTON HAD BEEN ABLE TO RELAX THROUGH THE next week when nothing major had happened. The tension between Bellamy and Kendra, however, had increased tenfold. There was no avoiding it now. Any time the two of them were in the same room, which was rare, it drowned Payton, but when they stayed in their separate offices, it was mostly manageable.

No one had said a word about what had happened in Kendra's office, and Payton could only assume Bellamy didn't know. From what she knew of Bellamy, if she did know, she would want to take immediate action in some way, shape, or form. Payton worked on keeping her head down and focused on the task at hand. She also tried to avoid Kendra as much as she could, but since Bellamy was typically gone to court or meetings or lunch things and Kendra wasn't, she was stuck with Kendra.

Payton got up to put a note on Bellamy's desk with an immediate meeting that needed to happen with Mr. Bildridge. When she was leaving Bellamy's office, Kendra stood in the doorway to her office, staring at her like she was prime rib for Christmas. Payton faltered in her step. She didn't want to ask Kendra if she needed something because she was pretty sure what the answer was going to be. With her heart racing, she tried to walk by and toward her desk, but Kendra put a hand on her belly to stop her.

"I need you in my office for a minute."

Payton didn't want to go into Kendra's office. Never again did she want to step into that office. Kendra took her hand and led her in, Payton's feet moving without her consent. As soon as they were inside and the door was shut, Kendra smiled. It sickened Payton, but there was nothing she could do to stop it. With a breath, she tried to focus on anything else in the room. Not Kendra's sleek pants, not her blouse that was unbuttoned too low, not the bright red lipstick she always wore, or the cool gray eye shadow painted on her eyelids or the quirk of her lips.

"I thought we could use some alone time to maybe pick up where we left off."

Payton swallowed. She had no idea what Kendra was thinking when she said pick up where they left off. There was nothing to pick up. Kendra stepped in closer, and Payton tried to move back, but Kendra's soft hand on hers forced her to stop.

"Maybe this time I can give you something."

Panic welled in Payton's chest. She had to find a way out. She was done with the job. She couldn't stay there and keep working if Kendra was going to continue on in this manner. Kendra's voice reached her ears.

"I talked to Bellamy about you. I thought perhaps you and her may have had something going on with all the late nights working, but she assured me I was incorrect."

"You are," Payton whispered, her voice quieter than she had anticipated, but she wasn't sure if speaking had made any difference.

Kendra grinned, her white teeth shining in the harsh light of the room. "Well, then I suppose that leaves you open for me."

Payton shook her head when Kendra took a step toward her. She couldn't do this again—she couldn't bring herself to be in that situation again. She was just about to say something when the door burst open and Bellamy walked through it. She halted sharply when her gaze settled on Payton. Bellamy's lips parted.

"Mr. Bildridge, he's got a case. It's huge. I'm going to need you in on it." Bellamy shifted her gaze from Payton to Kendra.

Kendra clapped her hands together and walked toward Bellamy. Gripping Bellamy by the cheeks, she planted a loud, fake kiss on her lips. Payton's heart clenched as she walked around the two of them and headed for the door. She didn't dare look Bellamy in the eye. She would know what had just about happened; she would see through everything.

Payton sat at her desk, panic still shooting through her chest. She had two interviews lined up. After the last week, she hadn't wasted time trying to find a new job, but she couldn't wait it out until she had one of them lined up. With tears in her eyes, Payton pulled up a blank document on her computer and started typing. She was resigning. Effective immediately.

She would wait until Kendra left for the day, she would finish out what she had open and what files Bellamy needed for the next week or two that she could do, but then she would give Bellamy her resignation when no one else was there. She wasn't going to face Kendra again. As much as she needed the income and the benefits, she was not going to stand for anything happening in that office.

She printed her resignation, folded it carefully, and slipped it into an envelope after signing it. She put it into the top drawer of her desk where she knew it would sit and wait for a few more hours. Bellamy and Kendra stayed in Kendra's office for hours, apparently talking strategy and the new case Mr. Bildridge was bringing them. Payton didn't know, and frankly, she didn't really care. If it hadn't been for Bellamy coming in unannounced, she had known what was going to happen, and she couldn't put herself in that situation again.

Staring at the one small picture of Liam on her desk that she had allowed herself, Payton let out a breath. Everything had to be for him, but it also had to be for her. She had to be healthy enough and strong enough to take care of him, and she couldn't do that with Kendra as her boss. If it was just Bellamy, then maybe, but Kendra was out of the question. With a huff, Payton turned to her paperwork to finish everything out. It was her last day at her new job, and as much as that hurt, she knew it was the right decision.

When Bellamy came out of Kendra's office, her cheeks were flushed, but she had a determined look in her eyes. She stopped in the middle of their offices and let out a breath before listing off a dozen things she needed Payton to do. Payton knew that she wouldn't get them all done by the end of the day, but she could at least get some of it finished.

With silence, she nodded and turned back to her computer to get a start. Bellamy went to her office, and luckily, Kendra stayed far away until she left. As soon as the door closed and Kendra was gone, the entire atmosphere of the offices changed. It was still high-paced and stressful, but the tension, the bad feeling, was gone. Payton relaxed, letting out a breath, and she was able to work far more quickly.

It neared eight when she printed the last of the filings she'd be able to complete that day. She grabbed her resignation and stood up from her desk after shoving her one picture of Liam into her bag. She was done. With a breath and a prayer for her nerves, Payton took everything and headed for Bellamy's office.

CHAPTER 7

Bellamy let out a breath when Payton walked into her office. "Oh good, you have it."

"Yeah." Payton handed the paperwork over but kept an envelope on top of the stack.

Bellamy stared at it, pursing her lips. She could push and get an answer, or she could not and let Payton come to her with whatever it was. Sighing, Bellamy shifted in her chair and pulled her glasses from her face, settling them down onto the desktop. She had a feeling Payton wanted to talk to her and needed her full attention. She'd come into the room with tension riding in her shoulders.

When Payton didn't budge, Bellamy pushed them both to talk. "Do you need something?"

"Uh . . . here." Payton shoved the envelope over and into Bellamy's waiting hands.

"What's this?"

Payton didn't answer, but Bellamy stared up at her as she opened the back of the envelope and pulled the paper out. She knew what it was before she even read the first line. Her stomach sank. Her head ached. Pursing her lips together, she skimmed the note, saw the words 'effective immediately' at the end and sighed.

"What happened?"

"It's all in there."

"There's *nothing* in here!" Bellamy tossed the paper on her desk and stood up, leaning over her desk, her hands against the papers as she stared directly into Payton's eyes. "Tell me what happened. I don't want platitudes. I want the truth. Whatever it was happened two weeks ago. I know that. You have not been the same since. Your work has faltered. Your attitude has changed. So what happened? Out with it."

Payton looked like she was going to cry. Bellamy backtracked. She hadn't wanted to cause any more harm, but for the first time in over a year, Kendra had actually managed to hire a paralegal who knew what they were doing and who lasted long enough to get a sense of routine and flow to their work life.

"I can't work here anymore."

"That's what's in this letter. I want to know why." Standing up straight, Bellamy put her arms across her chest and waited. She wanted to know why they kept losing paralegals, why no one lasted outside of the fact she and Kendra fought literally all the time except the last two weeks. Curiously, since the time Payton had changed.

Payton shook her head, tears unbidden sliding down her cheeks. This time, Bellamy didn't hesitate. When she saw Payton crying, she swung around the desk and wrapped her small form against her chest. She ran her hands up and down Payton's back and over the back of her head. She kept quiet while Payton clung to the fabric at her blouse, no doubt wrinkling it, but she didn't care. Something was very wrong. Her heart knew it as much as her head.

It took several minutes for Payton to calm, and Bellamy stepped away, cupping both of Payton's cheeks. "I'm going to shut the door, okay? Just in case anyone comes in."

They both knew who anyone was, that neither wanted Kendra to interrupt them. Payton nodded at her, and Bellamy moved to the door shutting and locking it this time. She then took Payton by the hand and led her over to the couch right in front of her large window.

As they sat, Bellamy let out a breath. "You have to talk to someone, Payton. I don't know what happened, but you know my door has always been open. I know you're dealing with a lot at home, and we can work around your schedule if you need more time to spend with Liam. I don't want you to neglect him. He is your priority."

Payton shook her head as more tears streamed down her cheeks, curling under her chin and dropping on her pants and the couch cushion. Reaching up, Bellamy wiped them away as much as she could, but she wanted to let Payton do the talking.

"She . . ." Payton's voice broke.

"Kendra?"

Payton nodded. Bellamy gripped Payton's fingers and squeezed. "What did she do?"

"I can't. I'm sorry."

"Payton, if you don't tell me, she may very well do it again. I can't do anything about it if I don't know what happened."

Nodding, Payton let out a breath then took a deep, steadying breath. "You're right. You can't, and this . . . it can't happen again."

"What happened?"

"About a month ago, Kendra wanted me to start scheduling your clients in ten minutes before they were to meet with you."

"What for?"

Payton pursed her lips and glanced up at Bellamy.

"Right. To steal them because she realized I was getting close to having enough."

"Having enough for what?" Payton's voice was stronger with the question, but it wasn't what they were there to talk about.

"Doesn't matter. You did it, of course, because you thought it would be your job."

"Kind of? I also made sure you knew they were coming in early, which kind of ruined Kendra's plans. She wasn't very happy about that."

"Okay, so that's not really an offense to warrant an immediate resignation. What happened after that? Because like I said, I know something changed a few weeks ago."

One more deep breath, and Payton staring at her shoes had the confession on the tip of her tongue. "She told me I had to—you know—in order to keep my job because I was not doing a good job."

"I don't know what 'you know' means." But she did. Bellamy knew exactly what it meant. Her heart shattered, but for her own sake and for Payton's, she needed to hear the words.

Payton's cheeks and nose reddened as she silently pleaded with Bellamy to not make her say it, but they needed the words. Bellamy's heart rapped a scared rhythm—her breaths came in short. If Payton confessed what Bellamy was pretty sure she was thinking, then she knew why all those other women had quit and she knew why Kendra only hired women.

"She made me go down on her."

Horrified. Heart-broken. Not for herself but for Payton. Hurt. Everything came at her at once, and she was overwhelmed. Bellamy let go of Payton's hands and closed her eyes, letting out a heavy breath. Those words were enough. With tears in her own eyes, she shook her head and stared at Payton.

"Do not *ever* think this is your fault. Please. I don't even know where to begin right now except there. This is *not* your fault, ever. I—"

"It's not yours either."

Taken aback, Bellamy closed her mouth confused. "What?"

"Don't think this is your fault either, Bellamy. You didn't

know. There was nothing you could do about it. Nothing at all. But I also don't want you thinking you can fix this either."

"I can." Bellamy was dead set. "I can, and I will fix this, as best as I can. She will not do this to anyone else."

"How? How are you ever going to be able to do that?"

Pursing her lips, Bellamy stared directly into Payton's baby blue and still innocent eyes. She loved that about Payton. She was so innocent and so mature, wise beyond her years and saddled with responsibility she never wanted or needed to have placed on her shoulders, but she was still so young. Cupping her cheek again because she couldn't resist, and if she was resigning, there was no reason not to. "I'm going to take her down. Divorce. The law firm. Everything. I've already been working on it for months, but this seals it. She is done for."

"Bellamy."

"No. Don't even. She dug her own grave on this one." This time when Bellamy stood, anger settled into her chest. She paced to her desk and back before shaking her head at Payton. "I wish you had told me sooner. I can't imagine trying to work with her around, being alone with her in here."

"You don't have a choice. You have to leave. You can't be here all the time."

Bellamy snorted. "Watch me. I will be now. I can move stuff around. It's about to ease up anyway for a little bit. I'll be here every second of the day. I won't let her do that again."

Standing up, Payton moved right in front of her. She was so strong. Bellamy recognized that strength, that tenacity, that ability to get back up after being torn down. "You can't hire another woman."

"I know. I'll have to find a way to hire someone else or no one at all."

Payton took a deep breath. "How long do you think it'll take you?"

"Take me to what?"

"File for divorce."

Surprised, Bellamy shook her head as she worked through a few quick calculations. She needed ninety percent of the client base in order to force Kendra to sell. She was at eight-seven. "No more than two months."

"I'll do it."

"No." Bellamy clenched her jaw. "No. Your resignation is valid, and I accept. The answer is no."

"You can't let anyone else be put in the position I was in and you need someone here so you can get to that point to file. I can handle myself."

Bellamy wanted to tell Payton the opposite—if anything of the last two weeks was true—but she didn't want to tear her down any more than she already was that night. She was vulnerable as hell, and Bellamy wasn't going to let her stay in a position like that.

"I can do this," Payton once again reassured her.

"No." Bellamy moved to her desk, reached over it and grabbed a piece of paper to make sure she could do this in two months, and as she skimmed it, she realized something was way off with the numbers. She did not want to make it any longer than necessary. When she stood back on both her feet, Payton was right there.

"I will do this."

"No."

"Bellamy."

"The answer is no, Payton. That's it."

Payton shook her head, tears starting in her eyes. Bellamy tried to hold her resolve. She couldn't put anyone in that position again. Aside from the liability issues, it was downright unethical. Payton knocked her chin up with a set look in her eyes. "I'm doing this."

Without another word, she gripped Bellamy's cheeks and brought their mouths together. Bellamy's stomach twisted with pleasure and fear, and she drew in a sharp breath as their lips touched. Payton pressed against her, a hand skimming down her side to her hip and holding on tight while her tongue tried to slip between Bellamy's lips, but Bellamy wouldn't let her.

Sadness ripped through Bellamy as she pushed Payton away. She let out a breath, her chest rising and falling sharply as she gave Payton a gloomy look. "Any other time, Payton, but after what you just shared? I'm not going to take advantage of anything. I'm not going to let you be vulnerable with me and then do this. I'm just not."

"I want to."

Bellamy let out a breath. She had known their attraction wasn't gone. She had wanted it to be, every day she walked into the office and smelled Payton's perfume she had wanted her allure to vanish. Instead, she avoided it as best as she could and played the role of the professional. "Payton—"

"This isn't anything new, Bellamy. Every time I see you I feel it. I can't stop it. I tried."

"You're over twenty years younger than me. You have a son to take care of. You have your whole life ahead of you." Bellamy laid the groundwork. She had not anticipated needing to have this conversation. While she knew they were both still attracted to each other, she had not thought it would come to this, especially on a night with the confession Payton had just given her. It was almost too much for her feeble mind to handle.

"So? That didn't matter months ago." Payton gripped Bellamy's hands, holding tight and stepping in closer.

Glancing to the ceiling, Bellamy let out a sigh as she reworked her reasoning. For someone who argued for a living, she was having a very hard time forcing herself to come up with rebuttals or at least giving them half-heartedly. "That wasn't . . . this is different. You know it is. I'm your boss now. That puts us in an entirely different situation. Not to mention, Payton, after what you just told me, my wife—the person I am legally married to, the woman I have been with for thirteen years—raped you. That isn't just nothing."

"You aren't your wife."

"Well, that's for damn sure. But no, Payton. The answer is no—to everything. We shouldn't even be having this conversation. You handed in your resignation. I accept it. This is the end of any relationship between us, at least . . . anything in the capacity of me being your boss and any potential personal relationship. I'm not going to do this to you."

"Do what to me?" Payton's voice rose in pitch.

Bellamy wasn't going to argue with her. She'd made her statement, she'd put her foot down, and she'd made the decision for both of them. There was nothing to grasp onto except a few last legs of sexual and physical attraction neither of them wanted to fully let go of.

"I'm done." Bellamy cut her hand across the air to signify an end to the conversation. "You can leave now, Payton. I will file your resignation with the rest of them, and I will deal with Kendra, assuming you don't press charges and deal with her yourself, which I really wish you'd do. She deserves it."

Payton's lips parted. "What do you mean press charges?"

Sighing, Bellamy softened her tone. "What she did was against the law. It's sexual coercion. You are free to press charges. I plan on reporting it not only to the police but also to the bar association, but these things take time, especially when they don't come from the victim themselves. You have the option to press charges if you want."

"I can't. I have enough legal battles to fight."

Furrowing her brow, Bellamy shook her head. "I'm going to come back to that in a second. Stay with me here for a minute. I'm serious. I want you to consider it. You have time to file a report. It doesn't have to be right now, but this is nothing to be taken lightly, Payton. It was wrong. There is no other conversation or opinion about it. There is no way to justify it. What Kendra did was reprehensible."

Payton swallowed.

"Do you understand that?"

Payton nodded ever so slightly but wouldn't look Bellamy in the eye. That move alone told Bellamy she had made the absolute right decision to put a stop to everything that had been about to happen, everything Payton had wanted to happen.

"Now, what other legal battles are you fighting? You haven't mentioned anything, and you work for a law firm. We're the perfect place for advice and to pick brains."

Payton ran a hand through her hair and moved back to the couch, collapsing in it. Bellamy made the quick decision to follow her, sitting next to Payton, although this time, she made sure to maintain her distance.

"It's my nephew."

"I surmised."

"His father's trial is next week."

"Trial?"

Payton let out a breath. "I didn't tell you why I had Liam, but when he was six weeks old, my sister called 911 because her baby daddy had gotten upset about the baby crying and shook him, hit him, and well, beat the crap out of a baby. He had both legs broken, a shoulder dislocated, and bruises everywhere. Obviously, Liam was taken by social services."

"That's how you ended up with him."

"Yes. After he was released from the hospital, he obviously wasn't going back there. My sister and Luis were arrested. They both confessed. She got a lesser sentence since she didn't do the actual beating, it was her first offense, and she called the appropriate services to get help. He, however, has been in jail ever since. He's signing over his rights as part of his sentencing to get a lesser sentence."

"Makes sense," Bellamy commented. She'd heard of that before, especially with certain judges. She wasn't sure she completely agreed with it, but she couldn't control what other people did. She had learned that lesson a long time ago. "And your sister?"

"Refuses to give up her parental rights. She's a drug addict, too. So as soon as she got out—which was before Liam was even released from the hospital—she insisted on reunification. She does this every few months. Insists on it, goes through the steps to stay sober for thirty days, gets one or two visits in, then starts using again. It's been this constant cycle."

Bellamy nodded. "And you have to stand by and watch. There's nothing you can do."

"I can sue her for custody."

"You can." Bellamy clenched her jaw. Taking a risk, she reached out and pressed her hand to Payton's knee. "You can do that if you want. I'll even help you if you want. But what about Liam?"

"What about Liam?"

"What story do you want for him? Do you want him to think you didn't give your sister every chance possible to make changes because you wanted him or do you want to give her all the chances possible knowing it will eventually end up in your favor?"

Payton stared at Bellamy near dumfounded. "I hadn't thought of it like that."

"Well, do, please, because it will make a world of difference to him if you give your sister every chance before her rights are legally terminated by the court against her will—and if she doesn't change, it will happen. You know it. I know it. CPS knows it. It's just a matter of time, which is something you have. You have the time to be patient."

Payton agreed. "You're right."

"But the offer stands. If you need legal help, I will do it."

Bellamy put her hands into the air, palms out toward Payton, and smiled. "Pro bono even."

Payton smirked. "Thanks. I may just take you up on that. Especially with how slow everything moves in family court."

"Ah, yes, it is tedious. They mostly want to make sure they're not making any detrimental decisions, which is stupid, because of course they are, and they make ridiculous decisions every day."

"Tell me about it."

Having fallen into an easier conversation, Bellamy relaxed a bit. She still planned on confronting Kendra when she had a chance because she was most definitely moving out of the master bedroom until their divorce was finalized and they figured out who got the house. Lost in her thoughts, she was surprised when Payton's hand touched her arm. Staring down at Payton's slim fingers and following the line of her arm up to Payton's eyes, Bellamy chided herself. She had to stop doing that just as much as Payton had to.

"I'll think about it," Payton's voice was strong.

"Think about what?"

"Filing a report and pressing charges."

"Good." Bellamy let a smile land on her lips because she truly was happy Payton would consider it. "And thank you for telling me. I know that wasn't easy, especially because she's my wife."

Payton shrugged. "Maybe by law, but you two don't act very wifely toward each other."

Snorting, Bellamy nodded her agreement. "You're absolutely right."

"I still want to kiss you."

Bellamy hissed at Payton's confession, because not-so-secretly, she wanted Payton to kiss her. Her body listed forward, but she stopped herself. "We can't. I'm serious, Payton. This is not the time."

"I understand. Doesn't stop me from wanting you."

Letting out a groan, Bellamy closed her eyes and remembered Payton's mouth pressed against her own just moments before and months ago. It would take her heaven and hell to ever forget that feeling. When she opened her eyes, Payton grinned at her.

"You want it, too."

Bellamy pointed a finger at her, a smile tugging at her lips. "Don't push your luck."

"Just admit it, and that'll satisfy me for months."

Bellamy lived into the silence of the moment. She knew she was playing with fire, but she couldn't help herself. Anytime someone told her not to touch, all she wanted was to touch. "I want to kiss you."

"See? That wasn't so hard, was it?"

"Enough. You need to leave." Bellamy pushed to stand and walk far away from the temptation right in front of her. "I'll see you around, Payton."

"Yeah, you will."

Bellamy turned to figure out what Payton meant, but she'd already slipped from her office and out of the door. Not wanting to risk it, she let her go, listening as Payton grabbed her stuff and left the office. After sitting in her chair for a few more minutes and staring at nothing in particular, she turned to her computer and let out a sigh. She suddenly had a lot more work and a lot more motions to file. Whether or not Payton pressed charges, Bellamy was going to do her damnedest to get justice.

CHAPTER 8

Bellamy got to the office early on Monday morning. She had worked as best as she could to rearrange her entire work schedule over the weekend, but she hadn't been able to finish everything without contacting some people who were only available during the week. She was moving everything to her office because Bellamy wasn't going to leave Kendra alone with anyone on her watch.

She had already contacted the bar association, she had contacted the police, she had filed the report, but she hadn't seen anything come of it—not that she expected it to in two days. With a breath, she shifted around a few more work things before she settled down to focus on paperwork and strategy for Mr. Bildridge's case. She'd need to find at least two more clients, depending on how big their caseload was, in order to finally file to buy out Kendra.

She wanted her firm. She wasn't going to give up all the hard work she had put into it, but at the same time, it was certainly something she could live without. She had no doubt the vast majority of her clients would follow her if she started up her own firm, but the idea of starting from near scratch was so unappealing, not to mention she wanted to stick it to Kendra for what she'd done.

The phone rang, shrilling through the quiet office. Kendra wasn't even in yet, not that Bellamy expected her to be. When she popped the phone to her ear, she was about to speak when she stopped. Someone else was talking on the line. Narrowing her gaze, Bellamy listened carefully.

Payton's voice echoed at her. Anger built in her chest, and Bellamy let out a breath as Payton finished the call, taking a message. Bellamy groaned. She should have anticipated this. Not only had she pretty much forced Payton out of the office, but Payton was as stubborn and as smart as she was. They were going to have to duke it out, but hopefully Bellamy had the upper hand.

She stood up from her desk and walked out her office, down the very short hallway to the open front office. Clearing her throat, she caught Payton's attention. When Payton turned to face her, she had a smile on her lips and a pink slip in her hand.

"I've got a message for you."

"I'm aware," Bellamy answered, keeping her voice firm and monotone. "My office, now."

Bellamy didn't wait as she turned and walked back into her office. It didn't take long for Payton to follow her in. Bellamy shut the door and spun around. Payton still had that determined grin on her face, but under the façade, Bellamy could tell she was worried about the conversation about to happen.

"What are you doing here?"

"I came in to work."

Bellamy crossed her arms. "You resigned."

"I took it back."

"No, you didn't. I accepted your resignation without contest. I filed it."

"Then where is it?"

"What?"

84

"Where is my resignation? If you filed it, where is it?"

Cocking her head to the side, Bellamy glared. "You didn't."

"Can't accept something that isn't in existence."

"Payton."

"No. Don't use that tone with me." Payton pointed her finger at Bellamy. "This is my decision to make. I changed my mind. I want to keep working here."

"You shouldn't. You shouldn't want it at all. You should want to run in the other direction and hide and forget this firm ever existed. I'm so sorry that this had to be your first experience in a paralegal position."

Payton stepped in closer to Bellamy, that smile back on her lips as she tilted her chin up and grinned. "It hasn't been all bad."

Bellamy's throat went dry. It was as if their entire conversation the Friday before had gone in one ear and out of the other. She didn't understand. Her wife was a monster, one who had no doubt hurt Payton in extreme ways, and yet there Payton was, standing in front of her and willingly wanting to be there.

"This is ridiculous. Get out," Bellamy ordered.

"Are you firing me?" Payton crossed her arms and set her jaw, her feet firm on the ground so Bellamy knew she wasn't budging without an answer.

Shaking her head, Bellamy swore. "Damn it, you know I'm not firing you. You quit."

"Says who?"

"Says you! In the resignation letter you handed me on Friday. Don't turn this back on me, Payton. You quit."

"I'm not going to abandon you."

Bellamy froze. Those words had been most unexpected. She had no idea what to say or how to respond. When she said nothing, Payton stepped in even closer, seeming to test the bounds of their willpower.

"I may have only worked here a few months, Bellamy, but I

think I figured out why you have stayed married to Kendra for as long as you have, why you have put up with a lot of the arguing, and why you are refusing to move forward."

"And why do you think that is?" Bellamy's voice was low, dangerous even. They were stepping close to the line she never wanted to cross. She towered over Payton, trying to intimidate her, but it wasn't working. Payton wasn't daunted by her attempts.

Payton raised an eyebrow. "You don't want to be alone. It scares you. You have this fear of people leaving. That's why you let Kendra handle the hiring and firing. It's why you have stayed here for so long and refused to divorce her. You told me that yourself when we first met. Why else would you put up with her?"

"Maybe I like the arguing."

Smirking, Payton shook her head. "You certainly like a good verbal battle, but you don't like this arguing. This is beyond what you enjoy. This is painful. So why stay in it?"

"I'm working on not staying in it."

"You don't need this law firm, Bellamy. You don't need to take it with you. You could have gotten divorced years ago."

"I *want* it. It's my baby."

Payton paused, tension filling the room. "I think that may be one of the most honest things you have ever told me about yourself."

"This place is my child. It's years of work, years of planning and building. It's not easy to run your own business, and to do it as a woman? It's even harder. To do it as an out lesbian in a world that is highly dominated by men? Next to impossible. But I've done it. For ten years I have kept this business afloat. I have worked my ass off to keep it ethical, to keep it as the go-to for litigation. I will not give it up."

Letting out a breath, Payton moved in even closer until they were only inches from each other. Bellamy could feel the heat from Payton's body. If she slid forward just a little their breasts would touch and she would be a goner. Payton had always been confident in her words and her actions, but this was the bravest Bellamy had ever seen her and it was beyond a turn on.

Bellamy's chest rose and fell rapidly. She was at a loss for words, and she was utterly captivated by the woman in front of her. Payton had captivated all of her attention. Still, she shouldn't be there. Payton needed to leave. It wouldn't be good for anyone if she stayed.

"I want to help you keep it." Payton's voice was even and strong, convicted.

Shaking her head, Bellamy whispered, "No."

Payton stepped back then around Bellamy, heading for the door. "Notice how you keep saying that word and how I keep not listening. You have a conference call in two minutes. Don't be late."

Payton left Bellamy's office and shut the door. Bellamy's jaw dropped as she stared at where Payton had just walked away from her. Flabbergasted, she was not sure what to do or say. The only way to get Payton out of the office was to fire her, and that definitely wasn't an option. Firing a woman who claimed their boss had sexually assaulted them? Yeah, because that wasn't opening herself up for a lawsuit.

Wordlessly, she moved to her filing cabinet and jerked it open with a little too much force. It halted with a loud clack. Sifting through the files, she searched for where she'd known she'd stashed Payton's resignation, except it wasn't there. Cursing, Bellamy dropped into her chair and closed her eyes. The one time she forgot to make a damn photocopy, not that Payton wouldn't have found it and taken it from her too, since she knew where everything was filed. She had no recourse. If Payton wanted to continue to work for them, she'd have to let her, at least for now.

Bellamy would have to put a plan into action to keep Payton

safe and Kendra away from her. She would not allow them to have any alone time together. Payton would not go into Kendra's office without Bellamy knowing. Taking the first step of action, she headed for her door and propped it. Open door policy had a sudden new meaning. Grunting, she headed for her desk and settled in to work on some files as anger coursed through her. What Payton was doing was reckless.

Bellamy focused on work as best she could because she couldn't let up on it any more than she had that weekend. She wasn't getting her way with Payton, she'd already figured that out, and if she dwelled on it too much, it was just going to piss her off even more. With a huff, she went about trying to find a new client. The faster she could get out of the marriage and buy out Kendra, the faster she could get Payton out of working for either of them.

PAYTON HAD CHECKED HER WATCH A DOZEN TIMES that day. Maddy had missed the last two visitations, and she finally had enough to file a petition for Maddy's rights to be terminated. Faith was supposed to join her at court to make it official. She'd already cleared it with Bellamy, who supposedly told Kendra about her absence, but Payton was still worried about slipping out of the office and not making too much of an impact while she was gone.

She let out a breath as she finally decided it was close enough to time that she needed to leave. She packed up her bag and shut down the front desk. She stood, with her bag on her shoulder, and was about to round the desk when Kendra's cold voice stopped her.

"Where do you think you're going?"

"I requested a half day today."

"You've been doing a lot of that lately. Too much, I should think, for such a new employee."

Payton's stomach dropped, and she paled. This was not something she could miss out on. She had to be there. If she wasn't, it would be bad for everyone. She started to plead. "I need to go. I can't miss this appointment."

"And what appointment is that?" Kendra sneered, her usually bubbly demeanor giving way to the anger that simmered below it for the better part of two weeks since they were last interrupted.

"I have . . . I have to go to court."

Kendra snorted. "You're not a lawyer. What could you possibly be going to court for? What's the charge against you?"

"Kendra," Bellamy's voice was smooth and commanding. Kendra spun around, her blonde curls flying around her shoulders before settling. "Her request was approved. I talked to you about it."

"I don't think she should be taking this much time off."

"Payton is a hard worker, and she works overtime consistently. Taking a few extra hours here and there to deal with some personal matters is nothing out of the ordinary." Bellamy nodded to Payton over Kendra's shoulder.

Payton let out a breath and was about to leave when she stopped again. Kendra's voice was getting desperate and even angrier. "How can she be a good employee if she continuously takes time off?"

Again, Bellamy remained calm. "This is neither the time nor the place for this discussion, but I assure you, Kendra, you are incorrect. Now, I have to go to court as well. You'll have to fend for yourself for lunch."

Payton made her escape when Bellamy gave her another nod, indicating she should leave. As she slipped out of the door to the offices, she saw Bellamy move into her office. It didn't take her long to get down to her car, but just as she was getting into the driver's seat, she heard Bellamy's voice.

"Stop, Payton."

She froze and turned, confused. Bellamy had her jacket on and briefcase in her hand, which she only ever had when she was going to court, but Payton knew for a fact Bellamy wasn't going to court because she made the schedule. Payton waited for Bellamy's heels to click their way over to her car. Bellamy grinned.

"We're taking my car."

"Wh-what?"

Bellamy chuckled. "Come on."

"I'm confused."

"I'm going with you. We're going to make sure this doesn't fail."

Bellamy grabbed Payton's wrist and dragged her down another row of cars to a black Lexus. Bellamy slipped behind the wheel, and Payton was utterly confused, but she followed along. As soon as they were at the exit of the parking garage, Payton turned and asked, "What are you doing?"

"I told you I would help you with this, so I'm helping."

"You don't have to."

"Don't start with me. It's the least I can do. Fill me in on what's going on today so I actually sound like I know what's happening if I have to speak."

Payton rolled her eyes. "My sister hasn't been coming to visitation. Luis' rights have been terminated, and they figured out last week, she's still living with him until he has to report for his sentencing. So in order to continue visitation, she has to sober up again and move out or live somewhere else because she can't be staying with the guy who hurt Liam."

"Understandable."

"Anyway, she doesn't want to. The social worker said if she doesn't show today, which is a strong possibility, then the judge might just go ahead with terminating rights or moving to a trial to do it or something like that."

Bellamy hummed, and Payton turned to stare at her.

"What?"

"They won't terminate today. But they may move to start the termination process. That takes time. If they do that, you'll have to be awarded custody in the meantime. Don't you have representation?"

Payton shrugged. She hadn't thought she needed a lawyer quite yet, at least not until she knew she'd have to petition for adoption or permanent custody. Faith hadn't told her anything of the sort, and it wasn't like this was something she was familiar with.

"You don't have a lawyer?" Bellamy was shocked and astounded.

"I didn't think I needed one yet."

Bellamy turned and sent Payton a pitying look. "Always bring a lawyer to court. Haven't I taught you that by now?"

"You work actual cases."

"I work litigation. But the same applies across the board. Any time you have to go in front of a judge, you talk to a lawyer. Tell me what Maddy has failed to comply with, not just this time, but overall."

"Three times she has tested positive for meth while supposedly sober and trying to earn back her custody through CPS. This is the third."

"She tested positive again?"

Payton nodded. "A week ago."

"Okay. I think we've got this."

"You sure?"

"Yup."

Bellamy pulled up outside the courthouse. Together they walked in. Even just having Bellamy there made Payton all that more confident in how the situation was going to go. As they stepped up to the front door, Bellamy stopped Payton with a hand on her arm. "I'm not going to say anything unless I think it's not going well, okay? I don't want to overstep."

"Okay." Payton let out a breath.

"Don't be nervous." Bellamy smiled at her and squeezed Payton's hand. "You've got this made. You've got a job, with good pay and benefits, and you've done a wonderful job taking care of Liam all year. You've got this."

Nodding, Payton bit her lip. She wished she could be as confident as Bellamy, but she wasn't. She was too nervous. Any time they had to go to court over this it made her nervous. Bellamy led her inside with a palm at her back until they were close to the courtroom. They waited to be let in, then they settled in the hard wooden seats to wait for their case to be called.

As soon as Payton walked through the double swinging doors to the front of the courtroom, her nerves were on full blast. They asked who everyone was, making them state and spell their names for the record. When they got to Bellamy, she said she was representing Payton.

Payton would have to thank her profusely as soon as she got a chance. Everything seemed to be going well until Maddy stepped through the doors. Her hair was a mess, and it was clear she was high. Payton tensed, her chest tightening as she watched Maddy walk toward the front of the room.

"Sorry I'm late. I got lost." Her speech was slurred, but she had shown up.

Payton gulped. This had to be her worst nightmare.

"Who are you?" the judge asked. Bellamy put a hand on Payton's elbow.

"I'm Madison. I am Liam's mother, and I want to make a statement."

"You may proceed."

Payton held her breath, no idea what Maddy was about to

say. Anything could come out of her mouth when she was high.

"I want Payton to adopt my son."

"What?" Payton asked, her voice shaking as she leaned against the table, Bellamy's grip on her tightening.

Maddy turned and nodded at her. "I want you to. Just . . . don't keep him from me all the time."

"Okay."

"I want to see him grow up."

Payton nodded, at a complete loss for words. Her heart thundered so loudly in her ears, she wasn't sure she would be able to hear anything else Maddy said. Maddy turned to the judge and stood tall.

"I want to terminate my rights as his parent if my sister will agree to adopt him. He needs stability, and I—I've come to realize I cannot provide that."

"That's very admirable of you," the judge answered.

The hand at Payton's back was firm and welcome. She let out a shuddering breath and blinked back tears. This had not been expected in the least. She missed the rest of what everyone was saying as she stared at Maddy, silently thanking God for whatever had changed her mind or made her realize what was best for Liam.

They were going to sign the paperwork for termination in the next week. Faith turned to Payton after the judge left and smiled at her. "Once she signs the termination papers, you can petition the courts for adoption."

"And you will need a lawyer for that," Bellamy added with a cocky grin.

"I . . . I don't know what to say." Maddy sent her a long look. Payton moved over and wrapped her sister in a hug, whispering in her ear. "I know this was hard, but it's the right decision."

"I know. I've got to go."

Without another word, Maddy left the courtroom. Bellamy escorted Payton outside, and they finalized everything with

Faith for that day. Once they were back at Bellamy's car, the shock must have worn off because Payton turned to Bellamy and grinned, throwing her arms around her shoulders and hugging her tightly.

"Thank you!"

"I didn't do anything."

"Doesn't matter. Just, thank you."

Bellamy rubbed a hand up and down Payton's back. Payton held close, not wanting to let go. It was the first time she had felt close to Bellamy in days. Staying in the moment as long as she could, she drew in Bellamy's scent, closed her eyes and held on to the moment.

"He's going to be mine," she whispered.

"He's already yours, Payton. How can you not see that?"

Blinking back tears, Payton let out a breath. "I have to call Mom."

"Then call. Don't let me stop you."

"It can wait. I just . . . thank you."

"Again, I didn't do anything."

"You did more than you know." Payton took a step back from Bellamy and smiled at her. "Really."

"Well, I'll take that, I guess, if you're going to insist. But now you have the rest of the day off to celebrate. I have to go back to work. I do believe I have court this afternoon."

Payton shook her head. "You don't. I make the schedule, remember."

Bellamy grinned. "New client. I slipped him in last minute so you probably didn't see."

"And you're already going to court?"

Pursing her lips, Bellamy shook her head. "He fired his last lawyer. I'm picking up right in the middle."

"Wonderful."

"Sure is! I'll drop you off at your car, then you can head out to pick up Liam early from daycare and spend the rest of the day with him. How does that sound?"

"Honestly? It sounds perfect."

"Good."

Getting into Bellamy's car, Payton couldn't keep the smile off her face. It had turned out to be an excellent day, and she had definitely made the right decision to stick it out working for Bellamy. She wouldn't let Kendra push her around again, and she knew Bellamy would back her up if need be.

When they got to her car, she had to resist leaning over the center console and kissing Bellamy. It was clear where the boundary line had been drawn—at least for now—and she didn't want to cross it. With one last grin at Bellamy after they got to the office parking garage, she slipped from the car and got into her own. She was going to make the most of the rest of her day.

CHAPTER 9

THE OFFICE HAD BEEN QUIET ALL WEEK BECAUSE Kendra had been gone. Payton had enjoyed the relaxed change. Bellamy had booked as much time out of the office as she could, so that left Payton largely to herself, taking notes and messages, answering phone calls, and emailing files and motions and everything of the sort to and from Bellamy's laptop as they tried to juggle an insane schedule.

Kendra was supposed to be gone through the weekend, and Payton had an idea. When Saturday morning rolled around, and Liam woke up bright and early just after sunrise, she got him dressed and fed. It was presumptuous of her, but at the same time, she wanted to see Bellamy again outside of work in a much more relaxed environment.

That day she'd shown up unexpectedly at the office in jeans and a T-shirt had just about been Payton's undoing. She shivered at the memory then gathered up a diaper bag, making sure she had everything she needed in it, and took Liam out to her car, tucking him into the car seat.

She enjoyed her weekends with Liam if she could keep to them and not get distracted by work, and she was determined to do just that, along with Bellamy. They both needed a break. After she had handed in her resignation and then taken it back, the tension in the office had skyrocketed. Bellamy hadn't left her alone with Kendra, and she knew it was because of what she'd told Bellamy that had happened. She had been surprised, but secretly, she had been glad for the buffer and the added protection against Kendra's advances.

Getting in her car, Payton let out a breath. She was taking a risk, but she wanted to do it, had to hope it would be worth it. It took her nearly thirty minutes to drive across town and get to the nicer part of Tacoma where she knew Bellamy lived. After that night in the car, there was no way to get the image of Bellamy walking up to her house tousled and smelling of sex out of her mind. She had memorized the address, willingly or not.

The house looked even more daunting during the day. It was huge with white stucco that stood out against the blue sky of late summer, one of the rare times they had blue sky in Tacoma. Pulling into the driveway, Payton parked her car behind Bellamy's black Lexus, glad to see it was still there and she wouldn't have to track her down at the office, where Payton was pretty sure Bellamy lived more than her actual house.

With a nervous breath, Payton pulled Liam from the car seat and slung the diaper bag over her shoulder. She tentatively walked up to the front door, leaning in with her whole body when she pressed the doorbell. It didn't take long before she heard footsteps coming toward her from inside, and she glanced around the rest of the neighborhood, knowing she stood out like a sore thumb with her ancient and rusty car, her biracial child on her hip, and her ratty jeans and a T-shirt because the seven outfits she owned for work were in the wash.

The door opened. Her heart stuttered. Bellamy stood on the other side, her long brown hair with a thick streak of gray right near her temple tousled around her shoulders, the curls loose and messy. Her brown eyes were wide with surprise that morphed into concern then back into surprise as her lips parted.

Payton took the chance and bounced Liam on her hip. "I brought a peace offering."

"You brought the baby as a peace offering?"

Shrugging, Payton gave a small smile. "You seemed to like him last time."

"I did. What are you doing here?"

"I thought if you had the whole house to yourself with Kendra still being gone that you would hole yourself up in an office either here or at work and literally work all day. So I came here to make sure you take a break."

"With a baby?"

"He's the bribe and the buffer."

Chuckling, Bellamy opened the door to the house wider and stepped aside to let them in. Payton stepped through the door and into a broad open entryway. The walls were stark white, like the outside of the house, shiplap lining everything. Paintings and pictures were placed perfectly every three to five feet, the proper size for every wall and all the themes matching.

"Your house is ridiculous," Payton muttered.

"Kendra." Bellamy knocked her head to the side. "She decorated it one year while I was gone at a conference for a week."

"Interesting."

"My house isn't very baby proof, you know." Bellamy pushed a finger at Liam's belly and made a face at him like she was trying to get him to laugh.

"He'll live, I assure you. He's a hearty breed."

"Good. I guess we could go to the den."

"You have a den?" Payton's eyes widened.

Bellamy sent a look over her shoulder with a grin and a roll of her eyes. "Yeah. This house is huge for two people, trust me. You could fit like six families in here."

Payton followed Bellamy down two hallways. Her gaze roved

over Bellamy's ass, thankfully once again in a tight pair of dark blue jeans. The shirt she wore this time wasn't a T-shirt but a loose peachy plaid semi-sheer tank top that billowed out around her waist and hips. Payton had to swallow when Bellamy turned to hold her hand out and let Payton walk into the den first.

The room easily could have swallowed up her apartment times three. Nothing made their income differential more obvious than walking through Bellamy's house and getting a first-hand look at how she lived. Her stomach clenched tightly, wondering if she had made a mistake or not. With a deep bolstering breath, Payton charged forward and into the room. She still wanted to see what might happen.

Payton set Liam on the floor in the center of the large and probably very expensive rug. She set the diaper bag next to the couch and turned to see where Bellamy had gone off to. With a sigh, Payton sat on the couch and waited while Bellamy awkwardly sat next to her.

Rolling her eyes, Payton leaned forward and patted Bellamy's thigh. "The entire point of this was for you to relax. You look like you're about to walk into an annual exam."

Bellamy snorted and shook her head. "You just surprised me is all."

"I should have called first."

"I would have told you no."

"You do like that word, don't you?" Payton narrowed her gaze in Bellamy's direction. Liam rolled from his butt to his hands and knees, squealing as he crawled toward them slowly.

Payton risked a glance toward Bellamy, who had bent down and grinned, holding her hands out for Liam to come to her. He changed direction and moved from heading to Payton to going to Bellamy. Payton's heart burst. Bellamy, whenever she looked at Liam, became a completely different person. She had seen it that one weekend and was witnessing it again.

When Liam got to Bellamy, she helped lift him up to stand

against her knees. He grinned at her, drool coming down his lips. Payton reached forward and wiped it off, rubbing it on her jeans. Teething babies were gross. It wasn't another two seconds before Bellamy lifted Liam up and bounced him in her lap.

"Hey there, cutie!"

Liam giggled. Payton leaned her shoulder into the couch and relaxed. She knew Liam could be the exact buffer she needed and wanted to win her way into Bellamy's heart or at least into her home for the day. With a sigh, she smiled at the two of them playing, Liam grabbing at the front of Bellamy's shirt, her gripping his hand and bouncing him. They played like that for a few hours before Liam's cranky and hungry side took over.

Payton grabbed the formula she'd brought, made him a quick bottle, and handed it over to Bellamy. She stared at it dumbfounded, but Liam grabbed her hand and brought the bottle to his lips. Payton smirked. "He knows what he likes."

"I guess," Bellamy answered. "How's your sister?"

"Maddy is Maddy. She always has been. Mom was just as surprised as I was about the hearing but pleased. She thinks it'll make everything a lot easier in the long run."

"I agree." Bellamy turned to look up at Payton, her dark eyes holding something close that she was hiding.

Payton licked her lips and asked a question she never thought she would have dared. "Why don't you ever talk about your family?"

Bellamy paled then turned her gaze back on Liam, refusing to look at Payton again. "Because they're not very nice people, and they don't particularly care for me."

"Hmm. I'm pretty sure anyone who doesn't care for you is either crazy or out of their minds."

Chuckling, Bellamy shook her head. "They live in their own world. My parents have been married since they were eighteen. I'm the middle child of five."

"Five? You're joking."

"No," Bellamy answered. "I'm not. I haven't spoken to any of my sisters in close to fifteen years. My brother, I think he called me once maybe six years ago, but that's the last I heard from him."

"Why don't they like you?"

"They think that I think I'm better than them."

"What do you mean?"

Liam dropped his head back, leaning into Bellamy's chest as he tilted the bottle higher, still using her hand to prop it up like he always did with Payton. Bellamy shifted on the couch to make it easier for him to lay down a bit. There was an awkward silence while Payton waited for an explanation.

"I went to college. I got not just one but two degrees. No one in my family had ever been to college before. My brother did end up going, finally. That's what he called to tell me. But he stopped after his associate's and technician's certification. He's an auto mechanic."

"So they're jealous?"

"I guess you could say that. They see education as not worth it. They make a fine living without theirs so why did I need mine? They just don't understand it."

"Or you, it seems."

Bellamy gave a wan smile. "Yes, or me. There's some other stuff in there, but it's neither here nor there."

Payton watched as Liam's eyes grew heavy. He would need his morning nap soon, then she and Bellamy would have one-on-one time together without him in the middle. She waited it out, trying to keep Bellamy talking.

"So why a law degree? If no one in your family went to school, what drew you to law?"

Bellamy's eyes lit up as she stared directly at Payton. "The money."

"Seriously?"

Shrugging, Bellamy glanced back down at Liam. "He's so cute."

"He is, and he's about to crash."

"I see that." Bellamy smiled. "I wanted a good paying job. I'm good with details and arguing. I do have four siblings, so I'm very well-versed in managing arguments and playing peace-maker. I like nuances in language. I was always the kid finding the loopholes in punishments and in rules. My parents hated it."

"Sounds like you."

"Yeah. What about you? Just Maddy?"

Payton shook her head. "I have a baby brother. He was an oops. He's twelve years younger than me. Maddy is three years older than me, and she's always been a wreck. My mom remar-ried when I was five and divorced again when I was ten. She has cancer, currently, so she goes for once weekly treatments for chemotherapy. Maddy is an asshole, and she always chose those days for her visitations because she knew she wouldn't have to see Mom. They do not get along. Maddy only talks to her when she wants something."

"That must be hard."

Shrugging, Payton watched Liam's eyes slip shut as he released the bottle. "Some days. Most days it's just normal."

Payton leaned forward then took the mostly empty bottle from Bellamy's fingers. She slipped it into the side pocket on the diaper bag before dragging out one of Liam's blankets. Laying it on the floor, she went back and slipped Liam's warm and pliant body from Bellamy's hands and settled him on his side on the blanket. He was so sweet when he slept.

Going back to the couch, she grinned. "Advantage to babies is they sleep a lot."

"And they're cute."

"Ha, yes, cute, except when throwing a tantrum."

"Oh, you know, have to take that to get the cute."

"You really do like kids, don't you?"

"I do." Bellamy gave Liam a wistful look then turned her grin onto Payton.

Payton's stomach dropped and twisted. Hope surged upward into her chest, and she let out a breath. She wanted desperately to lean over and kiss Bellamy, but she resisted for now. They were just getting to the good part of the conversation, and after their last talk, she wasn't sure how amenable Bellamy would be to that kind of forward action.

"Kendra didn't want kids?"

"God no, she hates kids. Says they're messy and take up too much time and space."

"Well, she's not wrong."

"She's not, but the difference is I think it's time well spent. Besides, it'd be nice to have a family again."

Payton grunted her agreement and risked a glance to Bellamy. "There's still time."

"You still think like a twenty-two-year-old." Bellamy laughed. "You want something to drink?"

"Sure. We can leave him here for a bit. He's not going anywhere for at least an hour."

"The kitchen isn't far."

Bellamy rose up, and Payton followed her down the hall. They walked into a stark white kitchen. Payton was beginning to sense the theme of the house was clean, white, and untouchable. The countertops were a white marble, the appliances stainless steel, which she knew would smudge with kid fingers in no time. Everything was neatly put away in its perfect spot like no one lived there at all.

Shuddering, she waited as Bellamy opened the fridge and brought out some infused water. She poured each of them a glass before leaning against the counter and taking a sip. Payton hesitated before drinking. She felt like it was now or never. Setting the drink off to the side on the counter, she turned her body and lined it up with Bellamy's.

Bellamy's lips parted in a protest, but Payton stepped in even closer, staring straight up into Bellamy's eyes. They were far closer to an even height level since Bellamy was barefoot instead of in three or four inch heels. Payton's heart pounded hard as she drew in a breath, Bellamy's flowery perfume taking over her senses. She gripped Bellamy's drink and set it down.

"You know, there's one thing I regret," Payton whispered.

"What's that?" Bellamy's voice was breathy, her chest rising and falling rapidly.

Payton leaned in closer, one hand on either side of Bellamy's body on the counter, effectively locking her in place. "That I have yet to properly kiss you."

Bellamy's breath hitched, catching in her throat. Payton took the opportunity and brushed her lips gently over Bellamy's, barely touching. The sigh that echoed from Bellamy spurred Payton on. Moving a hand to Bellamy's hip, she held still as she brushed their mouths together again, this time adding a little pressure. She kept her eyes open, staring straight at Bellamy with each breath she took. She wanted to see Bellamy's reaction, feel Bellamy under her.

"We shouldn't," Bellamy whispered, but she didn't move, didn't push Payton away.

Halting any forward motion, Payton waited to see what might happen. She wasn't going to kiss Bellamy if she truly didn't want it, but she needed to know how to proceed. Seconds ticked by, her thumb rubbing up and down against Bellamy's hipbone.

Bellamy made the next move. Fingers brushed over Payton's bangs, moving them aside until Bellamy cupped Payton's cheek, her hand sliding to hold her jaw and her ear. Payton still waited to see what Bellamy would do next. Closing her eyes, Bellamy pressed their foreheads together and drew in a deep breath.

"I'm married."

"I know," Payton answered.

"My wife . . ."

"Is not a great person."

"Yeah, that's a nice way of putting it."

"This isn't any different than what we did before."

Bellamy moved away at that comment. She regarded Payton with a deep look. Her lips quivered before she spoke. "This is vastly different, Payton. That was . . . that was physical."

"Hmm, I remember." A flush rose in Payton's cheeks. "You're right. This isn't only physical."

Bellamy stared at her for another minute. Payton could watch her mind working. She'd seen Bellamy do it every day for the past two months at work, and it was no different standing in the center of Bellamy's kitchen, pressed against her, hoping they could both break down the last of the walls.

"Bellamy?"

"Hmm?"

Payton dashed her tongue out against her own lips and let out a breath. "Are you going to kiss me?"

"I have no doubt of that, Payton." With a grin, Bellamy's gaze shifted from Payton's mouth to her eyes. "The question is how and when."

"Now. I mean now."

"I don't—"

"I want you to kiss me," Payton interrupted. "If that's your hesitation. I don't know how much more forward I can be."

Bellamy closed her eyes. "It's not about forwardness. It's about ethics."

"We've already kind of screwed the ethics playbook. Literally."

"That was before I was your boss, to be clear."

"Oh, I thought we were talking the marriage ethics playbook, since that's the one you keep bringing up." Payton snorted. "You want the boss one? All right. Your wife screwed that playbook. Now, Bellamy, *please*, kiss me."

"I . . . I want to, please don't think that I don't want to."

Payton shifted her stance, pressing her hips into Bellamy's to try and keep her attention focused on what they both wanted. "I want to, too. So what's the hold up?"

Sighing, Bellamy shook her head. "I don't even know anymore."

Bellamy took the next step, bending her head to capture Payton's lips. Payton groaned, falling into the embrace. Bellamy had a sharp taste as their tongues tangled and danced. Payton drew in a shuddering breath, moving one hand up Bellamy's back to press it firmly between her shoulder blades, bringing her in closer.

Nipping at Payton's lower lip, Bellamy cupped both of Payton's cheeks and kept their bodies pressed tightly together. Payton groaned and moved her other hand up the front of Bellamy's shirt, stopping short of finding her bra. Bellamy's skin was hot against her hand, and she lost herself. Her entire world became about Bellamy and that moment, the embrace, the two of them together, Liam sleeping in the other room.

Payton lost track of how long they stayed like that—lips touching, hearts beating against each other—as Bellamy leaned against the kitchen counter. When they finally broke apart, Bellamy pulled Payton back in for one last quick kiss, then smiled.

"This was quite an unexpected surprise," Bellamy whispered.

"A good one, I hope."

"Yes, but Payton, I can't stress enough that now is not the time for this. Today aside, I am still married. I haven't filed for divorce yet."

"But you're planning to."

"I am, but I don't want you to get tangled in my mess."

"I'm already in it."

Bellamy shook her head. "A little bit, yes, but not in every-thing. You don't understand what it's like to dissolve a marriage of ten years and a business partnership. This takes time and a lot of negotiations."

"I get it." Payton grabbed her infused water and took a drink. She walked back the way they had come so she could check on Liam. When she got to the door of the den, she could see he was still pressed into the same place she had left him, sleeping soundly. A smile flitted across her lips at the sight of him.

Bellamy's hand on hers surprised her. Bellamy tugged her in closer, coming right up next to her. "I don't want you to get hurt by all of this."

"I won't," Payton assured her. "I'm stronger than I look."

"I have no doubt of that," Bellamy answered. "But this is my mess, and something I need to deal with."

Payton rolled her eyes. "Look. I like you. I'm pretty sure you like me. We're not making any commitments to each other, at least not right now. But you said it yourself—your marriage has been over for years."

"Yes, but that doesn't mean I want to get a divorce and jump right into another marriage."

Narrowing her gaze, Payton smirked. "When did I say anything about marriage?"

Walking away from Bellamy, she headed into the den. Bellamy followed her a few seconds later. They avoided the topic again, and when Liam woke up, Payton took her leave, knowing he was going to need more than formula to last him through the day, and she had a birthday party to plan for him. Bellamy walked her out to the car two hours later and stood by as Payton slid Liam into his car seat.

As she shut the door, Bellamy cupped Payton's cheek and kissed her lips. It wasn't full of the passion and tension the kiss in the kitchen had been, but it was worth it. They were out in the open, neighbors could see, and she didn't want to push her luck. Getting Bellamy to think about being with her was harder than she had anticipated. When Bellamy pulled away, Payton grinned at her.

"I'll see you Monday, boss."

"Oh, shut it," Bellamy answered, rolling her eyes.

Grinning, Payton pinched Bellamy's ass as she turned to walk away. Bellamy yelped and twisted back around, shaking her finger in Payton's direction. "You may think about that Monday, but you may not do it."

"Eh, we'll see if you change your mind or not."

Bellamy sent Payton a fake glare. "You're flirting."

"So are you." With a laugh, Payton slid behind the wheel of her car and started the engine. Rolling down the front window, Payton whistled at Bellamy as she got to the door and sent her a broad grin and a wink before she pulled out of the driveway and onto the street. Visiting Bellamy had been a perfect idea.

CHAPTER 10

BELLAMY HAD HER DOOR WIDE OPEN, AS HAD BEEN her new practice. She'd heard Kendra's rumblings in the office, had heard her slam drawers and curse as she went about whatever it was she was doing in there. Bellamy largely ignored her except when she saw Payton go in and out of the office. In those cases, she twisted her chair to make sure the door was left open, and if it was closed, she walked closer to listen in so she could interrupt if need be. Nothing had happened since, which had been a blessing, but Bellamy was on high alert every day.

That week had been particularly brutal. Kendra had been awful at home but equally as bad at the office, which was rare for her. Usually she was pleasant to clients, but she'd been abrupt enough that a few had actually commented to Bellamy about it. It was Wednesday before there was a major blow up between Payton and Kendra. Bellamy had been waiting for it, knowing the tension was rising to untenable levels.

Everything Payton had done that week had ticked Kendra off in some manner. It was as if Kendra had taken all of her anger toward Bellamy and shifted it onto Payton. The more she observed, the more she knew why they had gone through so many employees recently.

When Payton walked into Kendra's office Thursday morning after only being in the office for an hour and after Kendra's shrill scream of her name, Bellamy shifted to sit straight up in her chair. Something felt different about this time than any of the other times. She listened, but when Kendra shut the door, she stood straight up and made a beeline for the door opposite of hers.

"What is this?" Kendra asked with accusation.

"The motion you asked me to look over."

"I see that, but you rewrote over half of it, and it makes no sense."

"I'm sorry." Payton's voice sounded so small compared to normal.

Bellamy's heart raced. She wasn't sure if she should go in or not. Payton had assured her she could handle herself, but Bellamy didn't even want to give her a chance to have to do that. When it got quiet in the room and there were mumblings, Bellamy opened the door. Payton gave her a look of utter fear, and Bellamy hardened her stare in Kendra's direction.

"What's going on in here?"

"Payton is not doing an exemplary job. In fact, she ruined my motion to the point I have to redo the entire copy."

Bellamy didn't believe Kendra for a moment. With her fists on her hips, she stepped into the office. "Payton, you can leave."

Without another word, Payton escaped. Bellamy glared at Kendra, shutting the door behind Payton and locking it.

"What the hell is your problem this week? You have been on a rampage since you stepped in on Monday."

Kendra snorted. "That's rich, coming from you."

"What are you even talking about?" Bellamy flung her hand out. "You need to cut the crap."

Nodding, Kendra came up closer to Bellamy and wrapped her fingers around Bellamy's hip to hold her. "Kiss me."

"What?"

"Kiss me. You're my wife, so kiss me."

"What are you going off about now?" Shocked and more than a little disturbed, Bellamy stepped out of Kendra's grasp.

Kendra snorted. "Did you forget that we have cameras in our driveway?"

Bellamy's heart jerked. Her shoulders froze. Her toes curled. Shifting her stance, she kept herself strong and fixed as she moved her gaze up to Kendra's angry and wounded eyes. "I'm well aware we have cameras in the driveway. We also have them at the front and back doors."

"And that every time the doorbell rings, a little notification pops up on my phone to show me who is there."

At that point, Bellamy knew exactly where the conversation was going. She'd had a feeling Kendra had figured it out but had kept her silence just in case. With a short breath, Bellamy gave Kendra a bold and confident stare. "So you know Payton came over."

"And I know you kissed her. What else did you do?"

"Nothing, not that it really matters since I am fully aware of what—and I mean who—you were doing while on your biannual trip to Cabo San Lucas. Don't think I know why it is you go down there with a new woman every time."

"Don't you dare equate what I do to what you have done. You have a broken this marriage," Kendra shouted, her voice reverberating around the walls.

Bellamy nodded slowly, drawing in a slow and deep breath. "When you want to talk about our marriage and how it was ruined, we can. But if you're going to throw accusations around, then I'm done with this conversation. We have both made mistakes, Kendra. I have slept with one other woman one time since I have been married to you. Can you even count the number you've fucked?"

Kendra's cheeks flashed with red, her nostrils flaring. She was about to scream, about to rampage. Bellamy put up a hand to stop her. It took everything in her not to yell back, not to start the argument she really wanted to have because it was only for some sick satisfaction knowing she would win.

"We will talk about this at another time, when there aren't clients in the lobby, when Payton isn't around to witness this. She has been traumatized enough by you." Bellamy started for the door.

"What does that mean?"

Bellamy twisted around, her face set. "You know exactly what it means. You touch her again, you will be hearing from more than just a divorce attorney."

She shut the door as quietly as possible just to piss Kendra off more. Releasing all her pent-up rage and anger—at least enough of it to focus on work—Bellamy walked out into the front room to find her client waiting. She held up a finger to tell them it'd be another minute before leaning over Payton's desk and whispering in her ear, "I need you to stay late tonight."

"How late?"

"Late."

"I'll see if Mom can babysit."

Bellamy touched Payton's shoulder. "If she talks to you again today, ignore any anger she has. It's not because of anything you did."

"I already ignore her ninety-percent of the time anyway."

"Good." Bellamy straightened up and plastered a smile on her face. Stepping toward Mrs. Jenkins, she held out her hand. "Mrs. Jenkins, good to see you again."

"You, too."

Bellamy led the way into her office, leaving the door open a crack so she could make sure Kendra didn't do anything stupid.

112

Focusing on her client as best as she could, Bellamy settled in behind her desk and listened to Mrs. Jenkins talk about the upcoming trial they were heading straight into.

THEY WORKED WELL PAST THE DINNER HOUR, AND IT was nearing dusk outside when Bellamy found even the slightest moment to hit the pause button. Mrs. Jenkins dropped a huge case in her lap—mostly unexpected, but welcome at the same time. It would solidify her suit against Kendra for the firm.

Bellamy dragged her laptop and more files from her desk to the coffee table in front of her couch. She needed a change of scenery. She'd asked Payton to order out dinner finally and expected it to arrive soon. She'd have to eat and work since personal matters instead of actual work had taken much of her time up during the day.

There would be no surprising Kendra anymore. She'd pretty much told her what her plans were when she'd left her office earlier. Luckily, Kendra had stayed very quiet the rest of the day. When Payton came to her door with a knock and food in hand, Bellamy let out a breath.

"Please tell me that's something greasy and fatty and so not good for me."

Payton shrugged. "It might be the cheapest Chinese I could find because it was the only thing open this late."

"Late?" Bellamy shifted her wrist up and twisted her watch around. "Damn. It is late."

It was after nine at night, and she hadn't anticipated that. The sun was just setting outside, but it was the middle of July. She'd forgotten how far into the evening it stayed light out in the middle of summer, mostly because she was always working.

"You joining?" Bellamy asked, raising an eyebrow as she shifted her papers around to clear a spot for the food. "Because if you didn't order enough for four people, we're going to have a problem."

Payton snickered. "I ordered enough. I wasn't sure if you could spare a few minutes to eat with me or if you needed to work."

"I always have time for you." Bellamy shifted her gaze to stare straight up at Payton, hoping her message was conveyed. "Besides, I need to talk to you."

"Well, that's never good." Payton settled the food down then plopped onto the couch next to Bellamy with a heavy sigh. "Lay it on me. What'd I do?"

Chuckling, Bellamy pressed her hand to Payton's thigh and squeezed. "You did nothing. Well, you did, but we'll get to that."

"You always say we'll get to it."

Bellamy raised her eyebrows. She couldn't lie—it was true. She would always come back to things after the fact when she found a more appropriate time to talk about them or when everyone was calmer.

"Let's eat first."

"Let's not," Payton responded. "I don't like waiting for conversations to happen."

Bellamy grabbed a container of food and popped the lid open. Shoving a forkful between her lips, she gave Payton a soft look. "Kendra's been on a rampage this week."

"Couldn't tell. I thought she was just acting her normal self." Payton reached for a fortune cookie and popped it out of the plastic wrapper. Bellamy watched curiously as she broke up the cookie and pulled out the fortune and read it. Then she took the other one and did the same thing.

"What are you doing?"

"Here. This one is for you." Payton shoved one of the fortunes in front of Bellamy.

It said something about a large sum of money coming into

her life. She snorted and shook her head—more like spending a large sum of money in order to get out of the life she had spent a decade building and avoiding. "You just read them all and hand them out as you see fit?"

"Why not? Can't leave fate in chance's hands. We'll never get what we want then."

"Fine. What's yours say?" Bellamy snagged the one Payton had kept and read it over. "'You will find love very soon.' Interesting."

"It's not quite accurate."

"They're never accurate."

Payton shrugged and popped one of the hard little cookies between her lips. "You were saying?"

Bellamy sighed and set the food container onto the coffee table. "I forgot we have cameras at the house."

"You have nanny cams in your house?" Payton's eyes widened in surprise, her face paling.

"No. We have security cameras by our front door—the doorbell, actually—and out by the garage, where you parked."

"So she—"

"Yes."

"Well, that explains a whole lot."

"I thought so as well." Bellamy grabbed her food and took another bite. "She knows I cheated on her that night when she left me at the restaurant, but she still has no idea it was you."

Payton gave no response.

"She's known for a while, and she cheats all the time. I'm well aware of what she does."

"I don't think she would have hired me if she'd known it was me."

"Probably not." Bellamy took another bite. "Anyway, after this week, and today in particular, I need to tell you that I filed for divorce this morning. She'll be served in" —Bellamy glanced at her watch again— "actually, she probably already has been served."

"You don't think she'll call?"

"She's too vain for that. She'll wait until I show back up at the house and beg me to stay."

"Will you?"

Bellamy froze. She shifted her gaze from her food to Payton's concerned and worried eyes. She hadn't anticipated that question, hadn't thought Payton would ask it. "No."

Payton didn't say anything else. She just grabbed a carton of food and opened it. Bellamy wasn't done though—something about the way Payton had asked that question felt like more weighed on it than her marriage. Reaching forward, Bellamy took the food from Payton and gripped her hands, both of them together.

"Why would you think I would stay?"

"Because you haven't left in ten years."

"That's fair." Bellamy nodded. She let out a breath she hadn't known she was holding and released Payton's hands. "I doubt the office is going to be cordial tomorrow or any time soon from here on out. If you want to resign, now is your chance. I wouldn't blame you."

"I'm in this to win it."

Smiling, Bellamy cupped Payton's cheek. "It's not your fight to win, Payton."

Bellamy stood up, walking around the coffee table and pressing the heel of her palm into her aching back as she stretched. She hadn't realized how exhausted she was until that moment, until she had let it release into the ether, until she had finally filed the papers that had been sitting in her desk for the better part of two years.

"I don't even understand why you are still here half the time, honestly." The confession left Bellamy's lips before she could stop it, but it was as if the floodgates had been opened, and she couldn't stop them. "I'm a mess. You're far more put together than I am in terms of life. Sure, I have a career and money, but I haven't done anything else with myself in twenty years. You, however, have everything to live for. You don't have to stay here and get berated day in and day out. You don't have to witness the arguments, the tension. Don't think I don't see you wince when we argue. I know what you think of me."

Payton stood then, abandoning the food and moving in closer to Bellamy. "What do you think I think of you?"

"What?" Bellamy's head whipped up.

Payton shrugged. "If you think you know what I think, then tell me. Let me tell you if you're right or not."

Sighing, Bellamy sat against the edge of her desk and closed her eyes. She didn't even know where to start. "Why on earth would I stay in a marriage that is as awful as you have seen it to be? It hasn't always been this way. There was a point when we actually liked each other."

"But not love?"

Bellamy sent Payton a sharp look. "We thought it was."

"Not every love is supposed to last." Payton stepped in closer, hands on Bellamy's upper arms. "But I don't think you're stupid for staying in a marriage. I've seen people do stupid things. I have very little tolerance for stupid—welcome to my relationship with Maddy. I think you turned a blind eye to how bad it actually was until you couldn't anymore."

Bellamy sucked in a sharp breath, tears in her eyes. "Perhaps."

"Hmm." Payton curled a finger under Bellamy's chin and lifted it up so Bellamy stared directly at her. "I think you didn't give up hope until today."

Tears spilled down Bellamy's cheeks. Payton wiped them away one at a time. "I just . . . I didn't think it would hurt."

Payton didn't say anything. She leaned down, pressing her lips to Bellamy's cheeks, kissing away the salty drops. On a shuddering breath, Bellamy reached up and pulled Payton into a deep embrace, their tongues tangling in a slow tango. She lost herself in it. This was what marriage and love were supposed to feel like. Nothing like what she and Kendra had been doing for at least six or seven years. When had she forgotten what it felt like to be the sole center of someone's attentions?

Bellamy didn't want to let go. Sliding a hand down to Payton's ass, she pulled her in tighter, spreading her legs so Payton could step right up next to her. Payton nipped her lip then grinned as she moved her mouth from Bellamy's lips to her jawline, then to her neck and down her chest between the open V of her blouse.

"Payton," Bellamy whispered, not sure why she said her name except it was the only word she could think of. Tears were no longer falling, but her heart thundered for an entirely different reason, and her weary body tensed in anticipation.

Payton moved up and pulled Bellamy's pearl drop earring between her teeth before letting it go. She whispered, her breath floating across Bellamy's cheek and into her hair. "If she already knows, what's the harm?"

Bellamy's chest tightened. Payton was right. There was no more use hiding anything. She had filed the paperwork. It was as good as done as soon as they worked out negotiations. They'd already ignored the ethics playbook. Turning her mouth, Bellamy found Payton's lips again and dragged her into a deep and heated kiss. She wasn't going to hold anything back any longer.

Her fingers worked at Payton's vest, then her blouse, pulling the cheap buttons through the fabric until she could palm Payton's breast through the beige and lacy push-up bra she wore. Bellamy groaned, reaching behind Payton to undo the clasp before she even had Payton's shirt all the way off. She just wanted to touch her, and this time she wanted her fully naked.

She ripped the emerald vest and light green blouse from

Payton's shoulders and dropped the bra to the ground after them. Running a hand up Payton's back and down again, she nipped at her collarbone and then covered her breast with her mouth, swirling her tongue around Payton's nipple. Everything in her focus was Payton. Nothing else mattered, nothing else even entered her mind.

Payton's hands were at her shoulders, then in her hair, tightening and loosening with each swipe her tongue made. Payton's nails scraped along her scalp, loosening the bun she had spent twenty minutes pinning to the back of her head that morning. When she glanced up, Payton grinned down at her. This was it. This was exactly what she wanted.

"I want to taste you." Bellamy pressed open-mouthed kisses down Payton's stomach, getting onto her knees.

Payton turned and took the place Bellamy had just vacated. Her chest rose and fell sharply, but something in her eyes made Bellamy stop. "Are you okay?"

"Yeah." Payton cleared her throat. "Yeah, I'm fine."

"Fine is not okay. Payton, talk to me."

"This is just . . . it's similar, but it's different. Please, don't stop because of that."

Bellamy's lips parted, her mind slow to catch up with Payton's words. "This is . . . Kendra?"

Payton bit her lip and nodded, staring down at Bellamy. "But don't stop. Please don't stop. I want this."

"But are you ready for it?"

"Yes. Please don't stop."

"Payton . . . I—"

"Don't. Stop. Listen to the words I'm saying. This is not the same, trust me. This is very different. I want this to happen. Please don't stop now."

Bellamy gripped Payton's calves and massaged the muscles as her mind whirred. She hadn't even thought about this, but she should have. They were only feet from where Payton was assaulted, the situation so similar. "No, I think we should stop."

Payton reached down, gripped Bellamy by her cheeks and slid onto her knees so she could face Bellamy. "I swear to you, Bellamy, do not stop."

Bellamy's heart raced. Payton pressed their mouths together. Bellamy slowly parted her lips to let Payton do as she wanted. She wished she knew what Payton was thinking, what she was feeling. She wished she had a window inside her head just so she would know what to do.

"Don't stop," Payton whispered again. When she stood back up, she unbuttoned her own pants and shoved them down to her feet. She slipped out of her flats, then out of her clothes completely.

Bellamy stayed where she was, her eyes feasting on Payton bared before her for the first time ever. The quickie in the car did not do her justice at all. She was beautiful. Payton sat on the edge of the desk and put one foot up on the arm of the chair Bellamy kept for clients, then she beckoned Bellamy to her with a crook of her finger and a sweet smile on her lips, the tension she'd had moments before completely gone.

"Don't stop."

Not needing to hear it again, Bellamy shuffled on her knees and skimmed her hands up the insides of Payton's thighs. Kisses followed, moving up and down each thigh with occasional nips here and there. She wanted to take her time unlike the first time they had done this. She wanted to savor every moment of it.

Payton pressed both her hands behind her, arching her back so her breasts jutted out, nipples hard as her lips parted on a breath. Bellamy was going to make this last as long as she could. She blew air across Payton's body and the small swatch of finely trimmed hair. Brushing with her fingers first, she made circles then replaced her thumb with her lips. Payton's voice echoed, and it was sweet as it filtered to Bellamy's ears. She didn't stop.

Payton gripped her hair, pulling the rest of the bun loose whether she meant to or not.

Bellamy's hands moved up and around Payton's hips, gripping onto to her ass to keep her close and the angle good. She buried herself in Payton, not letting up until Payton cried out her orgasm and shuddered around her. Licking her own lips, Bellamy sat back on her haunches as she stared up at Payton's flushed cheeks and chest. In that moment, there was nothing else she could have asked for.

Payton slipped from the desk down to Bellamy's level. They kissed. It was slow, tantalizing, and comforting. Bellamy groaned when Payton palmed her breast and began undressing her. Their chests crashed together as they each took deep breaths. Helping, Bellamy pulled her shirt from her body and dragged her bra off when Payton fumbled with the clasp.

"Stand up," Payton ordered.

Gripping the arm of the chair, Bellamy pushed herself to stand and let out a breath. She was half-naked, her high-waisted skirt suddenly feeling like it was too much. Ditching her stilettos, she reached behind her to undo the zipper, but Payton's hands on her wrists stopped her.

"Let me."

Turning, Bellamy stared over her shoulder and bit her lip as Payton slowly dragged the small zipper down then pressed her hands under the edge of the fabric to push it off her hips. It fell to the floor silently.

Payton's mouth on her shoulder and her back caused Bellamy to close her eyes. Sensations roiled around in her stomach and ramped up in her chest. She was consumed in everything Payton did to her. Payton's hand moved around to her belly, sliding down and under her thong to play with her. Bellamy leaned back, Payton's smaller but lithe form holding her up.

Bellamy's hips rocked back and forth in a slow rhythm,

moans escaping her lips as she closed her eyes and listened to her body, listened to Payton's movements. The softness was nice, but it wasn't what she needed or wanted. Reaching behind Payton's head, she drew her into a kiss and scraped her teeth firmly over Payton's lower lip. "Harder."

Payton increased the pressure, the firmness, the angle. But it wasn't enough. Whining, Bellamy clenched her eyes shut and tried to get closer to the edge, but she wasn't finding it.

"Harder, Payton. I won't break."

"Then lean down on the desk."

Payton's hands moved and guided Bellamy until her palms were pressed firmly in front of her on the desk. She glanced over her shoulder, but Payton had disappeared. Looking between her legs, she saw her kneeling down. The first bite to her inner thigh took her by surprise. Her core heated as she cried out, gripping the edge of the desk as she rocked back. That was exactly what she needed.

The next bite was on the bottom of her ass, and she knew it was going to leave a mark. Wet pooled between her legs. Bellamy grunted and pushed her butt back into Payton's waiting tongue and lips. Payton wasn't soft. She moved against her with a fury Bellamy hadn't experienced before. But it didn't last long. Payton bit her way up Bellamy's back, nipping at her shoulder blade then the top of her shoulder followed by the soft skin at her neck.

With her fingers between Bellamy's legs, Payton slapped her hard on her ass. "You ready?"

A groan was the first thing to leave Bellamy's mouth. She was beyond ready. She had been waiting months for this, waiting since the last time they had dabbled in anything similar, but this was so much more and so much better. "Yes."

Payton rammed her fingers inside her. Bellamy's body jerked forward. Each and every time Payton shoved into her, her body moved, her voice responded, her nerves endings fired. Her brain was muddled and confused. She bit her lip, tasting blood she'd done it so hard. The last time Payton moved in her, her release grasped Payton's fingers, bursting through her chest and surrounding her body in rapture of pleasure.

When Bellamy opened her eyes, she was still plastered to her desk, Payton behind her, running hands over her back and ass, dropping soft and sweet kisses here and there and all over. Payton chuckled. "I've heard you be that loud before, Bellamy, but never something that sounded so good."

"Cocky son of a bitch."

"You know it." Payton helped her to turn around and kissed her sweetly. "I think we should probably eat now."

The words were on the tip of Bellamy's tongue, but she held them back. They did not need any help going down that line of thinking. Bellamy pulled Payton in for another gentle kiss before testing the stability of her legs and standing on her own two feet. She was not likely to forget this night, ever.

After dressing, they sat down and finished the cheap Chinese Payton had ordered. With one lingering kiss, Bellamy sent Payton home and started on the next petition she had to file.

CHAPTER 11

BELLAMY GOT HOME SHORTLY BEFORE MIDNIGHT. Every single light was on in the house. When she pulled her car into the driveway, she sat in the driver's seat for a few minutes, readying herself for the battle about to happen. The papers had been served. She'd gotten confirmation, and so the argument they were about to have would no doubt last for hours.

She took a small envelope out of her briefcase and slipped it into the large pocket of her overcoat. Leaving her briefcase in her car, which she never did, she pushed her way out of the vehicle and headed inside. For the first time in years, she felt confident in her decision. It was the right choice to make, the right step. Perhaps Payton had been correct in why it had taken her so long to actually file for divorce. She hadn't been in love with Kendra for years. They'd been living and existing together but that was all.

Pushing open the door, she was surprised to see boxes upon boxes stacked through the entryway and spreading out into the living area. Clenching her fists, Bellamy stepped around them. She wanted to call out to Kendra, see where she was and what the hell she was doing, but she kept quiet, observing everything.

Some boxes were closed up, some were open and half-full of stuff and others were completely empty.

When she heard footsteps upstairs in the bedroom, Bellamy changed her direction and headed that way. Kendra was flitting to and from different places in the room, shoving things into boxes. Bellamy's shoulders squared when she realized it was her items Kendra was packing away. With wide eyes and a slight tinge of fear in her voice, Bellamy spoke. "What are you doing?"

Kendra jerked to a stop, her arms full of Bellamy's work clothes. Her eyes were wide, feral, her own fear written all over her. "You don't want to be married, so you don't get to live here."

"Kendra." Bellamy's shoulders slumped. She probably should have figured something like this would happen. Kendra was not without her flair for the dramatic. "I will move out of the house should you want it in the divorce, but for now, I'm staying here. At least tonight."

"No." Kendra dropped the suits into a large box and went back to the closet.

"That's not how this works, Kendra. And for Christ's sake, you cannot tell me you didn't see the writing on the wall."

"Oh, I saw it." Kendra popped her head out of the closet, her eyes wildly looking over Bellamy. "The moment I saw your reaction to Payton as soon as you walked into the office after I'd hired her. You didn't give two shits about me anymore. It's always been about her."

"This started well before two months ago, and you know that." Anger surged in her chest and all hopes of picking her words wisely went out the window. "You started cheating when, Kendra? Were we even married before your first affair?"

Kendra's lips thinned, and she straightened her back. Her voice was dead calm when she spoke next. "I never wanted to cheat on you."

"Like hell. If you didn't want to cheat, you wouldn't cheat. If you wanted to make this marriage work, this one between us, you wouldn't have so casually thrown it out. I don't have time for this conversation. "

"Don't act like I'm the only villain here."

"Yeah, I cheated. Once. Like six months ago. Like I said, this marriage has been over for a long time. Neither one of us was willing to make the final step. Well, I did. I'm tired of being stuck in this relationship where you think you can toss around a few good looks, a few apologies, and get away with whatever you want to do. I'm done with being walked all over."

Kendra's lips parted in surprise. Bellamy realized she had never been so forward in their relationship before. Sure, they argued and she gave as good as she got, but she'd never truly said what she was feeling. Shaking her head, Bellamy stepped into the bedroom fully and put her hands out to her sides.

"You take advantage of me every day. I carry the brunt of the work and income at the office. I'm the one who is stable and stays here to make the money to pay for this house. Don't think that I don't know I'll be paying alimony when this is final, that I'll still be supporting your deadbeat ass until the day I die because you are vindictive enough to never release me from that punishment. I am not someone you can just walk all over and use what way you will. Thirteen years of it is enough. I've had enough."

"Enough? *You've* had enough?" Kendra's voice was so low Bellamy almost couldn't hear it, and as she walked closer with a deadly look in her eyes, Bellamy felt fear for her well-being for the first time since they had met.

Bellamy's chest rose and fell in an even pattern as she held her ground. She would not give up on this one. With her jaw clenched, she tensed every muscle in her body as Kendra got even closer, her glare deepening as she came.

"I have put up with you working so many hours you don't even know what day of the week it is. I have put up with your cheating, your lying, your looking at other women. I have put up with you putting me down, constantly. Did you forget I have feelings? My feelings count!" Kendra's pitch rose until it nearly broke on the last sentence.

Bellamy drew in a deep breath. Kendra was trying to swing the conversation back around on her. She always did that. It put Bellamy in a place of defense rather than offense. It was a great tactic in court, where Kendra was amazingly good at arguing, but at home it left a whole lot to be desired.

Bending down so she was close to Kendra's face, Bellamy scrunched her nose and shook her head. "I have one more thing to give you. I'll be sleeping in the guest room tonight and the rest of the week, and I will move out by the end of the week if you really want this giant cold house to your lonesome self."

"What?"

"Here." Bellamy shoved over the paperwork she had slipped into her pocket. "I'm suing you."

Without another moment's hesitation, Bellamy grabbed a few clean outfits out of the box Kendra had just thrown them into to make sure she was left with clothes for the week since Kendra was about to explode. But Bellamy wasn't done yet.

Stepping in closer to Kendra, Bellamy made her tone firm and clear. "I'm taking this law firm out from under you, and frankly, Kendra, your license is in jeopardy."

"What?"

Bellamy gave her a hard stare. "I also filed a grievance with the bar association weeks ago. You should be hearing from them soon as I hear they're in the middle of a very detailed investigation into your conduct."

"My conduct?" Kendra put a hand over her heart, the color draining from her cheeks.

Chuckling, Bellamy nodded. "Yeah, your conduct. Sexual harassment. Sexual assault and coercion. We'll start there. I'm sure I'll find out more once I start digging into the financials of our firm that you have so insisted on doing yourself and keeping to yourself. Tell me, Kendra, why is it that I have ninety percent of the case load and my income hasn't gone up by more than four percent in the last five years?"

Kendra's lips parted in surprise. "You didn't file a grievance."

"I did. Not only is it illegal, it's utterly immoral, and I can't believe I'm still married to you. You're disgusting."

Without another word, Bellamy grabbed her clothes and shoes and left the room. She went to the guest bedroom the farthest from the master bedroom where she'd already been staying for the last couple weeks since Payton's confession. She did not want to see her or deal with Kendra if she could manage it. It took her an hour to fall asleep, but when she woke up at five in the morning, it was the most refreshed she had felt in years.

When Bellamy got to the office the next morning, she cleared her schedule of meetings and spent the day in financials. Kendra's lack of response to her accusation that there might be more than sexual harassment to report scared her. Before Kendra had a chance to hide anything, she copied everything to an external hard drive, changed passwords, and then settled in to really look through it all.

It didn't take her long to find inconsistencies. All she had to do was go back a couple weeks to when Kendra had gone to Cabo San Lucas, a trip which ostensibly was a business trip. Bellamy grunted her half-surprise and half-idiocy before rolling her eyes. She had been such an idiot, so blinded to what was happening because she was too damn scared to stir the pot. She was going to have to go through all ten years of financial records to figure out just how much Kendra had embezzled.

Her eyes should have been opened ages ago. Rubbing her

temples, Bellamy let out a sad sigh. She'd buried her head, let it happen, let it fester as she purposely ignored it. She didn't want to think Kendra was capable of being such an awful person. She wanted to think she made better decisions than that in her life. They made good income. Kendra could have had just about everything she wanted, especially if she herself had put a little more effort into working for it.

As soon as it was late enough in the morning, Bellamy made a phone call to a financial investigator and auditor. She needed another set of eyes on their records. She needed to know how bad it was and how much trouble she herself was going to be in from not catching it any sooner.

Payton came into the office at her normal time, the door opening and closing outside. She started up the music that was always present when she was around. Bellamy stood up and moved to the entryway out into the lobby. She leaned against the wall, her shoulder holding her up. Taking off her reading glasses, she dangled them between her fingers as she stared at Payton's back.

A smile lingered on her lips, memories of the night before flashing through her mind, plus all the moments they had managed to steal here and there to touch, to flirt, to be together when they really weren't. Payton was so young, but she had reminded Bellamy of all the dreams she'd once had, of the confidence she'd once had in herself and her own abilities.

"Payton," her voice sounded tired but she felt anything but. "Can I talk to you a minute?"

Payton turned and nodded. "Sure."

Bellamy didn't wait as she headed into her office. As soon as Payton was inside, she shut the door and moved to sit in one of the two chairs at the far end of her desk where clients usually sat. She slipped into the chair, crossed her legs and settled her glasses on her thigh.

"I don't know what Kendra is going to be like when she

comes in today, but if last night is any indication, it will not be good."

"Okay." Payton's blue eyes were wide, but she didn't seem all that surprised. "I guess we'll just wait and see."

"I'll take the brunt of it as much as I can. She's mad at me, not you."

Shrugging, Payton shifted in her stance and nodded. "I get that."

"But I also need to tell you that I did file a grievance with the bar association about what happened with you, and some other things, but mainly that. It's unconscionable, and whether or not you file a formal police report, there needs to be consequences for her actions and there will be an investigation, so you will likely be getting a call. She cannot ever use her position of power for something like that again." Bellamy knew, though she doubted Payton did, that whatever Payton said, accidentally or on purpose, could also take Bellamy down with Kendra, but it would be worth it if Kendra was barred from practicing law ever again.

Payton's cheeks paled. Bellamy rubbed her palms together before gripping the arms of the chair. She wanted to stand up, encompass Payton in a warm hug. She did any time Payton got that pained expression on her face, the one where her nose reddened and it looked like she was about to cry, and yet she was still so very strong in the face of all of it.

"I want to be as honest as I can be with you about what's going on since you are in some ways the center of it all."

Payton nodded. "I get it. Thanks. Is that everything?"

"Yeah." Bellamy stood up as Payton made a mad dash from the room. She wasn't quite sure where that left them or anything really, but she knew she was on the right track to reclaiming her life and her job. Sitting at her desk, she dove head first into the financial records again. She needed to know how big a hole they truly were in.

~

PAYTON HAD SAT AT HER DESK FOR ALL OF FIFTEEN minutes, processing. She wasn't sure she had ever thought Bellamy would file for divorce, but suddenly the possibilities were a little more open than they were before. Letting out a breath, she checked the schedule and saw Bellamy had already rearranged a bunch of things, giving her the rest of the week in the office. Payton did the same for Kendra's schedule if only to try and eliminate the fallout with some clients, but when the first client of the day stepped through the doors, Payton froze.

Kendra wasn't there. She hadn't shown up, and it was nearing ten in the morning. Payton grabbed the woman a drink from the mini-fridge they kept just for clients and asked her to wait. She rushed to Bellamy's office and let out a breath as she went through the door.

Bellamy turned to look up at her, glasses perched low on her nose. "What is it?"

"Kendra's not here."

Bellamy shifted to look around the partially closed door to Kendra's still shut office. "Okay. That's unexpected. Did she call?"

"No."

"Don't call her. I'll do it."

"Wasn't planning on it." Payton wrung her hands. "But . . ."

"Yes?" Bellamy obviously was thin on the patience, although Payton had no idea why. "Out with it."

"I wasn't able to change her schedule fast enough, and a new client has come in to talk to her. I think it's a small case from what I remember of the initial phone conversation, but Kendra isn't here to meet with her."

Bellamy blew out a breath and leaned in her chair. "Send her in here."

"Okay."

"Email me the intake first, though. I want to skim it."

"Got it." Payton slipped from the office and shut the door. She made it to her desk and emailed the form to Bellamy before she moved to sit next to the woman. "Kendra unfortunately wasn't able to make it in to the office today because of a family emergency. Bellamy, however, is here, and she will meet with you if you're okay with that."

"That'll be fine. They work closely together, right?"

"They do," Payton halfway lied.

"Okay."

"She'll just be a few more minutes."

Payton went to her desk. Bellamy finished the meeting with the new client in record time. When they emerged from her office, Bellamy had Payton set up a second meeting in the next two weeks so they could get into more details. As soon as they were alone in the office again, Payton went to Bellamy's office, stopping at the door. There was actually very little work for her to do since Bellamy had cleared her schedule and they weren't going to trial that week.

"Kendra won't be joining us this morning," Bellamy said without looking up from her computer. "Something about being sick."

"Really?"

Bellamy snorted. "My thoughts as well."

"Was she mad?"

"Livid. Pretty sure all of my personal items will be packed and ready to go by the end of the day. She was pretty close to being done last night when I got home." Bellamy did turn then and set her glasses on the desk.

Payton nodded. Glancing over her shoulder at the front door, she saw no one was coming through it and slipped all the way into Bellamy's office. She walked straight up to Bellamy, putting her hands on the armrests of the executive chair and tilting it back. Bellamy's lips parted in surprise, but Payton covered her mouth with hers before Bellamy could say anything.

Their tongues tangled, and Bellamy's hand came up into the short hair at the back of Payton's head, tightening on the strands as much as she could. Payton nipped at Bellamy's lower lip, knowing she seemed to like everything a bit harder, a bit rougher than Payton did herself. Moving into her even more, she took possession of the kiss, making it last exactly as long as she wanted and in exactly the way she wanted. When she pulled away, she grinned.

"I'm glad you finally did it."

"Did what?" Bellamy's breathing was ragged.

"Filed for divorce. I think you deserve to be free and happy."

"Payton, you don't think—"

"I don't, but thanks for assuming." Payton winked. "We'll have to explore everything on our own when you're more unencumbered."

Leaning down again, Payton pressed another long kiss to Bellamy's lips before leaving the office again. When she got to her desk, her cell phone rang. The number on it made her heart sink.

"Hello?"

"Hi, this is Liam's daycare."

"What's wrong?"

"Nothing major, but he's got a bit of a fever and isn't looking all that happy about life right now. But since he has a fever, we'll need you to come get him as soon as possible."

Payton sighed. "I'll be there as soon as I can."

It was the first time he had gotten sick that she'd had to truly leave work for it. Before, she'd always managed to switch shifts at the restaurant to cover her bases or her mom would be able to help. But her mom had taken a lot of time off from her own job already, not to mention, if Liam was sick, she didn't want him anywhere near her mom. Sighing, Payton trekked her way back to Bellamy's office. She knocked this time.

"What?" Bellamy's voice was sharper than it had been before, her voice echoing through the room.

"Sorry," Payton answered. "Daycare just called. Liam's got a fever, so I have to leave to go get him."

Bellamy's face went from one of annoyance to one of pity. "Oh no!"

"I think it's just teething. He's been chewing on everything lately, and he gets fevers sometimes when his teeth break through."

Pursing her lips, Bellamy glanced around the office. "There are no other clients coming in today, right?"

"No. We rescheduled them all. You don't have court until next week, so my load isn't very much right now. I can schedule delivery for lunch so you're not left high and dry for that."

Bellamy waved her hand. "If you really think it's just teething and not something else, just bring him back here if you want the hours."

"He'll be super cranky."

"Nonsense. It's your choice, but if it's a light day, bring him. He won't disrupt anything."

"You're sure?"

"Payton, I wouldn't have made the offer if I wasn't sure. Go get your kid, do what you need to do, but also feel free to take the day off if you want."

Payton froze, caught between wanting the alone time with Bellamy and knowing it wouldn't really be that. "Okay."

Dismissed, Payton grabbed her purse and keys and headed for her car. It seemed to be harder to read Bellamy by the minute. Before, she'd been able to read her emotions and what she was thinking pretty readily, but ever since she'd visited Bellamy's house, it'd been harder. They would have to figure out their own relationship, but until that happened, Payton was lost.

She knew Bellamy was going through a lot and that her ability to think about another relationship of any kind was probably zilch, and she didn't want to push her luck.

She liked Bellamy, liked just about everything about her. She was strong and confident in her job, but she was also soft and unsure in other areas of her life. She was clearly a self-made woman, someone who worked hard to get what she wanted, and Payton admired that. That was who she had wanted to be her entire life.

Sure there was a twenty-three year age gap between them, but that hadn't hindered them so far. They were kind of in different places in their life, but at the same time, they were in the same place. Both were starting out on a new adventure, Payton with being a parent and Bellamy with being single. Both had their careers to think about. Payton had been toying with the idea of going back for her bachelor's degree once her adoption of Liam was finalized, now that it was a reality and not just a prayer. She wasn't quite sure what she wanted to study yet, but bettering her life would be the first step to bettering Liam's.

As soon as she had him buckled in his car seat, Payton swung by to grab the lunch order and head for the office. After seeing him, she was sure it was just teething and he'd be fine by the next day. With food, diaper bag, and baby in her hands, she pushed her way into the office with her elbow and hip. Bellamy stood over the copy machine in the corner of the front office and dropped everything she was doing as soon as she saw Payton come through the door.

Bellamy grabbed Liam first and nestled him into her side as she grinned at Payton. "See? He'll be perfect here today."

"You may change your mind when he screams while you're on the phone, but we'll see."

Chuckling, Bellamy shook her head. "Never. He's too cute to scream. You don't cry, do you, little guy?"

Payton snorted. "If you truly believe that, I'm going to leave him with you all night so I can get a full night's sleep."

Bellamy halted her steps to the copy machine at that. She turned and faced Payton with worry etched onto her face. Payton shook her head and waved her hands in front of her. "I didn't mean anything by it."

Bellamy visibly relaxed. Payton was going to have to watch what she said more carefully. With a sigh, she dropped the diaper bag next to her work bag and brought the food into Bellamy's office. Bellamy had apparently been busy while she was gone. The room was cleared of small objects Liam could get into, random decorations were put up high and out of his reach, and there were extra blankets and pillows on the couch.

"I thought he might end up in here for a nap since it's quieter than out there."

Payton turned at Bellamy's voice with tears in her eyes. "I can't believe you thought of that."

"Why can't you believe it?" Bellamy bounced Liam on her hip as she bent over her desk to slip the papers she had just been copying onto it. "I like babies, remember?"

"Yeah, but this . . . I don't know. I haven't run into many people being kind about a young mother. I mostly get dirty looks, and a few not-so-nice comments here and there."

Bellamy looked offended. She put her hand along Liam's back like she was protecting him from the world. Payton didn't miss the move, but she wasn't entirely sure Bellamy was aware she did it. "You are a wonderful person and mother, and don't you let anyone tell you otherwise. That does remind me, though, I have some paperwork to file for you. I wanted to do it earlier, but I got distracted."

"Paperwork?"

Bellamy grinned. "Your petition for adoption."

Payton's chest warmed, her stomach swimming with joy. "My social worker says everything is set. We finalize soon."

"Sooner if I get this petition filed."

Bellamy smiled at Liam, then kissed his chubby cheek before handing him over to Payton. "I'll do it now, so I don't forget."

"Okay. Thank you again for doing that. You didn't have to."

"It's the least I can do, really." Bellamy sat at her desk and reached into a drawer. Payton kissed Liam and headed to her desk. The day was surprisingly quiet, but she knew tomorrow would bring with it all the drama they were waiting for.

CHAPTER 12

PAYTON GOT TO THE OFFICE A LITTLE EARLY THAT morning. She shifted her bag off her shoulder and slipped it under the foot of her desk before turning on her computer and checking the messages. Sure enough, there were a dozen left between the time she'd gone home the night before and that morning. Most were for Bellamy and only two were for Kendra.

Dutifully, Payton took down the messages on pink slips of paper. She started the coffee machine so they could all be properly caffeinated. With the pink slips in hand, she went into Kendra's office to place hers on her desk. She was still suspiciously absent. Turning, she went to Bellamy's door and stopped.

The lights were off. Pursing her lips, Payton cocked her head to the side. Bellamy was always in the office well before she was, unless she was in court. She was pretty sure Bellamy got there somewhere between five and six every morning no matter what day of the week it was. But the light was off, indicating she wasn't in the office at all.

Confused, Payton moved to the door and eased it open. She walked quietly inside and set the pink slips on Bellamy's desk, which was still scattered with work, but the computer was asleep. Straightening her back, Payton bit her lip. Bellamy's cell-phone sat dead center on the desk upside down. She almost reached for it but decided it would be better not to.

Turning to leave, she stopped short. Bellamy was curled up asleep on her couch, a throw blanket tossed haphazardly over her legs and hips. Her hair was undone and strewn behind her head, and her chest rose and fell in a steady rhythm. Payton had never seen her sleep before; in fact, she had an inkling Bellamy never slept with how much work she managed to accomplish.

Payton checked her watch, noting it was only fifteen minutes to nine, and Bellamy's first client was coming in—she had no other option. She walked quietly to Bellamy's sleeping form and brushed her fingers over her warm cheek.

"Bellamy, you have to wake up."

Bellamy barely rustled, her face moving against the rough fabric of the couch but her eyes remaining shut and her chest rising and falling in that gentle and easy pattern. Payton slid to sit on the edge of the couch and covered Bellamy's shoulder with her hand, shaking lightly.

"Bellamy, wake up."

It didn't take long for Bellamy's eyelids to flutter and her breathing to change. Payton leaned back to give her some room. When Bellamy blinked, she looked briefly confused before she figured out she was in her office. Sighing, she pressed her face into the back of the sofa.

"What time is it?" Bellamy whispered, her voice deep with sleep.

"It's almost nine."

"What?" Sitting upright and flinging the blanket off, Bellamy was fully awake in a millisecond, her eyes wide. Payton grabbed the blanket before it fell to the floor and pushed it down to the end of the couch.

"It's almost nine. I found you sleeping in here."

"Damn it." She sat up, swinging her legs onto the ground.

"Bellamy, why were sleeping here?" Payton tried to get her attention, but Bellamy was going a million miles a minute.

"I never sleep this late."

"You must have needed it," Payton commented while she folded the blanket and put it back where it belonged on the bottom shelf of one of the end tables. "You should sleep in more often, really."

"I don't need comments from the peanut gallery, thanks."

Payton rolled her eyes and bit her tongue. In the last few days, Bellamy had gotten very short with her. She knew it wasn't likely *her* Bellamy was annoyed with, that she was stressed with everything else going on her life, but it still stung.

Picking up, she organized the papers on the coffee table and brought them back to Bellamy's desk to at least make it look decent enough for the client. Bellamy moved to the small closet in her office and grabbed a new outfit.

"I'll be back."

"Sure." Payton didn't hold her breath. She threw out the food cartons from whatever dinner Bellamy had clearly had in the office and continued to put everything in its place. She realized Bellamy hadn't put any of the knick-knack decorations back after Liam had spent the day with them, so she started to put those where they belonged.

When Bellamy came into the room, she wore slacks and a suit jacket. Payton halted what she was doing for a moment. She hadn't ever seen Bellamy wear slacks before. Her hair was still around her shoulders, curled from being left in a bun the previous day, but not done up again.

Her makeup was smudged, but Bellamy swiped her hands under her eyes to remove what she could of it. She looked more beautiful in that moment than at any time Payton had seen her before—tousled, mismatched, and out of sorts. Payton grabbed the overflowing trash and took it to the main lobby. She would deal with it in a minute.

When she got back, Bellamy was leaning closer to the mirror on the far side of the wall. Payton rolled her eyes. "Stop it. You look amazing."

"I look a mess."

"Sure. You didn't answer my question earlier. Why are you sleeping here?"

Bellamy stared at Payton in the mirror and closed her eyes briefly before turning to face her fully. "I went home last night to new locks on the doors. She's boxed up my stuff and informed me there is a moving company coming to get it today, and I'm to tell them where to take it."

"Need a storage unit?"

"I guess I do." Bellamy put her hands on her hips. "And a hotel room."

"I can arrange that while you're in your meeting."

"Thank you. Oh, and Kendra won't be in today. She's apparently still sick."

"Sick of being a bitch, sure."

Bellamy snorted. Payton was glad to hear the sound, thinking that finally Bellamy was going to come out of her shell. "Thank you for waking me up. I didn't realize I'd forgotten to set an alarm."

Payton leaned over, grabbed Bellamy's cellphone and stared at the screen. She turned it so Bellamy could see it. "You didn't. You just slept through it."

"What?" Bellamy took the sleek device between her fingers and stared dumbfounded at it.

"Like I said earlier, you must have really needed the sleep. It's not healthy to run on five hours of sleep every day. Take it from the woman who is sleeping in the same bed as a teething one-year-old." Payton wasn't sure where to stand or what to do. Everything had suddenly become awkward, and her heart raced.

She wanted to see if Bellamy's lips were as warm as her cheek had been, but they weren't standing close enough for that, and it didn't quite feel like the right time.

Bellamy sighed and came closer, her heels making her stand far taller than Payton. When Payton tilted her chin up, she couldn't read the look on Bellamy's face. Her eyes looked sad and forlorn, but her lips were pulled tight and her entire body was tense.

"You have no idea how much I would love to trade sleepless nights."

Payton's heart ached. Reaching out, she gripped Bellamy's hand and squeezed to reassure her, to try and bring her some comfort, but she wasn't sure any of it worked. When Bellamy's look didn't change, Payton stepped in and cupped her cheek.

"There's always time. Don't think because your marriage is ending that you can't still have what you want, one way or another. It may take a bit more time, but you're pretty stubborn, and you work hard for what you want."

This time Bellamy did stare directly at her, big brown eyes near tears. When she parted her lips, they both heard the front door rattle. Payton looked over her shoulder even though she couldn't see the door itself. She had forgotten to unlock it to allow their clients to come in.

"I'll go get that."

"Payton, wait a second. Thank you, really. I know this is strange and unorthodox, and I don't know, but thank you."

"Any time."

The sad look that crossed over Bellamy's features again concerned her but the rattling door alerted her to the fact she had to go let whoever was on the other side of it in. She didn't wait any longer as she left Bellamy by herself and headed for the front.

Mr. and Mrs. Crighton stood on the other side of the door with sour looks on their faces.

"I'm so sorry," Payton started, "I forgot to unlock the door this morning, and I was in the other room when you arrived. Come on in."

She settled them in to wait for another minute or two, heading to Bellamy's office. She knocked on the door, finding Bellamy already seated at her desk with paperwork in front of her that she was skimming over, no doubt going over the initial case file for the Crightons before they sat down to talk with her.

"The Crightons are here."

"Give me two minutes."

"You got it."

Again that pained expression crossed Bellamy's features, but she didn't look up at Payton this time, continuing her work. With a sigh, Payton walked to her desk to let the Crightons know they were going to have to wait. She knew they wanted to sue a police officer, but that was as much information as they had given her. Mr. Crighton was a character to say the least, and the few times she'd been on the phone with him left a lot to be desired. She was glad when they left the lobby and headed into Bellamy's office for the next hour.

With Kendra gone, their day moved quickly and mostly quietly. It had been an odd sort of few weeks with Kendra absent for most of the days. It felt like an actual office and not like a law firm on the stage with Jerry Springer. Payton skimmed over one of the files Bellamy had sent her for correction.

After the Crightons left, a strange man came in. He seemed simultaneously intimidating and intimidated. Payton couldn't find his name on the schedule for that day no matter how much he insisted he had an appointment with Bellamy. Biting her lip, Payton shook her head at him.

"What did you say your name was again? I'm sorry, it was a long night."

"My name is Gerald Worthington. I'm a financial investigator."

Payton jerked her head up at that. "I'll go see if she has a minute."

Without another word, Payton slipped into Bellamy's office. "There's a Gerald Worthington here for you? He's not on the schedule, but you also don't have anyone due in for the next couple hours."

"Yes, I expected him. You can send him in."

"Okay." Curious and a bit concerned, Payton led the man into Bellamy's office.

"Shut the door, Payton." Bellamy sent her another sharp look that took her by surprise. Payton was in the process of closing the door when Bellamy's voice caught her attention. "And please go get the lunch order."

"Sure thing." With the door shut, her stomach was in knots. There was most definitely something going on that she didn't know about and that Bellamy clearly didn't want to share with her.

AS USUAL BELLAMY HAD GOTTEN TO THE OFFICE WELL before anyone else had, and by the time Payton arrived, she was already nose deep in work. Payton's chest constricted as soon as Kendra waltzed through the lobby, eyeing Payton sharply before sauntering into her office without another word.

The tension was about to hit an all time high, she knew, but she was more worried because she knew Bellamy had to go to court that day, leaving her alone with Kendra for the first time in a month. Bellamy having to reschedule and rework everything meant she'd be spending a lot of time out of the office in the coming weeks. It was unavoidable, and Payton was going to have to find a way to protect herself against Kendra.

Kendra and Bellamy said nothing as they walked around each

other. Payton had never felt more like the middle child than then. She had to keep the peace between them, had to be the go-between for them. She hated it. Her own stress levels were hitting a near max, but she knew she could handle it, at least for a little longer.

Liam's adoption hearing was coming up, and she could at least hold out through that, not that she felt she had to. She was pretty sure Bellamy would follow through with everything even if she did quit. Rubbing her lips together, she drew in a sharp breath when Kendra came in and leaned over her desk, her breasts almost in full view.

"I need you to contact Mr. Bildridge for me and set up a meeting."

"Okay. Any preference on time?"

"As soon as possible."

"Okay." Payton pulled up his contact information on her computer while Kendra stayed exactly where she was. Kendra watched her and listened the entire time Payton made the phone call and did as Kendra had asked.

Payton couldn't understand why Kendra couldn't just make the phone call herself but whatever. She did as she was asked, trying not to stir the pot more than it already was. Bellamy must have come out of her office because Kendra leaned forward even more and had a sly look on her face.

Letting out a breath, Payton tried to focus on the document on her screen and finish out her own work while the two of them did their silent battle over her. She really wasn't in a mood to deal with them. Bellamy said nothing to Kendra and Kendra said nothing to Bellamy, but it was clear to Payton that Kendra was trying to use her against Bellamy as much as she could. She was relieved when they both left the lobby and she was cast into actual silence.

When Bellamy went to court in the afternoon, Kendra didn't wait long to call Payton into her office. With heavy feet, Payton made her way only to find Kendra waiting at the door. She shut it but didn't lock it this time.

"Come in, sit down."

Payton swallowed the bile rising from her stomach and sat on one of the hard chairs near Kendra's executive desk. "What can I do for you?"

"You can do a lot, actually." Kendra sat across from Payton in her own chair and leaned down again. "I need to know what Bellamy is planning."

"I think you know what she is planning."

Kendra's eyes scrunched and her lips pressed together. "I know some of it, yes, but you have far more access to her thoughts right now than I do. I need to know what exactly she is doing."

"Other than filing for divorce, I don't know what she's doing. It's not something she's really shared with me."

"I find that hard to believe." Kendra pressed her arms across her chest and stared Payton down. "I saw you kiss her."

"I'm aware." Payton paled despite not wanting to. She couldn't prevent her body from reacting to the words. "That was my fault. I shouldn't have done that. It was inappropriate and uncalled for."

Kendra narrowed her gaze then shook her head. "I don't believe you."

Payton grunted. "I really don't care if you believe me or not."

Her patience had worn thin faster than she had anticipated. Perhaps she wasn't as over everything that had happened between the two of them as she had thought. Seeing Kendra in the office was far more triggering than anything Bellamy had done. Payton twisted her hands together in her lap.

"I'm not going to spy on Bellamy for you, and the same is true for her. I will not be used by either of you for either of your gains. This is your personal problem, not a work problem."

"But it is a work problem. We own this firm together, thus should we divorce, this firm goes under."

Payton stared directly at Kendra. "I can find another job."

"Not as a paralegal you won't. I will blacklist you faster than you can blink. If you don't do what I am asking, you won't find another job as a paralegal in this entire county."

Standing up and leaning over Kendra's desk, Payton sneered. "I'll find another job. There are plenty of jobs out there, Kendra. I don't need to be blackmailed into staying here, and frankly, I won't stand for it again."

Without another word, Payton walked out of Kendra's office, shutting the door behind her. She let out a breath as she went to her desk, satisfaction filling her chest. She had never talked to a boss like that before, but it had felt damn good. She wasn't going to let Kendra take advantage of her in any way again, and she'd taken the first step toward that.

However, it made the rest of her day a living hell. She had pissed off Kendra by not doing what she wanted, so Kendra's vindictive nature came out full force. Anything Payton did was wrong, whether it was actually wrong or not. No matter what she sent to Kendra—it was wrong. Kendra watched her like a hawk with any phone call or email she sent. She'd never been so micromanaged before.

As soon as the end of the day came around, she packed up her stuff and rushed out of the building. She did not want to stay there longer than she had to. As soon as she was in her car, she checked her phone and smiled at the message on her screen.

Bellamy had texted, knowing either Kendra had left or Payton had left, asking how it had gone and if anything had happened. Payton responded that all was good and no major developments had occurred. With the response from Bellamy telling her to get Liam and enjoy her night, Payton decided to do just that. She drove straight to the daycare to pick him up and take him home.

CHAPTER 13

SOMETHING HAD BEEN OFF FOR DAYS. PAYTON HAD barely seen Bellamy at all. She'd either been at court, out at meetings with clients, doing something she didn't want to talk about, or holed up in her office. For the first time since Payton had confessed what Kendra had done to her, Bellamy's door was shut, every day. She was unapproachable, which was the first time ever since Payton had met her.

Sighing, Payton brushed her fingers through her hair as she stared at the clock on her computer. She had one hour until she was leaving for the day. She honestly wasn't even sure if Bellamy remembered why she'd requested part of the day off or when she was going to be gone. They hadn't talked about it beyond the initial request and approval of the time. Letting out a shuddering breath, Payton shifted through some more work and tried to ignore the fact Bellamy had completely changed in the past few weeks.

The woman she had admired, the woman she had been attracted to, the woman who had done so much for her was gone, and she had no idea if this was the true Bellamy finally coming out now that social conventions didn't mean she had to play up being the nice one against Kendra's evil side or if this was still a manifestation of everything going on in her personal life. If it was the latter, then Payton had no idea what to do to help, and every time she tried to do something or take a step in that direction, Bellamy shut her off and put her down.

It was exhausting, especially because Bellamy refused to communicate with her and tell her what was going on. Payton finished up what she was working on, checked the messages, ran a couple new ones to Bellamy's empty office, and ran one to Kendra's office.

"I'm leaving in ten minutes," Payton said. "Is there anything you need me to do before I go?"

"Leaving?" Kendra's shrill voice echoed in Payton's ears. "I never said you could leave early. The day is only halfway over."

"I requested time off weeks ago. It was approved."

"Not by me it wasn't."

"I've never had to request my time off with both of you before."

Kendra's upper lip pulled into a sneer. Payton stood strong. She was not going to miss her court date even if she got fired or quit. She would not miss it for anyone or anything. Bellamy was supposed to meet her there since she was already at the court-house for the day, but again, Payton had little hope Bellamy would even remember. She should probably text her to remind her, but she didn't want to seem nervous or overbearing.

"You can't leave."

"I'm leaving for a few hours to go to court for the final adoption hearing for my son. You can try all you want to make me stay here, but I am not going to miss this."

Kendra pouted, full out pouted. Her lips moved together, and her nose scrunched up. Instead of saying anything, she waved Payton off. Payton rolled her eyes as she turned toward her desk and grabbed her things. She had to go get Liam from daycare before she headed to the courthouse. Initially, she had wanted to take the whole day off to celebrate, but her mom's infusions had been changed, so they would do court that day and the party over the weekend.

With a deep breath, Payton slipped out of the door to the office and headed to her car. It didn't take her long to grab Liam from daycare and head back into the downtown area to go to the courthouse. She met up with Faith, her mom, her brother, and Maddy, and they waited outside of the courtroom to be called in. Bellamy was nowhere in sight.

Nerves ramped up in her stomach, and her foot tapped insanely hard on marble flooring. Denise grabbed her hand and shook her head. "What's got into you? Everything will be fine."

"It's not that," Payton whispered and shook her head. "It's something else."

Faith turned to both of them. "Did your lawyer say she was going to be late?"

Payton shrugged one shoulder up and let it drop. "She has to be here for it, right?"

"Yes."

Reaching into her purse, Payton grabbed her phone to see if she had any messages from Bellamy but there was nothing. She tried to remember which case she was even in court for, but she couldn't bring it up in her mind. She opened her phone and searched through the online schedule to see if it was one that was going to take Bellamy a long time or if something unexpected had come up.

When she saw what was written in the time slot, she knew Bellamy wasn't in court, but she had no idea where she was. It said she was in court, but unlike all the scheduling Payton put into the calendar, there was no reference number for a case, no name next to it, no time, and no judge. Everything was blank. It just said 'court' which told her absolutely nothing.

They were all ushered into the courtroom, but there was still no sign of Bellamy. With her stomach twisting and turning into knots bigger than she imagined, Payton grabbed her phone again. Perhaps she should call Bellamy. She didn't want to have to reschedule everything because Bellamy couldn't be bothered to show up. She was just about to hit call when the door opened and Bellamy slipped inside.

Payton had to do a double take. She did not look herself. Her clothes were not pressed clean and perfect like they typically were, her hair was again around her shoulders rather than pinned into a tight bun at the back of her neck. Her eyes had large and dark bags under them like she hadn't slept in two days. Payton's jaw dropped as Bellamy pushed right next to her, saying nothing.

Faith grabbed Payton's arm to direct her attention to the judge who was already coming into the room. Somehow she had missed that. Bellamy pulled out papers and stood, leaning against the table in front of them. Payton drew in a deep breath, her mind and her body attuned to the woman on her left, her arms wrapped around the child on her hip. Bellamy hadn't even greeted Liam.

She did everything she was told to do. She introduced herself and Liam to the court. She listened as the judge talked about adoption and how it was permanent. She stared at Bellamy, trying to pay attention to the judge but so focused on the stranger next to her. When it was her turn to stand up and answer the questions the judge asked, she did so with Liam in her arms.

It wasn't much longer before the judge made his decree, signed a piece of paper, and they were dismissed. They managed one picture with all of them—the family, the judge, Faith, and Bellamy. But as soon as the moment was over, Bellamy grabbed her briefcase and tried to slip out of the door. Payton charged forward, keeping Liam with her.

It took her halfway down the hallway to catch up with Bellamy. She gripped her hand and spun her around so they were facing each other. Payton's mouth was dry, and she was at a loss for words. Her breath escaped her as she truly got a good look at Bellamy. Whatever was happening, something was wrong, massively wrong.

"What's going on?"

"Nothing. Take the rest of the day. Go celebrate."

Payton shook her head. "Bellamy, stop avoiding. Where were you this morning?"

"Court."

"You were not at court. Why do you keep lying to me?"

Bellamy drew in a deep breath. She squared her shoulders, removing her wrist from Payton's grasp before she shifted the briefcase from one hand to the other. "You have your adoption finalized, Payton. You should celebrate."

The words died on Payton's tongue. She wanted to celebrate with Bellamy, one of the few people who had been truly supportive of her during the time she'd been going through the custody hearings and reunification process. Payton took a step forward, but Bellamy stepped back.

"Go celebrate."

"Where were you this morning?"

"It's none of your concern, Payton. I'll see you at the office tomorrow." Without another word, Bellamy turned in her four-inch heels and left Payton standing in the hallway by herself with Liam falling asleep on her shoulder. Confused and hurt more than she could put into words, Payton went back to the courtroom to grab her stuff and find her family. Her mom would take Liam to daycare while she went back to work, but she couldn't stop thinking that something major was about to happen, that Bellamy had finally broken, that life had caught up with her in a way she couldn't keep up with.

As she got into her car to drive to the office, she let out a breath. So much had changed in the past few weeks. Whatever glimmer of a hope she thought she had with Bellamy was gone.

She hadn't been naive enough to think they would run off into the sunset, but she had hoped they could at least explore a little of what they might have, because clearly there was something there. Without that hope, her job looked a whole let less appealing than it had the day before.

∼

SHE WAS ONLY FIFTEEN MINUTES LATER THAN SHE had expected because her mom had wanted to talk to her, but when Payton walked into the office, Kendra was waiting for her. The phone was ringing, there was a client sitting in a chair, and Payton let out a sigh as she walked toward the desk and answered the phone.

"Bellamy isn't in the office at the moment, can I take a message and have her call you back when she returns?" Payton wrote down everything Bellamy would need and hung up the call. When she turned to face Kendra, she really wanted to ask why she hadn't just answered the phone herself, which would have made everyone's life easier, but since there was a client sitting in the chair not far from the desk, she restrained.

"Do you need something before your meeting?"

"No, I was just wondering when you were coming back."

Kendra popped her hip to the side as she walked around Payton to call her client into her office. She ignored Payton as they disappeared into her office, shutting the door. Thankful for at least a few minutes of silence, Payton checked emails and phone messages since she doubted Kendra had answered it even once while she was gone. Sure enough there were two more messages.

She wrote down notes and put them on Bellamy's desk, then stood up straight, fists on her hips. She knew Bellamy didn't have anything scheduled after her finalization. They were supposed to meet back at the office, but Bellamy was still missing, and Bellamy had left before her. Sighing out her frustration, Payton went to her desk and sat down. Notes littered the desktop with Kendra's handwriting all over them, correcting things she was doing for Bellamy along with things she had done for Kendra.

When she opened up the computer again, there were two new emails—Kendra cyber-yelling at her for not doing something to full completion even though Kendra had *asked* her not to, and once again for being gone when she had already requested the time off. Payton groaned as she ignored the rude emails, redid the papers Kendra had changed her mind on again, and sent them back. At least she would have an hour of quiet while Kendra was in her meeting with the client.

Kendra emerged from her office with a smile on her face and the client two steps behind her. She had Payton set up another meeting for them before ushering them out of the door. Then Kendra turned on her, the smile gone, replaced with a glare. Payton's back stiffened—her chest constricted. She had a feeling she was not going to like what was about to happen.

"You were late coming back."

Payton's lips parted. "I'm sorry. Court took a bit longer than expected. It was only fifteen minutes, and I'll make it up tonight before I leave."

"No." Kendra stalked forward, the line of her body offering no reprieve and no hope for Kendra easing up on her. "You will not make it up before you leave tonight because you will not be working here."

"Excuse me?" Payton's heart thudded hard.

"You don't work here anymore."

"You're firing me?" Her stomach jumped into her throat, bile rising. She had never once been fired from a job in her life. She had never once even been written up before either. But in a small firm there were far fewer safeties than working for a larger company or even a chain restaurant. Payton's fists clenched tightly, her nails digging into the palms of her hands.

"You are being insubordinate. You don't show up when you're supposed to be here, leaving me to do your job and mine. You are incompetent. The amount of work I have to redo because you do it wrong is out of control, and you're not showing any sign of marked improvement. I've put up with this for long enough, and I need someone in this position who can actually do the job."

Payton's mouth went dry. Her lips parted in surprise. Bellamy never complained about her work. If there was something she did wrong, which was rare, she sent an email with a correction and asked Payton to redo it. Those had come less and less since she had figured out how Bellamy worked. With Kendra, there was nothing she could ever do that was right, no matter how many times she tried to follow directions.

Pushing to stand and lean against the desk, Payton stared at her with wide eyes. "So you're firing me?"

"I need someone who can do the job."

"You know what?" Slapping her hands on the desktop, Payton let loose. "I quit. I'm done. I don't need this kind of crap in my life. I don't need you for a boss. I can get a job anywhere, and I don't need your incompetent and insatiable jerk of a personality trying to undermine my work at every step."

Grabbing her purse and her bag, Payton slung them over her shoulder. She grabbed the one picture she had of Liam on the desk and shoved it into her bag, taking out the files she had for Bellamy in there and slamming them down onto the desk with as much force as possible. With her jaw set and her lips pressed firmly together, she walked around the desk to get into Kendra's face.

"You have literally been the worst boss I have ever worked for. Thanks for nothing."

She made it to the front door to the office and wrenched it

open only to find Bellamy standing right on the other side, about to open it herself. Payton glared. She had no time for any of it anymore. Bellamy had been right. She should have kept her resignation when she had initially turned it in. She should never have tried to continue to work there when she knew how bad it was.

"What's going on?" Bellamy asked, still disheveled, still looking exhausted.

Payton pursed her lips and pushed beyond Bellamy, saying absolutely nothing as she turned and walked toward the elevator. She pushed the button and waited impatiently for the elevator to arrive. She had to get out of there.

Bellamy's hand on her arm caused her to stop and turn, looking up into Bellamy's dark and now unreadable eyes. She shook her head at Payton. Suddenly their roles were reversed. The elevator doors opened, and Payton broke Bellamy's grasp as she entered. Bellamy, however, followed her inside.

"What happened?"

"Well, she tried to fire me for being late. Told me I'm incompetent and unable to do my job and that she needs someone in there who can do the job properly, and you know what? I'm just done, Bellamy. I'm tired of it all. I can't keep doing this."

"Doing what?"

For the first time in weeks, Bellamy's voice had concern filtering through her tone. She put her briefcase down against the wall as they stood face to face, the elevator door closed but not moving.

"Any of this," Payton let out a sigh. "I need a new job, one that doesn't have so much drama with it."

Bellamy let out a sigh and closed her eyes, her chin knocking down into her chest. She didn't say anything for at least thirty seconds, and Payton wasn't sure what to say or do. She stepped around Bellamy and hit the button on the elevator to bring her down to the walkway over the street so she could get to the parking garage.

When she moved, Bellamy's eyes were sad, devastated almost. Payton stared at her, again not sure what to do or say. Bellamy stepped closer, cupping Payton's cheek and tilting her chin up to press their lips together in a gentle kiss. Payton let her, drawing in a deep breath of her scent. Closing her eyes, she fell into the moment, using it for what comfort she could. The kiss felt like a goodbye, like a last moment between the two of them. When she walked out of the job, Payton hadn't meant to end their relationship—whatever there was of it, friendship or romantic—but that had certainly been what she'd done.

Bellamy shifted, pecking Payton's lips twice before she pressed their foreheads together. "I'll give you a glowing recommendation for whoever you want to work with, but I strongly suggest contacting Robinson, Schraeder, and Hamilton. I already called them and put your name in for a position over there."

"You what?" Confused, Payton stepped away. "Why would you do that?"

Bellamy's lips parted as if she was going to say something, but the doors opened and she stared outside. "You should go. Let me know if you need that recommendation."

"Bellamy."

"Go, Payton. I'll see you again, I promise."

With her heart thudding hard, Payton followed instructions and left the elevator. She turned around to watch the doors shut as Bellamy stared at her. Everything felt final, like the very end. Biting her lip, Payton blinked unexpected tears that blossomed in her eyes. She stayed, standing and staring at the elevator for longer than she wanted to admit.

Finally heading to her car, she slipped behind the steering wheel and pulled out her phone. Curious, she searched for the law firm Bellamy had told her about and called it, speaking directly with one of the lawyers there who knew exactly who she was. Surprised, she set up an interview for an hour from then since they had been anticipating her call.

More confused than ever, Payton left downtown Tacoma and headed for the larger law firm that sported its own building. It had many different lawyers, it focused on litigation, which was what Payton had been doing, but this time, she would be able to focus completely on being a paralegal without any secretarial duties. It would be a dream if she could land herself the job and start almost immediately.

She grabbed herself a quick lunch, checked how she looked in the mirror of the fast-food bathroom. She had to find herself some sort of income so she could pay the rent on the run-down one-bedroom apartment she could barely afford on her own. She knew she had to do this. She had to leave Bellamy and that hell-hole of an office behind and find something better for her and for her son.

Her son.

Payton smiled at the term. Liam was officially her son, forever. There was no going back on that, not that she would ever want to. He had been hers almost from day one, but now it was official and legal. Bellamy had helped her with that, and she would be forever grateful for the added help and for not having to pay lawyer fees for all the filings it took.

With a lighter step, Payton got into her car and drove to the new law firm, ready for an interview—ready to start over on a better track for her life. She was a mother now, and that made a whole world of difference in how she saw her life and what she should do with it. Whether or not Bellamy was a part of the changes would remain to be seen, but after their conversation in the elevator, she was pretty sure any connection or relationship they had was over.

CHAPTER 14

BELLAMY WAS READY FOR WAR. ENTERING THE OFFICE she shut and locked the front door, hitting the lights in the lobby. She didn't want any disruptions for the argument that was about to happen. She moved to her office and set her brief-case on her desk, then headed straight for Kendra's office. When she opened the door, she found Kendra at her desk with the phone pressed to her ear.

Bellamy waited. She wasn't going to drag this out any longer. She didn't care one way or another, but she wanted Kendra to sign the divorce papers before everything went down. They had randomly texted back and forth what each of them wanted. Bellamy pretty much didn't care so long as she got the firm all in her name because she knew she'd get everything in the end anyway. She agreed to pay a reasonable alimony because in order for Kendra to claim she needed more money she would have to fully admit she wasn't earning any of the income at their firm— something Kendra would never confess to.

Crossing her arms, Bellamy sat in one of the chairs and waited Kendra out. She seemed nonplussed to have Bellamy sitting there, listening in on an obviously flirtatious conversation. With a sigh, Bellamy rubbed her lips together and waited as patiently as she could. She had wanted Payton to find another job ever since she had handed in her resignation. Bellamy had wanted to find an opening for her to go to when she finally decided to leave, as Bellamy knew she would.

No one who was sane would stay working for them longer than necessary. It was going to take Bellamy years to rebuild the disaster of a reputation they had developed. In some ways, it would be easier to start over, but she didn't want to. Bellamy picked at invisible lint on her pants as she continued to wait for Kendra to finish.

She was losing her ability to keep still as Kendra continued the talking, but she'd already been sitting there twenty minutes. She wasn't about to give up now. Just as she had that thought, Kendra hung up and set the phone on her desk. She turned to face Bellamy, her lip curling into a sneer.

"That was rude," Kendra stated.

Bellamy grunted. "So is trying to fire someone for something they didn't do. You know she didn't deserve it."

Kendra shrugged. "Got her out of here, didn't it? I don't need her here to ruin more of our business."

"If anything, Payton increased our business by being consistent and highly organized. I sent her to Robinson—"

"You did not."

Bellamy raised an eyebrow at Kendra, daring her to continue. When Kendra's jaw snapped shut, she knew she had won. "I want a divorce."

"I don't," Kendra's voice turned soft, and shock rang through Bellamy's chest and spine.

This was a complete change from any conversation they'd had in the past week. Bellamy stopped fidgeting with her clothes and shifted to sit up straighter in her chair. "You don't want a divorce?"

"I love you, Bells."

Keeping silent, Bellamy clenched her jaw and waited for the other shoe to drop. There was always something Kendra wanted, and it was whether or not Bellamy would give in that would determine how bad an argument was going to get.

"I want you to come home. I miss you."

"House too big for one person?" Bellamy snarked. "You packed up all my stuff and paid movers to take it to a storage unit. You don't want me home. You're just not quite ready for the single divorced life yet."

Kendra shook her head, her blonde curls bobbing around her face and her bright red lips forming into a pout. "No, that's not it, Bells. Really. I miss you. The house does feel empty, but it's more than that. I feel empty. I haven't . . . we haven't really talked in a week, and I just don't know how to handle it."

"It has been far longer than a week since we really talked. Try years. And I've tried to talk to you. I've tried to make this work. I tried to get you to love me even, but I'm tired of trying. I'm tired of being second best to whatever new fling you've got going on. I'm tired of being the steady one at home who provides everything you want. What about what I want?"

"And you want Payton?"

Bellamy shook her head slowly. "No. I don't know. What I don't want is this. What we had? It's long gone. It's time for us to accept that and move on. I want a divorce, and I want you to sign the papers now."

"Papers?" Kendra's head jerked up. "You have them?"

"Yes. With all the specifications you asked for." Bellamy's heart raced, hoping the calm they had managed to keep so far would remain. She wanted to be able to talk about this like civilized adults who might care for each other. "You get the house, the cars—minus mine—everything you wanted. I'll give you the alimony you wanted. But I added one clause into it."

"What's that?" Kendra turned her chair and stared directly at

Bellamy, her lips parted slightly and her eyes wide with surprise and curiosity.

This was going to be the difficult part. Kendra would no doubt read over every inch of their decree, making sure everything was perfect and exactly as she wanted it. It was the curse of being lawyers. They knew the ins and outs of how to make things turn out better for each of them.

Bellamy folded her hands in her lap, crossing one knee over the other. "I put in a clause that you will not contact Payton and you will not tarnish her name. You will not slander her. She's innocent in all of this, and you know that."

"You can't—"

"It's that or we can take this to mediation and maybe even before a judge if you won't agree to it. I just want a fresh new start, Kendra." Bellamy stared directly at her. "We can both have that if we do this the right way. We're going to have enough of a battle over the firm. I'd rather fight you there than here."

Kendra lifted her chin and stared down her nose at Bellamy as she contemplated. Bellamy gave her the time to think, the time to really understand—except Bellamy knew she'd have the firm all to herself easily enough and Kendra signing the divorce decree was added evidence for the suit she had filed. Kendra was completely unaware of what Bellamy knew, but she could hold out a little longer before revealing that.

"Fine."

"Fine, you'll sign?"

"Yes. Under one condition."

Bellamy sighed. There were always conditions when it came with Kendra. There was always one more thing she wanted. When Bellamy didn't answer, Kendra stood up and came around her desk. She bent down over Bellamy's chair, her hands sliding along the armrests to block Bellamy in, and it was the first time Bellamy had ever truly felt trapped with her.

Their mouths touched, briefly, but enough. Bellamy parted

her lips in surprise and in sadness. If her kiss with Payton had been a goodbye, this one was forever. She allowed Kendra to kiss her, to take whatever it was she wanted from that moment, but she gave nothing in return. She had no heart left for their relationship, no heart for what they had once hoped and dreamed. When they'd first signed the lease for their office, they had stayed there the whole night dreaming of what it would look like and what it would become.

It was the same with the house. After dreaming together, Kendra had decorated everything to her liking while Bellamy worked to bring in the money to make it possible. Bellamy closed her eyes. She should have seen it then. She should have seen how her future was going to unfold, but she'd turned a blind eye to all the warning signs, all the nasty quips Kendra made, the flirting with other women, the cheating so very early on in their marriage.

When Kendra leaned back, she smiled. "Go get the papers."

Bellamy pushed herself up from the chair. She came in with the paperwork and together they signed, one by one, going through each form to make sure everything was as it should be. When they finished, they put it into an envelope. "I'll file this tomorrow morning."

"Thanks," Kendra whispered. "About the firm—"

"We can talk about that another day." Bellamy took the envelope and stood up, awkwardly staying in place for another minute. "One problem at a time."

"Okay."

Bellamy went to her office, shutting the door behind her. As soon as she heard the click of the lock, she let out a breath and leaned her shoulders against the door as tears streamed down her face. She hadn't expected this. Sorrow swept into her chest and took over. Her marriage had been over for years. Everyone around them had known that, had seen it, but still, signing the papers was so final.

Picking herself up, she moved to her couch and collapsed into it, tossing the divorce decree onto the coffee table and curling into a ball, sobbing. She let everything out, let every emotion pound into her on one side or the other. She just felt— for the first time in so many years—she felt everything she should have been feeling. Exhaustion. Pain. Hurt. Weariness. Sadness. Brokenness.

By the time she was done crying it was dark outside, and her eyes were itchy and no doubt red. Her makeup had long since streamed down her cheeks and created streaks of black on her face. With a deep breath, she picked herself up and cleaned her face in her mirror. She moved to her desk to get some work done but sat there for an hour while accomplishing nothing.

She did get one email message that she made sure to check. It was a note from Carol Robinson, saying they had hired Payton on the spot and she was starting the next day. A warm sensation filled her heart and a smile flitted across her face. At least she had managed to do one good thing through all of the drama and pain. She had managed to secure Payton a position that would be to skillset in a firm that would appreciate her. Sending a short reply to Carol, she closed her computer, left her briefcase and headed for her car. She needed a hot shower and a stiff drink. She needed to let loose everything she had been bottling up for years.

SHE MADE SURE THEY WERE OFFICIALLY DIVORCED before she finished her investigation into their law firm. Bellamy had told Kendra not to hire anyone else until they figured out what they were doing with the firm, and Kendra—to her surprise—had agreed. Something had changed in Kendra since they had signed the papers. Suddenly she had become far more like the woman Bellamy had met all those years before.

She was kind, she was thoughtful, she was hard-working, and she was considerate. She'd bring Bellamy coffee in the mornings when she came in to work, knowing Bellamy would already be there. If Kendra had been this way the last seven years, there might have been hope for them yet, but Bellamy maintained their relationship was not one that should be continued or revived. Kendra flirted with her often, and Bellamy would occasionally flirt back, but she knew what was coming. She knew the end of it all was in sight.

It took two months for everything to process. They hadn't discussed the buy out of the firm in the intervening time, and Bellamy wondered if Kendra thought she'd given up on that dream.

When the front door to the office opened, Kendra went to see who it was. Bellamy's office door was propped open, and she waited with bated breath when she heard the detective's voice. She had spoken to him several times in the last four months as the investigation got underway. Her heart was in her throat, her stomach flip-flopping like a dying fish in her belly.

"I'm Kendra. What can I do for you today, Detectives?"

"We're here to take you down to the station."

"What for?"

Bellamy chose that moment to stand up from her desk. Her knees were weak, and she had to force herself to stand upright and keep her breathing even. She bit her lip as she slipped from her office into the hall and stood at the vertex of their offices and the lobby. Kendra turned to look over her shoulder at Bellamy and gave her a confused look.

"You are under arrest for embezzlement, for theft. You have the right to remain silent. . ."

Bellamy tuned them out, her gaze completely focused on Kendra's frightened eyes, her quivering lip as they pulled her arms behind her and handcuffed her. Bellamy's chest constricted when Kendra shook her head.

"What did you do, Bells?"

Swallowing, Bellamy moved forward as soon as the detectives were done with her Miranda rights and stopped right in front of Kendra. She stared her down, the fear in her chest giving way to joy and freedom. With a deep breath, Bellamy shook her head at Kendra in disbelief.

"You can't honestly think that you could steal close to a million dollars from our firm over the last six years without me discovering it—without consequences for your actions. What I don't get is how I didn't catch on until this year."

Kendra wisely said nothing. Bellamy let out a breath as she watched the detectives lead Kendra out of the office. She shut and locked the door, pressing her forehead to the cool glass and closing her eyes. The largest chapter of her life was closed, the one thing she had hoped would never end. But she wouldn't lose her license. She wouldn't lose her firm, at least not yet. She'd still have to fight to get Kendra's name off of everything, but she could and would do that.

Sliding to the floor, Bellamy rested her back against the door and stared into the completely empty office in front of her. She was alone, truly alone, for the first time in decades. She wouldn't likely see Kendra again until sentencing. Her law firm was hers. Everything was hers. She had won, and Kendra had lost, spectacularly.

Hitting the back of her head against the door, she let out a snort. Why did being alone feel so awful? She had thought it would feel good to finally have everything she had wanted, everything she had needed. She'd even managed to find herself a nice little two-bedroom apartment that she'd already moved into.

With open eyes, Bellamy knew what was wrong. She didn't have what she wanted. The divorce, the law firm, they were all byproducts of what she really wanted. She wanted to be happy. She wanted to enjoy life. She didn't want to be working from five in the morning to midnight every night, seven days a week. She wanted a family. She always had.

Bellamy dragged herself up and back to her office. She forced herself to finish the day's work and call in a locksmith to change the locks on everything that had Kendra's and her name associated with it. Kendra wouldn't get back in without her knowing. She filtered through the applications for a new paralegal, pulled out three good options and set up interviews with them for the coming week.

She'd no doubt have to finish her lawsuit against Kendra to get her name off the company, to buy her out completely. It would take time, but it would be time well spent. Sighing, Bellamy gave up on work shortly after eight in the evening, grabbed her keys, and headed out of the office.

Alone in her new apartment, she grabbed the bottle of her favorite whiskey that Kendra had managed to angrily pack into one of the boxes that fateful night. She didn't even bother with a glass as she brought it over to the brand new couch she had purchased, collapsing into its cushions. She had wanted a new start to life, and she had managed to give herself a hell of a new one.

She closed her eyes. The whiskey burned as it slid down her throat at first, but she kept drinking. It had been two months since she'd gotten so drunk she couldn't see straight. Two months since everything had really started. Two months since she'd said goodbye. But it wasn't Kendra she was thinking about. Payton's blue eyes, her sharp and smart haircut styled right across her eyes in a professional punk look, her smile, her voice—especially every time she talked about Liam. Just her very presence, the calming effect she managed to have on Bellamy's racing nerves no matter the situation.

Payton was who Bellamy thought of. Not her ex-wife—who was no doubt having the worst night of her life sitting in a jail cell while she waited to see if she could meet with a judge to post bail. Surely not her ex-wife—whom she'd had arrested. Sweet Payton—the woman who had somehow managed to steal her heart without her even noticing. Dragging the blanket over her legs, she flicked on the television, turned off her phone, and drank herself to sleep.

CHAPTER 15

IT HAD BEEN A YEAR SINCE BELLAMY HAD SEEN HER—A
year of legal battles, of quiet nights and even quieter days. It had
been a year of thinking about Payton. As she sat in her office on
Friday, she couldn't get her mind off Payton—wondering just
what she had gotten up to, where she was, and how cute Liam
would be now. He'd be two years old if her memory served,
though she could just look up the legal paperwork if she wanted
to find out for sure.

Saturday morning, she took a risk. She'd woken up early as
usual and gone into the office for a few hours of work, then
decided to take the rest of the day off. She pulled out the file for
Payton's employment record and hoped nothing had changed in
the last year. With a deep breath, Bellamy locked up the offices
and headed for her car.

Kendra was still in prison. She'd been sentenced to five years
and reparations, which Bellamy was pretty sure she'd never
actually see—she'd essentially be paying herself because of
alimony. She would try to get out of that when Kendra got out
of prison.

It took her twenty minutes to get to the small run-down

apartment complex after stopping by a department store. If Payton still lived there, she would hopefully be looking for a new apartment soon enough. It wasn't the greatest part of town, and surely with a full-time salary for a year, she could find a better place for her and Liam.

Holding her breath tightly in her chest, Bellamy stepped out of her car and headed for the front door to the complex. She was sure it was supposed to be locked, but it was propped open with a giant rock. Sighing, she stepped around it and through the hallways until she found the apartment she was looking for on the fourth floor. Suddenly nervous, Bellamy pulled her hair into a ponytail then smoothed her sweaty palms over her jeans. Her heart thumped as hard as her fist when she knocked on the door. She waited and waited.

Biting her lip, Bellamy hoped Payton was still there, that she hadn't gone anywhere, that she was still available and wanted to be available. The present she had bought for Liam felt awkward in her hand and a bit like a bribe, but she wanted to celebrate him. He deserved it as much as Payton did.

When the door finally opened, Payton's bright face shone through the small crack. Her baby-blue eyes were wide with surprise. Her hair was far longer than it had been the last time Bellamy had seen her, but it was still cropped around her face in a sweet pixie cut, making her look more mature and older than she actually was.

"Hey," Bellamy said when Payton said nothing. "I come bearing gifts." She held up the present for Liam, the bag swinging on her fingers as she put it in front of Payton's face. "It's for Liam, for his birthday."

"I'm sure he'll enjoy it." Payton reached forward to take it but didn't open the door any wider to let Bellamy in.

Taking a deep breath, Bellamy figured she was going to have to do some serious groveling in order to get her toe inside. She wrung her hands together, pressing her thumb into the palm of her hand and using the pressure from her fingers to center herself.

"Can we talk?"

"About what?" Payton's voice was sharp and firm.

Bellamy lost her gumption. It had taken her twelve months to get to the point of even wanting to show up at Payton's door but the less than warm welcome made her want to turn tail and run. "You know, never mind. This was a bad idea."

She spun on her heel and headed for the stairs to leave, but Payton's hand on her wrist stopped her. Bellamy turned to look over her shoulder, her eyes wide and her heart in her throat. She had no idea what she'd been thinking. Surely after an entire year, Payton would have moved on and found someone else, someone far more suitable for her than a cranky, divorced lawyer twenty-three years her senior.

"Don't go," Payton's voice was soft. "I'm sorry, that was rude of me. But why are you here? I think that's a very reasonable question to ask."

Bellamy turned around to stand, facing Payton. She stared at the door as it opened slightly and Liam popped his head out to see them. She smiled and stared down into Payton's eyes. "We have an audience."

Payton grinned. "He doesn't like to be too far from me."

"I can see that. To answer your question, I'm not sure I really know what I'm doing here."

Payton glanced up at Bellamy, stared deep into her eyes and nodded. "Okay. Come inside then."

Payton's hand never left hers as she led the way through the door and into the tiny one-bedroom apartment. Payton shut and locked the door behind them, shooing Liam toward the living room. Bellamy followed, her wrist still imprisoned by Payton as she was dragged to sit on the second-hand couch in the middle of a toy-filled living room. Payton handed over the present Bellamy had brought, and he dug into it.

He pulled out the sleek action figure and squealed, bringing it over to Payton so she could open it properly. He turned to Bellamy and uttered "Thank you" in a cute little tone that absolutely melted her heart. Liam took the toy and immediately set about playing with it, running around the living room like he had just won a prize. Bellamy grinned at him, glad to have made him happy at least.

Payton's hand found its way back to Bellamy's, and she squeezed lightly, bringing Bellamy's attention to the conversation they had yet to have. She sighed and shook her head. "I didn't even know if you would still be living here since it had been so long."

"I think we'll move next year when I have enough saved up. Hoping to put a down payment on a house. That's if my sister stays sober this time."

"She's sober?"

Payton shrugged. "For now. She's pregnant. She managed to stay sober when she was pregnant with Liam, so maybe she will this time too."

"Oh! Liam's going to be a big brother. That's wonderful news."

However, Payton didn't look too happy about it. Her lips were thinned and her face set. "We'll see. If this new one is born addicted, I've already agreed to take custody."

"Really? You're such a strong and wonderful woman. I'm not sure what I would do in that situation."

Raising one shoulder up and dropping it, Payton let out a sigh. "I'd rather keep them together than separate them."

"I can understand that."

"But you didn't come here to talk about Liam and Maddy."

"No, I came here to maybe talk about us, but really just to see you again."

Bellamy leaned into the couch and stared directly into Payton's eyes. She had missed these moments, when they could read each other so easily, when they didn't necessarily have to speak. She missed hearing all about Liam and everything he was doing. Walking and talking were clearly two of those things. She distracted herself by watching him as he moved. She had no idea where to start, and it would be especially awkward if Payton had found someone else.

"I've missed you," Bellamy whispered, glancing in Payton's direction. "I really have."

"I've missed you, too, though I can't say I've missed that office."

Bellamy wrinkled her nose and smirked. "No, I didn't think you would. Kendra is in prison, by the way, so the office is much quieter these days."

"Prison?"

"Embezzlement among other things. She confessed. Just over a million dollars in the span of six years. That's what I couldn't talk to you about toward the end. I was meeting with police and investigators and lawyers and financial people all trying to figure out where the money had gone, what she'd done with it, and how I could stay out of trouble. She also hadn't been paying taxes. I'm still paying off that bill."

"Jesus, Bellamy. She was really screwed up, wasn't she?"

Bellamy snorted. "Yeah, she was, and still is in some ways. But now it's just me in the office with a new paralegal. Though I'm thinking of hiring a junior associate to help with some of my caseload."

"Do you like being your own boss and having no one to answer to and no one to try and make you do things you don't want to?"

"Absolutely."

"Is it weird?"

"Is what weird?" Bellamy bit her lip and stared down at Payton's lips, wondering if they tasted the same.

"Being on your own."

Shaking her head, Bellamy shrugged. "Honestly, in a lot of ways, it feels the same. Less stressful for sure, but I was pretty much doing everything anyway."

"That's true."

"What have you been doing? I hear you're still at Robinson Schraeder. You liking it?"

"Yeah, I am. They're great to their employees, and they've been really flexible with my time for Liam, which has been good. He's needed some physical and occupational therapy because of what happened after he was born. They're going to help with my bachelor's degree, too. I go back to school in a month."

The question burning on the tip of Bellamy's tongue wouldn't leave her mouth. As much as she tried to force herself to say it, she couldn't bring herself to hear the answer if it wasn't what she wanted. Payton, in her usual flair, read right through her.

"I suppose you're here for an actual reason, though."

"Yes," Bellamy whispered, her voice catching in her throat.

"The answer is yes."

Confused, Bellamy shook her head. "I'm sorry, I don't—"

But she didn't get to finish. Payton cupped her cheek and brought their mouths together in a sweet, slow kiss. Bellamy hummed as her body listed forward into Payton's, her hand landing on Payton's waist to hold her still. Their tongues tangled in a gentle, calm dance, one they had never really managed before. Liam squealed over something, but neither one of them moved to see what.

Payton pulled Bellamy's hair out of its ponytail and let it fall around her shoulders, skimming her fingers through it before gripping and tugging to hold Bellamy's head in place so they could deepen their kiss. Bellamy groaned and closed her eyes, falling into the moment. When Liam touched their thighs, Bellamy jerked back and smiled down at him as he grinned up at them.

"That's a yes, I'm single, and yes, I would like it if you kissed me."

Bellamy's lips quirked into a smile. "I had no idea how to ask."

"I know. It's not usual for you to be at a loss for words. Perhaps you really have changed a lot in this last year."

"Maybe. I haven't stopped thinking about you. Every time I go into the office, I can't help but wish you were there. Not that I want to work with you again, but I want to see you again, that often. I've had a whole year to think about it, Payton, and I was stupid in a lot of ways, the least of which was hanging on to a bad marriage, but the biggest of which was not recognizing what was right in front of me."

"And what was right in front of you?" Payton bent to pick Liam up and set him in her lap. He shoved the toy in her face, and she took it and ogled at it before handing it back.

Bellamy shrugged, holding out her hand for Liam. "You."

Payton nodded slowly. "I'm not sure I want to date you."

"Which is perfectly fine." Bellamy's heart broke. She hadn't been expecting those words, but she would in no way pressure Payton into anything she didn't want to do. She swallowed, not quite sure what to do with that answer and figuring she should probably leave some time soon.

"I mean, there is a lot of drama that comes with you."

Chuckling, Bellamy nodded. "That happens when you sleep with married women. I should have known better than to allow that to happen."

"Hmm, well, to be fair—the first time, we thought that was going to be it and there wouldn't be anything after that."

"I was shocked to walk in that day and see you in my office. You know that, right?"

"Absolutely. I was just as shocked."

Bellamy smirked. "Talk about a coincidence, but I'm glad

Kendra did hire you. If only for the fact it revealed who she truly was and how much I really needed to act."

"Well, you're welcome for that, I guess."

They lapsed into a silence while Liam climbed off Payton's lap and wandered around the living room to play with various toys. Bellamy watched him move and enjoy his toys, still not quite sure what to say or what to do. The conversation seemed to be nearing its end, so she patted her legs and moved to stand.

Payton followed her to the door. Bellamy turned to stare down at Payton before placing her hand on the knob and turning it. Liam came over, his hands held up. Bellamy wasn't sure what he wanted, but instinct told her to pick him up. She reached down, and he moved into her arms. She placed him on her hip and nuzzled his cheek, his jet-black hair long around his ears so that it tickled her nose.

"He's grown so much."

"He has," Payton answered. "Is your number still the same?"

"It is." Bellamy bounced Liam on her hip and grinned at him when he laughed. He pressed his chubby hand to her cheek and stared into her eyes, and she was lost in them as much as she was lost in Payton, though she was pretty sure it would never happen romantically for them at that point. Friendship would have to be enough. God knew she needed more friends, people who weren't also lawyers.

Payton reached for Liam and took him from Bellamy, shifting him onto her side. "I'll call you then, if I change my mind."

Bellamy already missed the warmth from Liam's body, the weight of him in her arms. She put a hand on his back and leaned in to kiss his cheek before she straightened and opened the door. "I'll see you around, maybe."

"I'll see you."

Leaving the apartment was harder than she had expected. After the kiss, Bellamy had some hope that perhaps they could rekindle some sort of relationship and really start fresh and new, but the mood had turned so melancholy afterward, she was pretty sure she would never see Payton again.

When her phone rang in her pocket, she was surprised. Lifting it, she narrowed her eyes at the number she didn't recognize and answered. "Hello?"

"Hey, it's Payton. Is that offer for a date still available?"

"Yes?" Bellamy spun around as soon as she got to her car and stared at the front door to the apartment complex. Her heart raced, her stomach gurgled with renewed hope and the smile on her face would not leave. "When?"

"Now. I just have to drop Liam at Mom's."

Payton walked out of the apartment building with the phone to her ear and Liam on her hip. She waltzed right up to Bellamy, hanging up the phone and pressing her mouth to Bellamy's in a heated but quick kiss.

"Come on, I'm parked over here."

Bellamy followed, almost as confused as she was before. Once they had Liam in the car seat and they were in the car themselves, she turned with a bewildered look. "What changed your mind?"

"First, I did not expect you to show up today of all days, or really ever again."

"I told you I would see you again."

"Forgive me if after a year I didn't believe you."

"Fair enough." Bellamy licked her lips. "And what's second?"

"That kiss . . ." Payton rolled her eyes as a blush touched her cheeks. "You do know how to kiss."

Laughing, Bellamy rested her head on the headrest as Payton drove. "Same goes for you."

It didn't take them long to get where they were going. Payton reached over and gripped Bellamy's hand before she got out of the car. "If you want to come in, you are welcome to."

"You want me to meet your mom?"

Payton shrugged. "You've already met her, technically."

"As your boss."

"Yeah, so. Mom also gets to talking and I often get stuck in there for an hour. I figure if you come in with me then I'll be able to get away faster."

Bellamy stared at the front door to the small quaint house, anxiety rising in her chest. This she had not anticipated from the day. When she turned to Payton, she gave a slight nod. "I guess."

Anticipation swelled in Bellamy's stomach. She moved slowly to make sure Payton was going ahead of her. As soon as they got to the door, Bellamy tried to plaster a smile on her face, but she so did not feel ready for any of this. When Payton opened the door and walked inside, she hesitated and almost didn't follow, but the sweet smile Payton sent over her shoulder beckoned Bellamy. The house was warm, and voices from a television filtered to her ears from the other room. Payton led the way, and Bellamy shut the door behind them.

"Mom!" Payton called. "I need you to watch Liam for me today."

"Oh?" Denise popped her head into the living room from the kitchen, a grin forming broadly on her cheeks as she saw her grandson but faltering when her gaze moved over to Bellamy.

Bellamy had no idea what if anything Payton had told her mother about what had happened, but she suspected Denise's opinion of her was probably rather poor. She had only met her once, during the final adoption hearing, and Denise hadn't said a word to her. It had not been a good day.

"Mom, this is Bellamy. You remember her?"

"Yes, I do." To her credit, Denise extended her hand in an olive branch offering.

Bellamy reached forward and took it, nodding in affirmation of remembrance. "Good to meet you again."

"You too," Denise answered but with a hint of suspicion in her tone.

Taking a back seat to the conversation, Bellamy stepped behind Payton who set Liam on the ground. "We're going to go out, and I don't want to drag Liam with me everywhere."

"How late will you be?" Denise asked.

Payton glanced over her shoulder again with a questioning gaze at Bellamy. "You know, maybe he should just stay the night in case it's really late."

Denise looked from Payton to Bellamy, worry etched in every feature. Bellamy's stomach dropped. Whatever Payton had told her must not have been good for her mom to be that worried about them spending even one afternoon together. Payton must have sensed it too because she grabbed her mom's hand and lowered her voice. "It'll be fine. I promise. We're just going to talk."

With one more long stare, Denise nodded her head in Bellamy's direction. "All right. But you text when you get home."

"Mom, I'm not sixteen anymore."

"No, but you're still my baby."

Payton rolled her eyes. "Zane home?"

"No, he's out playing Magic with some friends."

"Okay. Thanks again, Mom!"

There was no more waiting. Payton grabbed Bellamy's hand and spun them around and out toward the car. Bellamy let out a rush of air as she made it to the car and slid inside. They were halfway down the block before Payton turned with a huge grin on her face and asked, "What are we doing today?"

"I have no idea," Bellamy responded. "I didn't think that far ahead."

Payton giggled. "Then it's my choice."

"Lead on."

Bellamy was surprised when Payton's fingers slid over the center console and along her thigh. They were warm against her jeans, and the tightness when she squeezed brought another surge of hope through her belly. They had one day to test the waters again, to see if maybe Payton had been right and twenty years didn't make a whole lot of difference, to see if they could work through the past to potentially have a future. Suddenly, Bellamy wasn't nervous anymore. Payton's confidence and jubilation flowed from the driver's seat to her, and once again, she was wrapped up in Payton's world.

CHAPTER 16

PAYTON UNLOCKED AND PUSHED OPEN THE DOOR TO her apartment with Bellamy hot on her heels, carrying a bag full of snacks and alcohol. They'd raided the local liquor store after having a nice meal at a local diner. Payton couldn't wait to spend some actual one on one time with Bellamy that didn't involve work or an ex in some form or fashion. It really would be their first chance to spend that kind of time together since they had met a year and a half before.

In some ways, Payton couldn't believe it had been that long. It felt almost like yesterday that she'd been waitressing and working her way through junior college to get her associate's and her certification to be a paralegal, when she'd just been thrown the fact she was going to have full temporary custody of her nephew and all those legal proceedings began.

Laughing, she tossed the bag of kettle corn into the microwave and hit start. Bellamy stood next to her and popped the tops on a couple cans of beer before taking a sip and shaking her head with a disgusted look on her face.

"Jesus, it has been a long time since I've had beer, forget the last time I had cheap pisswater beer."

Payton snorted. "Been living it rich too long."

Chuckling, Bellamy nodded. "You're probably right." She took another long drag from the can and set it on the counter.

Payton bit her lip and looked Bellamy up and down. She looked good. Bellamy didn't have that gaunt and ghostly look or that haunted sense about her any longer. Her color was brighter in her cheeks, her eyes wider and more full of life and hope than Payton had ever seen since she'd known her. Whatever had happened since the last time they had been together, it had been good for Bellamy in the long run.

As the microwave whirred its gentle hum next to her, Payton couldn't help but to move forward and press her body into Bellamy's. Bellamy pressed both her hands to Payton's hips, holding her in place as she looked down at her with a curious look in her eyes. Payton touched the palm of her hand to Bellamy's stomach and leaned in, brushing their lips together, barely touching.

Her heart picked up steam as it thumped along. Her mind lost track of the popcorn as it focused only on Bellamy's plump lips that tasted faintly of beer and had a cold chill to them from the edge of the aluminum can. When she moved against her again, Bellamy sighed and relaxed into her, which was all she could have asked for.

"I want to kiss you," Payton said, their lips touching with every word. "But I'm not sure if I should."

"Why not?"

Bellamy's eyes were closed, but Payton kept hers open. She wanted to see every reaction as it flitted across Bellamy's face, every small change in her body as they talked.

"I don't quite know where we stand."

They stared at each other then, Payton's heart racing and her chest rising and falling sharply. Popcorn popped next to her, but she ignored it as she focused on the woman leaning against her counter. Bellamy felt so out of place in her tiny apartment but so right at the same time, like she fit in perfectly in all the oddity that was Payton's life. Nothing was normal for Payton. She was raising her sister's son, she'd had to grow up way faster than anyone else in the family. She was the responsible one, and yet all she wanted to do was rip Bellamy's clothes off and have sex with her in a bed—an actual bed—something they had yet to do.

"Where do you want to stand?" Bellamy whispered, her voice pulled tight like she feared the answer.

Payton moved away slightly then so she could look her directly in the eye. She blushed when the answer popped immediately into her head. It wasn't something that required much thought. She hadn't been able to stop thinking about Bellamy either. At least once a week, she vividly remembered their last moment together in the elevator, the sadness permeating the entire conversation. Bellamy hadn't been mad Payton had quit—she had been resigned to it, had planned on it even. Payton had spent the months trying to figure out exactly what Bellamy had been thinking, but she'd never been able to quite put her finger on it.

"Why did you call Robinson Schraeder to hook me up with a job?"

Bellamy sighed and slipped from the counter and Payton's grasp. With the beer back between her palms, she stared at it, not looking in Payton's direction. "As much as I loved you continuing to work for me while I figured out life and Kendra, it was not ideal for you, and you needed to be someplace that would support you, someplace with fewer memories, someplace that made you a priority. We couldn't do that."

"You did."

Shaking her head, Bellamy answered with a sad tone, "No, I didn't. If I had, I would have insisted on accepting your resignation. I never would have allowed you to walk back into that office. It was a toxic environment."

Payton sighed and stepped in close to Bellamy again, taking her hand and squeezing. "It was toxic for you, too."

"Yes, but that was of my own making. I wasn't about to drag you down with me."

"Drag me down?"

"You didn't know what Kendra was doing, what she had been doing. I couldn't share that with you. I didn't even know at the time if I'd still have a firm to claim as mine when all was said and done. I wasn't going to take you down that road with me."

"You don't have to protect me, Bellamy."

"I want to."

The confession rang true in Payton's chest, and she took one more step in to press her forehead to Bellamy's shoulder, closing her eyes and deeply inhaling Bellamy's scent—that scent she had missed so very much. "I made you cross boundaries."

"None I wasn't willing to cross," Bellamy responded.

"But I pushed you."

"And I went willingly. Payton, none of what happened was your fault. If anything, it was mine. I cheated on my wife. I was your boss. I'm twenty-three years older than you. I knew better."

"I knew better, too. That night in the car? I knew you were married. I didn't care. Same with that night in your office. Rules be damned, Bellamy. Sometimes rules are meant to be broken, and I was willing to break them for you."

Bellamy's breath caught in her throat. Payton reached and ran two fingers along Bellamy's lips.

"But we don't have to break the rules anymore," Payton whispered.

"So why don't you kiss me then? Because I think you just answered your own question." Bellamy's breathing increased, her pupils dilating.

Payton grinned. "I suppose I did."

"The real question, I think, is if there is anything left if there are no rules to break."

Swallowing, Payton blinked slowly, looking from Bellamy's deep chocolate eyes to her lips. "I think there is. I always thought there was. I missed you, Bellamy. For what it's worth, I didn't want to quit that day. I wanted to stay and be with you, I wanted to stay and support you."

"I know," Bellamy murmured, her fingers coming to cup Payton's cheek. "But it was better this way."

"Perhaps." Payton turned when the microwave sounded its completion. "What do you want?"

"I'm sorry?"

"What do you want from me? What are we doing here? Because I've got to tell you, as good as the sex is, if it's just sex, I'm not sure I want any part in it beyond tonight." Payton grabbed the popcorn bag, pulled the top open and dumped it into a plastic bowl she'd grabbed from the dishwasher.

Bellamy gripped Payton's wrist and set the bowl on the counter next to her abandoned beer. Without a word, she tugged sharply so Payton crashed into her chest. Her head bent, and her mouth descended onto Payton's. Their lips pressed together in a bruising kiss, Bellamy guiding it as she pushed Payton into the counter, lifting her up to sit so Payton was above her.

Payton's eyes fluttered shut as her mouth stayed connected with Bellamy's. Bellamy gripped Payton's shirt and held on, her nails digging into her skin every once in a while. When they finally broke apart, Bellamy's lips were red and swollen, her eyes were wide, and her mouth parted as she drew in deep breaths.

"Don't think this was ever just about sex. It may have been that first night, but after five seconds with you in that car, I knew it was more than just sex."

Grinning, Payton bent and kissed her loudly. "Then dating?"

"Yes."

"Maybe more?"

"We'll see."

Payton hopped off the counter and kissed Bellamy again before reaching around and squeezing her ass sharply, making Bellamy jump in surprise. "I'll take that. Now, let's start this movie, eat popcorn and make out like teenagers on a first date."

"We have beer, so we are most definitely not teenagers."

Lifting one shoulder in a half-shrug, Payton grabbed the popcorn and headed for her small living room. "Just means we don't have a curfew and sex in a bed is still a strong possibility. We don't have to screw in the back seat of a car like teenagers again, because while that was fun and all, I want to be able to stretch out and see you."

Bellamy's cheeks were bright red as she sat next to Payton on the couch. "I'm inclined to agree with you."

"See! We're doing good already." Payton giggled as she reached forward, turned the television on and found the movie they'd already agreed to watch. She started it, digging her hand into the popcorn bowl to eat while she had the chance.

SOMEWHERE HALFWAY THROUGH THE MOVIE, BELLAMY curled up onto her side and pressed her head against Payton's shoulder. Payton threw her arm around Bellamy and tugged her in closer. Their empty beer cans, only two each, were left on the coffee table along with the empty popcorn bowl.

By the end of the movie, Bellamy was snoozing lightly against Payton's shoulder. When Payton turned to look down at her, she smirked and combed her fingers through Bellamy's super soft, fine brown and gray hair, pushing it behind her ear and over her shoulder before dropping a kiss to the top of her head.

"Is it done?" Bellamy's sweet and sleepy voice flitted up to her.

"Yeah. You missed the end."

"I'll watch it again some other time." Bellamy shifted to sit up and rubbed her eyes to get the sleep out of them. "What time is it?"

Payton glanced at the clock on the microwave. "Just past ten."

"It's only ten? Feels like I pulled an all-nighter."

Snorting, Payton gripped Bellamy's fingers. "I'm betting you still work eighteen-hour days."

The flush running up to Bellamy's cheeks told Payton the answer, which meant Bellamy taking the day to spend with her meant all that much more. Payton curled a finger under Bellamy's chin and lifted her face. She didn't hesitate this time as she pressed their mouths together in a soft, warm and comforting kiss.

She wanted to sleep with Bellamy, like actual legitimate sleep. She wanted to see if Bellamy hogged all the blankets, if she snored, or if she talked in her sleep. She wanted to know if Bellamy was the one who would twist and turn all night or if she was out like a light as soon as she lay down. When Payton pulled back, she knew what was going to happen. She knew what her morning would look like, and it was the sweetest way she could think to wake up.

"Stay the night," Payton whispered.

"Here?"

"Yeah."

Bellamy's lips parted slightly in surprise, her eyelashes heavy when she glanced up into Payton's eyes. "You're sure?"

"Yes."

"Maybe—"

"Stop finding excuses, Bellamy. You're too good at that sometimes. Stop trying to protect me. I make my own decisions."

"You've told me that before."

Payton nodded. "And why don't you believe me yet?"

Bellamy drew in a long breath, but she didn't answer. Instead, she nodded and leaned in for a kiss. This time their kisses were heated. Payton tugged at Bellamy's shirt, pulling it over her head then immediately reaching for her breasts. She flicked her thumb over Bellamy's nipples as soon as she had her bra off.

Pushing up, her knees pressing into the couch cushion, Payton moved over Bellamy until Bellamy was completely under her. She feasted on every inch of exposed skin she could reach. Bellamy writhed under her, her body moving with every new touch, her lips sighing with every nip of her skin. Payton pressed her teeth into Bellamy's shoulder, marking her, pulling the red, angry flesh between her teeth until she knew there'd be a purple mark by morning if not before.

Then she moved down. Over Bellamy's breasts, leaving hickeys every place she could reach and think of. For the first time in their long and strange courtship, she didn't have to worry about not leaving marks, about not being rough, about holding back. Bellamy liked it rough, enjoyed it.

Payton's fingers worked at Bellamy's jeans, pulling down the zipper and moving apart the button with a deftness she herself was impressed with. She didn't wait as she slid her hand down Bellamy's pants and cupped her, pressing her fingers into her warmth and rocking her wrist hard. Bellamy gripped her shoulders, her lips parting as small noises escaped her. When she came that first time, her body clenched tightly around Payton, and it was a surprise to both of them how quickly it happened.

Bellamy breathed hard, her body going lax on the couch as her eyes closed briefly. When she stared up into Payton's eyes again, she grinned. Carding her fingers through Payton's hair with a gentle touch, Bellamy pulled her down for a long, sweet kiss.

"I never thought this day would turn out this way," Bellamy whispered.

"What way?"

"That you would even give me a second glance after everything."

Payton snorted and nuzzled her face into Bellamy's neck. "There's something about you I can't quite put my finger on yet, but something about you that keeps me saying yes to your crazy ideas."

"I'm pretty sure you're the one with all the crazy ideas—like the car and the desk and now the couch."

"Me? Never." Payton kissed Bellamy's neck, nipping at the soft skin at the juncture of her neck and her shoulder. Bellamy sighed and tightened her grip in Payton's hair while shifting her legs to cradle Payton's body more fully.

Giggling, Bellamy fumbled with Payton's pants as she tried to push them down her hips. "Do you have something against beds?"

"No, not at all. Why do you ask?"

"Because we have yet to make it to a bed."

"Oh, well, we'll get there eventually." Payton moved down Bellamy's chest to her nipples, swirling her tongue in circles around the hard little nubs. She wanted more of Bellamy before she shared of her own body. Palming one of Bellamy's breasts, she massaged the skin while working the other one with her mouth.

She stayed there until Bellamy scratched her nails along the back of Payton's head and pushed Payton's head down. Grinning because she was getting exactly what she wanted, Payton sat up and helped Bellamy tug off her jeans and underwear, tossing them to the floor before she dove back down.

Payton used her tongue, her lips, her fingers, everything she could think of to bring Bellamy over that edge again—harder than last time. She slammed into her with her fingers, sucking hard and focusing all of her energy on one purpose. Bellamy's voice grew louder, ringing over the through the small apartment.

When she cried out her release, Payton licked her thoroughly before moving to lie on top of her, kissing Bellamy's lips lazily. Bellamy turned her cheek, deepening their embrace in a sleepy, sloppy kiss. She combed her fingers through Payton's hair, down her shoulder, then tsked.

"What?" Payton asked, her voice rough.

"You're way too overdressed for this."

Snorting, Payton pushed herself to sit up and grabbed the edge of her T-shirt, pulling it over her head. She finished with her bra then stood because the couch definitely was not wide enough for her to lie next to Bellamy and wiggle out of the rest of her clothes. As soon as she was as naked as Bellamy herself, she went to lie down, but Bellamy stopped her with a hand on her hip.

"No, up here."

"What?"

"Sit on me."

Payton raised an eyebrow at her but did as she was told. Bellamy curled her arms around Payton's thighs and hips, shifting so they were lined up perfectly. Payton gripped the arm of the couch as Bellamy reached her tongue out and touched her the first time. Heat surged through her body, and her hips rocked with pleasure. She wasn't going to last long either. She hadn't been celibate since she'd been with Bellamy by any means, but Bellamy knew how to touch, knew how to entice, knew how to tease her body in the best way possible.

The room was cast in silence. Payton stared out of the window into the dark night and then closed her eyes, focusing solely on everything Bellamy was doing to her. She wanted to feel it all, remember it all, just like the two other times they were together. This was so different. This wasn't for comfort. It wasn't for distraction. This was because they both genuinely wanted to be together, they wanted to test the waters, they wanted to see what they could bring out in each other.

Payton bit her lip and leaned back slightly, giving Bellamy a better angle. She gripped the back of the couch cushion with one hand to keep herself in that position, her hips undulating as pleasure built in her core faster than she had anticipated. She knew she was nearing her end, knew Bellamy would taste her soon. She grunted, trying to hold back just a little longer to make it last, but she couldn't. Sliding through her orgasm, Payton's nipples hardened, her chest tightened, her body coiled until Bellamy slowed her ministrations and allowed her to relax.

As soon as she could, Payton moved from where she kneeled and laid alongside Bellamy's body, tracing slow circles along the skin on her chest and closing her eyes. She hummed her contentment as Bellamy gently rubbed fingers along her arms and sides.

"You know what I want?" Payton asked.

"What do you want?"

"I want to sleep in a big giant bed with you. I want to go to bed with you and know you'll be there in the morning when I wake up."

"Hmm, that does sound nice." Bellamy dropped a kiss into Payton's hair. "Do you have a big giant bed?"

Payton snorted. "Absolutely not. I had to fit a crib in that room."

Bellamy chuckled. "Maybe next time then."

"Why? Do you have a big giant bed?"

"It's big. I'm not sure I'd call it giant."

Payton pushed herself up on one arm and stared down into Bellamy's eyes. "Come on. Let's go to bed."

"Yes."

Turning the television off, Payton grabbed Bellamy by the hand and led her into the one bedroom the apartment boasted.

Liam's crib sat in the corner and her small full-sized bed sat against the wall without a window on it. Her room was a mess, but she didn't care, and she hoped Bellamy didn't either. She pulled aside the blankets and slid under them, waiting for Bellamy to join her. As soon as they were lying next to each other, Payton pressed her lips to Bellamy's in a slow, sleep-filled kiss. She was ready for the first night of the rest of her life—at least she hoped that's what this was.

CHAPTER 17

BELLAMY'S EYES FLUTTERED OPEN, BUT SHE CLOSED them against the warm sun shining through the window. She turned her face into the pillow, her hair in her eyes. Sighing, she pushed it out of the way and stretched her legs. The warm body at her back surprised her, and when she turned her head to get a look, she was happy to find Payton pressed up against her.

Smiling, Bellamy snuggled into the blankets and closed her eyes again. She reached for Payton's hand at her waist, tangled their fingers together and scooted back against Payton's hot skin, their bodies melding together. She couldn't remember the last time she woke up in bed with someone, someone who had wanted her to be there, who had worshipped her body over and over again, someone she felt a sense of hope with.

Payton's palm splayed across her belly, and she moved behind her, lips pressing into the nape of her neck. Bellamy grinned, wanting to turn over and see Payton in the morning sunlight but also not wanting to lose the feeling of her body pressed up behind her. Payton's hand slipped up and cupped one of her breasts, pulling her in tighter against Payton's front.

Air rustled across her skin when Payton spoke. "When is the last time you stayed in bed long enough that it was daylight when you woke up?"

"Really?" Bellamy chuckled. "That's the question you ask?"

Payton shrugged. "You were always at the office and deep in work before I even got a chance to show up. Don't tell me you weren't getting there until five minutes before I did."

Biting her lip, Bellamy closed her eyes and relaxed. "I wake up between four-thirty and five every morning, typically."

"So I repeat, when was the last time you were in bed until after the sun came up?"

Bellamy shifted so they were facing each other and pressed her hand to Payton's heart. Her eyes were downcast, and she didn't dare look at Payton's face. "When I got so drunk that I physically couldn't get out of bed until well into the afternoon."

"You? Drunk? Somehow I have a hard time believing you got drunk."

Bellamy paled. She traced a singular finger down Payton's chest to her hip, gripping her hip but still not looking into her eyes. "In college I used to drink all the time."

"But now? Never. You're prim, proper. You wouldn't dare get drunk and lose control."

Chuckling, a smile played at Bellamy's lips. "You might be surprised at what happens when I lose control."

"When do you lose control?"

"Really?" She did look into Payton's baby blue eyes then. She curled a finger through her soft hair that was just long enough to curl twice. "Do you not remember anything of working for me? I lost control all the time."

"Never. You fought back."

"Hmm, that may be what you think."

Payton pressed a kiss to Bellamy's forehead. "When did you get so drunk you didn't get up until afternoon?"

"The last time I saw you." Her words were a whisper, and for a moment, Bellamy wasn't even sure whether she had said them out loud or only in her head. She stared at Payton's lips as they formed into a surprised 'O' and her tongue dashed out to wet them.

"Why would you get drunk then?"

Bellamy turned onto her back and threw a hand over her head, closing her eyes. She didn't really want to remember that day—that had been the point of getting so drunk she might not remember. But she remembered everything, every vivid moment of it from signing the divorce papers, to crying on the floor of the bathroom with her bottle of Johnnie Walker Blue Label clutched to her chest as she knew—just knew—she would never see Payton again.

She'd been wrong, of course, but she wouldn't have if she hadn't been the one to take that first step. "It doesn't matter."

"It does." Payton shifted up the bed and turned Bellamy's cheek so they looked at each other. "It does matter."

Bellamy let out a breath. "That was the day we signed the divorce papers. It was the day your final adoption hearing was done and over with. I couldn't keep you with me any longer. I had nothing to tie you back to me. I knew you were going to quit, and if you didn't, I was going to try and get you to quit. You needed to be somewhere else, anywhere else but in that hellhole. But I wasn't sad because of Kendra, I was devastated because of you."

"Me?" Payton's eyes were wide with surprise. "Why would I devastate you?"

Bellamy's heart clenched. The words were on the tip of her tongue, but she swallowed them down. It wasn't time for those words yet, and she wasn't even sure if she believed them herself. Letting out a breath, she tried to change the subject. "I should probably get some work done today."

"Don't do that," Payton stated, propping her head on her hand, her elbow pressed into the pillow by Bellamy's head.

"Do what?"

"Close off like that. You were just opening up."

Bellamy rolled her eyes, but she'd been caught. Sighing, she bit her lip, still not wanting to look Payton in the eyes. She was scared Payton would be able to see everything she was thinking, everything she was feeling before she could even put words to it herself.

"Let's go on a proper date this week," Bellamy tried this time.

"Okay, but you're still skirting around what you were saying."

With a huff, Bellamy answered, "I wasn't thinking of my broken and failed marriage. I was thinking of you and everything I had done to hurt you, to put you in harm's way, in ways I couldn't protect you, in things I was oblivious to. I was thinking about you that day."

"Why would you get drunk thinking about me?"

"Payton, just drop it."

"No. I'm not going to drop it. This seems important." Payton put her thumb to Bellamy's lips, stared directly into her eyes. "Tell me why you would get drunk thinking about me."

"No." Bellamy tried to push up and out of the bed, but Payton was surprisingly strong.

With a raised eyebrow, Payton smirked. "I wrangle a two-year-old into diapers on the daily. Trust me when I say I can hold you here if need be."

"I don't want to talk about it."

"You brought it up."

"Payton, now is not the time."

"You always say it's not the time."

"Fine. I didn't think I would ever see you again. Everything felt so final, so finished. I didn't think you would ever want to see me again, but I could not stop thinking about you. I never have been able to, not since the night we met. You were the most unexpected thing to walk into my life a year and a half ago, but you gave me the courage to live how I wanted to live, for me and not for anyone else. But I was scared, Payton. Scared you wouldn't want me. Scared you wouldn't see me. Scared that everything I had just given up, everything I had just done, was going to ruin me. And you *weren't* there."

"Because *you* wouldn't let me."

"Because you couldn't be there, Payton. All of that was something I had to do on my own. I couldn't involve you in it. I couldn't drag you down with me."

Payton pursed her lips. "You keep saying that, but I really thought you were going somewhere else with that confession."

"What?" Bellamy turned, staring up into Payton's eyes, but she knew exactly what Payton was going to say, exactly where Payton had thought she'd been going, because to be honest, she was going there. She was just really good at avoiding it.

Payton bit her lip. "I thought you were going to say you loved me."

Bellamy's heart clenched tight, tension building in her chest. She stared directly into Payton's eyes, saying nothing. She didn't want to confirm or deny, but everything she had learned as a lawyer about arguing a case one way or the other slipped from her mind. She had no words to hide what she truly felt. Instead, she reached up and pulled Payton down into a kiss, a deep kiss, one she hoped would be very distracting.

Running her hands over Payton's bare skin, enticing and heating, she turned on her side and slid a leg between Payton's, pressing her thigh hard against Payton's core and rocking lightly to test the waters. Her nails scraped down Payton's chest. She could distract. If she couldn't admit, deny, or work around the conversation, she could and would distract.

THEY'D BEEN OFFICIALLY DATING FOR THREE WEEKS before Payton's first day of school. In that time, Payton had seen Bellamy at least three days a week. She'd come by for dinner, helping to finish making it while Payton occupied Liam or vice versa, and she'd come over nearly every weekend, staying almost all day each time.

Something had changed in her since their conversation the morning after Bellamy had shown back up in her life. Payton couldn't quite put her finger on it, but Bellamy was giving more of herself and her time to Payton than she ever had, than Payton even thought was possible.

Nerves rampaged in her belly as she gathered up her bag from work to book it to the daycare before heading home to drop Liam at the sitter and drive to school. Her life had become an insane list of places to go and things to do, and she hadn't even started classes yet. She didn't have her full schedule of assignments, and she knew it was going to be next to impossible to finish.

Night classes were one thing but staying up late to finish the homework and read for each class she attended was going to be harder than she ever imagined, especially with a two-year-old running around. When Liam had been an infant that was different. He slept through most of it, but at two he not only craved her attention, he needed it. She didn't want to do him a disservice just because she wanted a degree and an education.

She had just pulled up outside the daycare when her phone rang. Seeing the sitter's number flash across her screen, her stomach dropped. She answered before she went inside. "Hey, Alicia."

"Hey. I'm so sorry, but I can't watch Liam tonight. Cici came down with hand, foot, and mouth. It's a five-day quarantine period after the fever stops, and you know the others are going to get it, so it looks like I'm not going to be able to sit for at least a couple weeks."

Payton had a really smart retort on the tip of her tongue, but she managed to hold it back. "All right. Thanks."

"I'm so sorry."

"I know. I'll see if I can figure something out." Hanging up, Payton pressed her forehead into the steering wheel and let out a groan. Alicia had never been reliable, but she had been the only person available. Her mother was sicker with chemo than before since they'd changed it up when the other one stopped working, and she wasn't going to put it on Zane to watch a two-year-old.

She was just about to go in and get Liam when her phone buzzed with a text message from Bellamy. Clenching her jaw, she stared at the daycare center as she debated. Bellamy liked Liam, and Liam liked Bellamy, but Bellamy also had her own life and often worked well into the evenings. Payton was vividly aware of that fact. Biting her lip, she dialed Bellamy's cell phone instead of answering in a text.

"Hey! I just texted, did you get it?" Bellamy's voice sounded confident but distracted. Payton knew she was likely bent over her desk working on something while she was talking.

"I did. Thank you. But I . . . I have a favor to ask."

"What is it?"

Payton sighed. "My sitter just cancelled. It's the first day. I can't not show up to the first day of classes. I might as well just not show up at all."

"What time is class?"

"Six-thirty."

"I'll see you at six."

Payton's chest released all the tension it had held. "Are you sure?"

"I wouldn't say I would see you at six if I wasn't sure. I've got some things to finish up here, but I'll be there. Don't worry. I've got you."

A smile slid across Payton's lips. "Thanks."

"Anytime. See you soon." Bellamy hung up.

Payton tapped her phone on her palm before she got out of her car and headed inside to grab her son. She could do this. She hated asking people for help, but she may just have to in order to accomplish everything she wanted in life. With Liam in her arms, she headed to her vehicle and put him inside. She'd make an easy dinner for both of them, then go to class, knowing Bellamy would be able to take care of him and put him to bed. Bellamy knew his routine, so the only thing amiss would be her being gone. It was ultimately a much better plan in the long run than hiring Alicia.

As soon as she got home, she started making dinner and gathering up her school supplies. Nerves wracked through her stomach as she grabbed a notebook and multiple pens so she had back ups. It had been almost two years since she'd been in school properly, and she had been in a completely different place at the time.

She'd had support from her mom, who hadn't been diagnosed with cancer yet. She hadn't been a parent. Well, she had toward the end, but not officially until well after the fact. She'd had a job where she could be more flexible with her hours, but she'd also never had someone help to pay for her school like her new firm was. And she hadn't been wondering if her sister was going to sober up or not and make her a second-time mom after the New Year. She shoved the pens into her bag and closed the flap on the satchel.

It would take some getting used to for sure, but she wanted it so badly. She wanted to be able to run her own business, but most importantly, she wanted to be able to look back on her life and say she had accomplished something big, that she had worked hard for her degree, and that Liam could look forward to that too.

When the knock echoed at the door, Liam turned and ran toward it, shouting, "Door, door, door," over and over again until Payton peeked through the peephole to see Bellamy standing on the other side. She was early. Unlatching the lock, she opened the door with a smile.

"You're early."

Bellamy shrugged as she leaned in and pecked Payton's lips. "I figured I could do work here instead of trying to finish it at the office. I can do it after he goes to sleep. Hey there, little guy!" Bellamy bent down and put her arms out. Liam ran directly to her and climbed into her arms. When Bellamy stood up, she had him with her as he grinned and giggled at her.

Payton's stomach did something weird. It felt lighter, and her heart thudded a few extra times. Shutting the door behind Bellamy, she headed to the stove to check on the boiling pasta. She mulled through her mind exactly what she was feeling, but she couldn't quite put a finger on it. When Bellamy pressed up against her from behind and kissed her neck, she sighed and leaned into her. Liam grabbed her hair and tugged. Payton glared at him as Bellamy moved his hand away.

"We don't pull hair, Liam," Bellamy chided.

Payton quickly retorted, "Well, I mean, you don't, but I get the feeling you might like it if I pulled on your hair during certain situations."

Bellamy froze as she glanced over Liam's arm at Payton. Her expression was almost unreadable before she cracked a sly smile and shrugged. "Maybe I would like that."

Snorting, Payton shook her head and drained the pasta. "I'll have to try that next time."

"So there will be a next time?"

"I should think so."

Bellamy took Liam and moved to stand by his booster seat at

the table. She rocked him back and forth and made smiling faces at him. Once again, Payton's stomach did that funny thing it had taken to doing when she glanced over. It was such an odd image —Bellamy dressed to the nines in a tight skirt with a slit straight up the back that threatened to be too showy, her blouse pressed and tucked into her waistband, her hair pinned perfectly into the dreaded bun Payton always wanted to mess up at the top of her neck with a baby in her arms, laughing and giggling like she was a teenager with a secret admirer.

Payton shook the thought from her head and added in the pasta sauce. "Strip him down, would you? I'd rather not be scrubbing stains out of those clothes for the next century."

Bellamy set Liam on the table to stand and tugged at his shirt and pants, leaving him in nothing other than his diaper before settling him into the booster seat and strapping him in. They had both learned the hard way that he needed to be strapped in, otherwise he would escape. Payton shoved a plate with food on it in the freezer to cool it rapidly, then made up two more for her and Bellamy. When she turned back around, Bellamy was right there to take the plates from her.

"Besides, if I come early I get dinner with my two favorite people." Bellamy spun around in her heels and sat at the messy, cluttered, and still sticky table, scooting her chair in.

Payton let out a breath. "Right."

She was going to have to figure out what it was her body was trying to tell her because the signals it was sending were utterly confusing. She'd always been headstrong and didn't think about her feelings too much, but ever since Bellamy had waltzed right back into her life, knocking on that door, Payton had struggled to keep up with everything she was feeling.

"Your classes are just two days a week, right?" Bellamy asked around a bite of food.

"Yeah. I'm taking three this semester, but one is online, so that one's pretty easy."

Bellamy set her fork down and pointed to Liam's fork. "Use this, kid. It's harder but less messy."

He stared at her like she had three heads before grabbing the fork and trying to stab the pasta. Bellamy smiled at him, and Payton was lost in the strange image of her prim and proper girlfriend chastising a food-covered toddler.

"I was thinking that if you don't have a reliable sitter, I could rework my schedule to be here those days. It'd save on paying a sitter, but really, I'd just love to spend more time with this guy." Bellamy poked at him, not turning to look at Payton.

Payton couldn't decide if she didn't dare look over because she was nervous about asking or if she thought it wasn't the wisest idea. She took a bite of her pasta and chewed slowly, thinking it over. If Bellamy watched Liam for her, then they would see each other even more often than before. The cash savings would be nice too, but that was the least of her worries.

"My sitter is out for a couple weeks because of her kids being sick."

"See?" Bellamy turned with a grin. "We could try it out while she's gone."

"Are you sure? Kids are a lot of work."

Bellamy gave her a sharp look. "I think I can handle babysitting for a few hours while you're in class, Payton. I may not have any kids of my own, but I very much know how to take care of a toddler."

She couldn't figure out why she was hesitating. Everything in her heart told her to say yes, to let Bellamy watch him and get know him better, but at the same time, she had trusted Bellamy like that before, had given her those opportunities, and while she'd come through in the short term, the long term hadn't worked out.

"Okay." Payton gave in. "For the next few weeks, then we'll see what Alicia is doing."

Bellamy's responding grin was almost her undoing. She

melted and gripped Bellamy's hand with a tight squeeze before going back to shoveling food down her throat. She only had ten minutes before she had to leave to get to class on time, and she wanted to make sure she didn't have park a mile away and run the rest of it.

CHAPTER 18

NOTHING EVER SEEMED TO GO RIGHT FOR PAYTON that semester. Halfway through it, she'd had to meet with her advisor to figure out what classes she would need after everything was officially transferred from her junior college, and one of the requirements she had somehow missed was a foreign language. Two full semesters of it.

If there was one class she had barely passed in high school, it had been Spanish class. She just could not understand the language to save her life. Groaning, she closed her laptop, as she couldn't stand to stare at the class options any longer for the next semester. She was trying to figure out what she was going to do about it because she was pretty sure if she couldn't get out of taking a foreign language, she was never going to graduate.

"What's wrong?" Bellamy asked from the couch where she was playing with Liam.

"Nothing."

Bellamy chuckled. "Doesn't sound like nothing."

"How's work going for you?"

"Excellent. Don't change the subject."

Payton sighed. "I need to take a foreign language."

"And?"

Getting up from the kitchen table, Payton walked around the couch and plopped down on it, pressing her head to Bellamy's shoulder. "And I suck at languages."

"You learned law language pretty well, and quickly. A foreign language should be nothing."

Payton scoffed. "You would think. Hey, so I heard from my sister. She wants me to go to her ultrasound next week, and she wants me to bring Liam."

"Is this the big ultrasound?"

"Yeah, I guess." Payton picked at invisible lint on her jeans. "I don't know why she wants me to go."

"She probably wants Liam there. He is the brother of this baby. It's sentimental to have him there when she finds out the sex of the baby, to celebrate. She hasn't gotten to raise him, so maybe she wants to try to include him as best as she can."

"Maybe."

"Is she staying sober at least?"

"I don't know," Payton muttered and turned her face into Bellamy's neck and pressed her lips to the soft, hot skin she found there. She dashed her tongue out to taste Bellamy's salty flesh before she hummed and pressed her cold nose into her. Bellamy tried to move away, but Payton reached over and held her close.

"Have you talked to her about it?" Bellamy asked, clearly giving in to Payton's nonverbal demands.

Liam tottered over and put his hands out. "Up. Lap."

Snickering, Bellamy drew him into her lap and relaxed into the couch. Payton leaned forward and kissed his chubby cheek. "He's getting really good at words."

"And sentences," Bellamy added. "He really likes that one book without pictures in it. No idea why, but he makes me read it to him about five times every night before I can convince him to go to bed."

Payton licked her lips. "Interesting. He won't let me read to him."

"Weird." Bellamy bounced her knees up and down. "You're still avoiding."

"I know. I don't know what Maddy is up to. I haven't really talked to her much because I just don't know what to do with her. It's either hot or cold."

"She's Liam's mother."

"Yeah, but she's not his parent."

"Right." Bellamy turned and stared directly into Payton's eyes. "But you need to keep her in your life, whether or not this other baby ends up in your care, Liam is yours, and you need to keep those connections open. He'll have questions someday, and you'll want to be able to answer them."

"I know." Payton drew in a deep breath and let it out slowly. "Can we go back to this foreign language credit thing for a minute?"

"Sure." Bellamy chuckled as Liam climbed down to go get into something else.

"What language did you take?"

"Latin."

Payton rolled her eyes. "Of course you took Latin. You couldn't take like a normal language?"

"I needed Latin for law school, and trust me when I say it was useful. If you wanted to become a lawyer, you could take Latin too, you know."

"I don't want to be lawyer. Working with lawyers has taught me that much."

Bellamy stiffened, her muscles tightening under Payton's hands. Instantly, Payton regretted her choice of words. Everything that had been happening between them made her do stupid things. Pressing her head back into Bellamy's shoulder, she closed her eyes.

"I'm sorry."

"Don't be."

"No, really, I am. I didn't mean that like it came off."

"Payton, just drop it." Bellamy pushed to stand up. "I really should be going anyway. I've got to be up early to prep for a hearing."

Payton shot straight out of her seat, worried she had offended Bellamy to the point she wouldn't come back. Panic gripped her heart. "Bellamy, stop."

She was already bending to grab her bag and slip her heels on. Payton raced to her and gripped her hands, pulling her to a stop. She stared up into Bellamy's dark eyes, trying to read everything in them, but unable to figure out what she was thinking.

"Just stop a minute."

"Payton, I have a lot of work to do."

"This isn't about work. What are you thinking? What did I say?"

"It's nothing."

"It's not nothing. Please, what did I say?"

Bellamy sighed and closed her eyes. She bit her lip then shook her head. "You just remind me sometimes—starkly mind you—how young you truly are and how old I am."

"I don't understand."

"You have your whole life ahead of you, Payton. Everything. You have kids, family, marriage, dreams, career—everything is ahead of you. For me everything is behind. I . . . I've already done those things. And some of them didn't work out, some of them did. But I know what to expect from life."

"Do you?" Payton stepped in closer. Liam moved to try and wedge himself between them, but Bellamy reached down to pull him up into her arms before Payton could even think about it. "Because I don't think you do. I think you want to know what to expect from life. You want everything to fit into your plan, into the neat little boxes you put them in, and I think that I really screw that up for you."

Bellamy's lips parted, but she didn't say anything. She nuzzled her nose into Liam's head and gave him a soft kiss. She was setting him down, still reaching for her bag, when Payton stopped her again.

"No, you don't get to leave in the middle of this conversation."

"I told you. I have work to do."

"You can do it later. This is important."

"Why? Why is it important?"

"Because I love you, damn it. Can't you see that?"

Whatever Payton had said this time had knocked the wind out of both their sails. Liam moved around them on the floor, trying to get Payton's attention to pick him up, but she ignored him. Her gaze stayed on Bellamy's face—her heart pounding so loud she was sure Bellamy could hear it.

"I love you."

"You love the idea of me."

"No. Don't do that. Don't put words in my mouth. I don't love the idea of you. In fact, I'm not particularly fond of some of the ideas of you. I love you, Bellamy. The whole package you come in. It took me a while to admit it, you know. But you're this weird conundrum, you always have been. This outside persona you put on, this put-together woman you think you have to be, it's not who you are in here." Payton pressed her palm flat against Bellamy's heart. "In here you are just as vulnerable as the rest of us, and you let me see that every once in a while, and I love that. I want to see it more often."

"Payton—"

"Shut up. I let you have the last word once, and I'm not going to do that again. I love you, Bellamy. All of you. The weird woman who eats out more than she cooks but who can cook a mean dish. The woman who loves cleanliness and organization and lines and plans but who also drops everything to come over and watch a two-year-old because she weirdly loves him, too. I love *you*, Bellamy. And I really cannot say that enough."

Silence cascaded over the room. Payton finally reached down and grabbed Liam, popping him on her hip. He played with her shirt and her necklace while she stared directly into Bellamy's eyes, waiting for some kind of response, any kind of response. This wasn't how she had meant for this conversation to happen, but it was how it came out. Nothing with them ever went smoothly, but Payton was sure she was always going to be the one to have to go first.

Bellamy finally spoke, her voice barely above a whisper. "I don't know what to say."

"You don't have to say anything, really. But I love you, that's a fact, counselor."

Laughing, Bellamy set her bag down again. She grabbed Payton's shirt right in the center of her chest and pulled her in tight so their lips touched. Payton let out a breath, tightening her grip on Liam so he wouldn't move or use his weight to pull her away. He put his chubby hands on both of their cheeks as their lips met, and he giggled.

Payton moved back and smiled at Bellamy. "Are you staying or not?"

"Yeah, I'll stay."

"Good . . . because someone is stinky."

Bellamy rolled her eyes, but she reached to take Liam out of Payton's arms. "You get the next one."

"Sure." Payton chuckled as she watched Bellamy move into the bedroom where the changing station was. She was no doubt going to have to start potty training him soon, but she could deal with that another day. Sighing, she sat on the arm of the couch and pressed her hands together.

She had just confessed the one thing she had been hiding from Bellamy for months, ever since she'd agreed to let her start watching Liam on a more regular basis. It hadn't taken her that long to figure out, as soon as she'd taken the time to sit in the emotion. She had loved Bellamy almost from the start, but they had taken a long, roundabout path to get where they were. After everything they had been through, Payton wasn't about to give up so easily, and she wasn't going to let Bellamy's need for control and comfort let another eighteen months pass again before they took the next step.

A MONTH HAD PASSED SINCE PAYTON'S CONFESSION of love, and Bellamy had managed to avoid a response. However, the tension was still there with unmet expectations. Payton had told her about the family Thanksgiving dinner more times than Bellamy dared to count, but it wasn't until Payton asked if she was coming that she realized it had been an invitation. Bellamy had told her she'd think about it before avoiding the conversation for the rest of the night, but Thanksgiving was tomorrow, and she really couldn't evade it any longer.

Bellamy let out a sigh as she finished out her day of work. She'd sent everyone home already, giving them the extra time for the holiday, but she kept finding work for herself to do to avoid going home. Holidays were not something she enjoyed in the least. Each year Kendra had left for the holidays, in the beginning to go to her family and toward the end to take some extravagant trip where she'd no doubt meet up with other women.

When Bellamy had left home, she hadn't really been welcomed back. She still hadn't spoken to her parents or her siblings in so many years she wasn't even sure she would recognize them if she saw them on the street. She could be an aunt for all she knew, but no one had ever really shared that with her.

Even when she was young kid, the holidays had not been the

most pleasant time in her house. She was the odd family member out, the one who didn't enjoy loud football games or big crowds. She always wanted to hide away in her room, read a good book, or get a jump-start on her homework. She wanted to avoid all the drama that came with family and relationships she didn't really care too much about one way or another.

She finished her motion and closed it up for after the holiday when she could file it with a judge. Opening another document, she started in on that one. The world outside was darkening, the streetlights coming on as the sun set over the Sound. She didn't know how to tell Payton that the holidays were not something she enjoyed and were really something she would much rather just forget even happened. She knew Payton wouldn't take very kindly to it if she even understood.

It was late in the evening when she finally finished her work for the day and headed to her apartment. It was cold when she entered and she turned the heat up, letting it warm the frigid tile floor. She settled her bag in the chair she had claimed for it by kitchen table and opened her fridge to see what was inside it. Payton was right—she didn't have any food. They spent most of their time at Payton's apartment rather than hers, simply because it was easier and all of Liam's things were there.

She spent the rest of her night avoiding her phone and the last text message Payton had sent, asking if she was coming or not. She really didn't want to answer. She wanted to just go in to the office in the morning, finish out some paperwork, then drink by herself at her apartment while she ate takeout from whatever place she could find that was open.

Climbing into bed, she closed her eyes and decided that was exactly what she was going to do. She wouldn't go to the big family dinner, and she wouldn't disrupt Payton's joyous celebration with her family and put a damper on the mood. Pulling the covers over her head, she let sleep consume her.

~

IN THE MORNING, BELLAMY PULLED ON HER FAVORITE pair of blue jeans and a loose T-shirt under a sweater from her Alma Mater. She grabbed a light breakfast and waited until the sun at least peeked over the horizon before she got into her car and headed in to the office. She was three hours into work when there was a loud knocking on the door.

Confused, Bellamy pushed up from her desk and glanced around the corner of her office, flashing to the many times Kendra had done similar. With her jaw clenched, she waited for the knocking to start up again, which it did. Her heart thumped hard as she walked barefoot through the lobby to the front door. She was just about to touch the handle when Payton's voice echoed through the door.

"I know you're in there, Bellamy. Open up."

Relaxing, she turned the lock and opened the door. Payton came right in like she owned the place and shut the door behind her, turning the lock back in place and crossing her arms. "I never thought I would see the inside of these offices again."

"Not much has changed," Bellamy commented, ignoring the fact they both knew why Payton was there. "Where's Liam?"

"With Mom. And it has changed. You changed the paintings."

"I like this better." Bellamy moved away from the front door and headed toward her office. She settled into her chair and pulled out more work, trying to distract herself from the argument they were no doubt about to have.

Payton didn't hesitate in following her, but when Bellamy tried to write something on a piece of paper, Payton stole the pen from her fingers and set it down on top of her desk. "You're going to talk to me."

"I don't see what there is to say."

"Are you coming to dinner or not?"

Bellamy put her hands in her lap. "Obviously not."

"Why not?"

"I don't want to."

Payton crossed her arms and glared. "Bellamy, you have to do better than that. You've been closed off for a month now. What gives?"

Bellamy closed her eyes, avoiding the unmet expectation again. "I don't like big holiday get-togethers. I don't go to them, ever."

"Oh." Payton's face softened, and she came around the desk, sitting on the edge of it right in front of Bellamy. "Because you don't have family."

"Yeah, but even before then. My family, they're not exactly the family everyone dreams of having. They get into arguments all the time, and they fight with each other. For holidays we never knew who was coming or where we were going because we didn't know who we were supposed to be mad at that year."

"How awful. Was there never one good thing about Thanksgiving or Christmas?"

Bellamy pressed her lips together as she thought. Truthfully, the only thing she could think of was that they ended. Christmas was always longer when she was in school because of vacation, but Thanksgiving was the precursor to that. It was what set everything in motion for the rest of the year.

"Honestly? No. I never enjoyed anything about the holidays."

"Not even watching the parades?"

"No." Bellamy sighed. "But you go and have fun. I don't want to spoil your Thanksgiving."

"Bellamy." Payton drew Bellamy's chin up with a finger. "Remember what I told you about a month ago? That I love you and all the weird contradictions that come with you?"

Bellamy stared directly into her eyes. She remembered like it was yesterday, and there was Payton to cut through her avoidance.

"I still love that about you, and this is just one more part of that. But . . . I'm going to make you do something you don't want to do."

"What's that?"

Payton sighed and kissed Bellamy's lips briefly. It felt weird, like she was using it as a distraction herself. When Payton straightened her back, Bellamy knew they were in for a serious conversation. She didn't know what she was going to say or do if Payton gave her an ultimatum. She wasn't ready. She hadn't planned for any of this. Drawing in a deep breath, she tried to stand up and move, but Payton grabbed her hands and pulled her back down.

"No. Sit and listen. I need something from you in order to keep doing this."

"Doing what?"

"Our relationship."

Bellamy's heart clenched. Everything she feared smacked her right in the face. She hadn't been expecting this from ignoring Payton's texts or avoiding Thanksgiving dinner with the family. She hadn't thought it would end in a breakup.

"I need a commitment from you. I need to know that this is something you want to keep doing, because while I love dating you, Bellamy, and I love you, I don't know how you feel or what you want half the time. We used to be able to read each other so well, but now I think that was just because we had to in order to survive in here." Payton motioned to the room.

Bellamy had no idea what to say. Her voice caught in her throat. She couldn't say those words, not like Payton did. She wasn't ready for them, as much as she wanted to say them, she wanted them to be absolutely true when she did. She didn't want to hesitate, and she certainly didn't want to feel forced into it.

Payton must have sensed her panic, because she slid off the desk and into Bellamy's lap, cupping her cheek. "I'm not asking you to profess your love, Bellamy. Chill out a minute. Take a breath. What I want from you is to know that you are in this thing with me. I want to know that you're in it for the awkward family dinners, for the family drama that I come with—not just the fun stuff with Liam. That's all great, but I want to know that you're in it for when I have to decide if I can care for Maddy's daughter and deal with even more fallout in our relationship when it inevitably comes that Maddy is unable to care for her. For when my mom might die because her cancer isn't getting better."

The tears sprouting in Payton's eyes broke Bellamy's heart. She wanted to be there for all of that, wanted to be it in for everything. She loved the time she spent with Liam, but Payton was right. She wasn't there for everything, for the doctor's appointments, for the therapies, for the aunts who said one too many wrong things when they showed up once a year for the family dinner they all hated. She hadn't been there for any of it, and she had neatly avoided any part of Payton's family other than Liam.

Brushing her thumbs across Payton's cheeks, Bellamy nodded. She cleared her throat when her own tears sprang to her eyes. "Okay."

"Okay what?" Payton bit her lip.

"You're right. So okay, I'll go to dinner. I'll do the family drama. I'll do the dates and the fun stuff, too, but I'll be more involved in everything."

"Thank you." Payton grinned. "Now, was that so hard?"

Bellamy chuckled. "Yes, actually, and dinner with everyone is going to be even harder. So please recognize that when I want to leave early."

"We can leave early, and you know what else?"

"What?"

"Liam is spending the night at Nana's."

"Really?"

"Yeah, so I thought, maybe, we could try out that big giant bed of yours."

Bellamy flushed. "Sure, we could do that."

"Good. Let's go. I like my mimosas strong and early in the morning." Payton grabbed Bellamy's hand and dragged her to stand.

Bellamy slipped her shoes back on and grabbed her sweater. Payton stopped her as soon as they left her office and put a hand on her neck, drawing her down into a deep kiss. Bellamy lost herself in the moment. Whatever was happening between them, it felt good. It felt far different from her relationship with Kendra. Payton was so different, and no matter how many times she seemed to screw up, Payton was right there to talk to her about it and not yell.

Groaning, Bellamy stepped forward, her mouth increasing pressure on Payton's lips until Payton's back hit the wall. She skimmed her hand down Payton's side then nipped at her lip. "Some day, we're going to use this wall."

"Now who is wanting sex in weird places other than a bed?" Payton grinned and curled her leg around Bellamy's to pull her in.

"You're quite an influence, what can I say?"

"Say you won't make me fight you on Christmas dinner."

Shaking her head, Bellamy pecked Payton's lips. "I'll try not to fight you on Christmas dinner. Is there a New Year's dinner?"

"No."

"Thank God." She grinned and moved in to Payton again. Maybe if they stayed that way long enough Payton would forget all about the dinner and mimosas and parades.

Payton hissed when Bellamy worked a hand up her shirt and cupped her breast. Payton groaned and knocked her head back into the wall, but her voice was clear when she whispered. "You can take me right here all you want, Bellamy, you're still not getting out of dinner."

"Fine." She kissed Payton loudly. "Then you'll have to wait."

Payton pouted as she straightened her shirt, but then she smiled. "Come on, Scrooge."

"Wrong holiday, kid. You're getting your classics mixed up."

"We'll see." Payton dragged Bellamy toward the door by her hand and didn't let go until they got into their respective cars and drove toward Denise's.

CHAPTER 19

THANKSGIVING HAD BEEN UNEXPECTEDLY PLEASANT, with very little drama. Bellamy couldn't stop thinking about how much she had enjoyed spending the time with Payton and her family, getting to know the ins and the outs of how they functioned, and hearing fun stories about Payton when she was younger—and the food had been fantastic.

Sighing, she sat at her desk on a Saturday morning wondering just what she was even doing there. As much as she used to love going in to work on days when no one else was there, she was finding she'd much rather spend that time with Payton and Liam—that she'd rather be in Payton's run-down one-bedroom apartment than in her high-rise getting ahead on work.

She sighed as she leaned back in her chair, crossing her arms and staring out the large windows to the high-rises around her. It was an odd feeling, one she wasn't sure she had ever experienced before. Her life had been about work and advancing her career ever since she'd dreamed of going to college. Her parents had never understood her desire for a better life.

Bellamy glanced around her office, realizing how cold it seemed. She had no family pictures. She had nothing given to her by someone else. She'd bought everything, bought it specifically for the design of the room, to make it professional but still nice-looking for all her clients. Each painting had been specifically chosen to keep with the theme, but she had nothing to show her clients what she was like other than professional.

To be fair, what was she other than a lawyer? For so long she had focused only on that. Even when married to Kendra, she never really thought of herself as Kendra's wife but as her partner in a law firm. When Payton had worked for her, she'd kept one small picture of Liam on her desk and that was it. Granted her desk was in a much more public area than Bellamy's office and she had no walls to put pictures on, but even Payton understood the need to show a little bit of herself to everyone around her.

She wanted to be a woman who was completely in love with her partner, but Bellamy knew somewhere in the back of her mind and the depths of her heart that her entire life could never be about another person. That wasn't her at all. Yes, she loved Liam, and if she admitted it, she may very well love Payton, but changing her entire life so it centered around two other people seemed so far-fetched that she struggled to make the final leap.

Kendra and she had always worked well together. They'd always let each other live life as they wanted and connected when they could, which should have been her first hint their marriage wasn't going to work. But she didn't want that with Payton. Like she had promised at Thanksgiving, she wanted to commit to her and Liam, wanted to be there when he went to his first day of preschool the next fall, when he went to kindergarten, when he graduated from high school.

"Huh," Bellamy whispered and bit her lip.

She wanted to be there when Payton graduated, when she

figured out what she was going to do with her degree. She wanted to be there for everything. Grabbing her phone, she called Payton, who picked up on the first ring.

"Hey, sexy, what's happening?"

Bellamy's cheeks flushed like they did every time Payton said something like that. "Are you studying today?"

"I am. Finals are next week."

"You have Liam. I can hear him." Bellamy shoved everything she'd need for the next two days into her bag, grabbing her keys at the last minute after tossing her jacket over her shoulders.

"I do."

"Want some Liam-free time so you can actually study?"

"I would love that, but does that also mean Bellamy-free time?"

"I'll have to bring him back at some point."

Bellamy locked the door to her offices and headed to the elevator with her heart in her throat. She wanted everything, but she wanted it with Payton, and with how the last few months had gone, she knew Payton wasn't about to ask her to give up who she was just to be someone else. That's what made Payton so different from Kendra.

"I'll even come back with dinner."

"I don't know. What are you going to do with him?"

"It's a surprise. Come on, don't you trust me?" That was her test. She'd never taken Liam anywhere without Payton. Any time she watched him, she'd done it at Payton's apartment, and since it was so close to bedtime, they very often just did dinner, bath, and bed. She would work for hours afterward until Payton got home from classes, but she wanted the one-on-one time with him, wanted to know she would be allowed to play that role in his life.

"Of course I trust you," Payton's bubbly voice echoed. "I'm just curious as to what you're doing."

Bellamy smirked when the elevator chimed its arrival. "Well, right now I'm getting into the elevator. I'll be there in twenty minutes."

She hung up. On the drive there, she knew she was doing the right thing. Payton had wanted commitment from her, and Bellamy was going to give it. She wanted to give it. They'd dated, they'd gotten to know each other in a completely new capacity, but it had been nearly two years since they had met that fateful night at the restaurant, and Payton was right, they needed to take the next step.

When she got to the apartment, Payton opened the door with a suspicious look on her face. "You're still not going to tell me, are you?"

Bellamy grinned and didn't answer as she cupped Payton's cheek and turned her chin up into a deep albeit quick kiss. Liam raced over to her, his feet moving far more quickly than they'd ever thought would be possible after everything that had happened to him. Bellamy reached down and picked him up, tossing him into the air a little bit before settling him on her hip.

Once he was there, she leaned in and kissed Payton again, this time lingering. "I'm going to need the car seat."

Payton narrowed her eyes but grabbed her keys from the hook by the door. "Fine. But I still want to know what you're doing."

"Nope. Mums the word. Isn't that right, little guy?" She tickled his belly as she bent down to grab his shoes and his jacket. "You want to go with Auntie Belly for a drive?"

"Yeah!"

"Get your shoes on then."

Liam sat on the floor and worked at pulling his shoes over his socks, whining when he got one on and it was clearly the wrong foot. Bellamy bent down, her warm black jacket surrounding her. Payton grabbed her own jacket while Bellamy slipped his shoes on the right feet.

As soon as he was ready, she held his hand and they walked to the stairs. He insisted on walking down them himself, so of course it took an extra ten minutes to make it to the bottom of the four flights. Bellamy had parked near Payton's car, knowing they were going to have to move the car seat to her vehicle. Speaking of which, she might just buy a spare while she and Liam were out, if it would make life easier.

Payton had the seat installed and Liam buckled in faster than Bellamy could even think about how it was done. When she turned to head to the driver's seat, Payton grabbed her hand and pulled her in for another kiss. "When will you be back?"

"Dinner? That gives you five hours to study all you want."

"He'll need a nap—"

"We'll be fine. I know his routine."

"Yeah. Okay." Payton let out a breath. "I wish you would tell me what you were doing."

"If you must know, Christmas is coming up, is it not?"

Payton narrowed her eyes. "It is."

"So, we're going Christmas shopping. Not to mention, isn't Maddy's baby shower next weekend?"

"Ugh, don't remind me."

Bellamy gripped Payton's fingers and tugged her in for a kiss. "I'm going to remind you because you have to be there and you have to be supportive."

"Doesn't mean I have to like it."

"Nope, but you're going to be an auntie again, so be excited as much as you can be."

"I'm trying."

"Okay, we're off. I'll see you for dinner. Don't waste the five hours, Payton. I want to spend some actual time with you tonight."

"Yes, boss." Payton saluted before she turned and headed inside.

Bellamy's heart clenched. Yup, she was doing the right thing. As soon as she was in the car, she started talking to Liam about all of her plans for the day. The first stop was going to be a department store. As soon as she got him into the cart, he giggled at her and covered her hands on the cart with his, thinking he was the funniest thing in the entire store.

Leaning down, Bellamy put her nose up to him and smirked. "You think you're the cat's meow, don't you?"

"Yeah," Liam answered, then his voice became worried. "Shoe!"

He pointed down as his shoe almost fell off. Bellamy grabbed it and tossed it into the basket of the cart instead of putting it back on his foot. He would no doubt lose it multiple times throughout their trip. The first things she put in her cart were two car seats, one for Liam and one for Maddy and the new baby. She checked the registry and bought two more small things on it before focusing on Liam.

They spent two hours in the store, and by the time they checked out, Bellamy knew Liam needed a snack. She grabbed them a quick lunch before heading to the one place she had really wanted to go to with him. Pulling up outside the small jewelry store, she took Liam out of the car seat and held him on her hip. She was not about to let him run around in a store like this unsupervised.

Taking him in, she let out a breath as soon as the scent hit her. Everything smelled faintly of metal, and of some weird candle they had burning on the back counter. There was no one else in there, but it was her favorite jewelry store. She hadn't been there in over a year, but the owner recognized her immediately and came right over to her, a smile on his face.

"Bellamy, good to see you again."

"Likewise, Gibson. I'm here for a special piece today." Liam wiggled in her arms, and she struggled to keep him on her hip.

"What can we help you with, then?"

"I need an engagement ring."

He raised his eyebrows at her as he froze, then grinned. "For you or for someone else?"

Bellamy flushed, but she smiled at him. "For this little guys mama, actually."

"Found yourself a family, did you?"

"You could say that." Bellamy clenched her jaw.

"Put him down, let him move, Bellamy. He's not going to get into anything on that side of the counter."

"All right." She set Liam down, and he pressed immediately up to the glass, pointing at the rings and necklaces inside.

"Tell me more what you're looking for, and we'll see what I have."

They spent an hour picking out a ring, and Liam helped her make the final decision. With the ring in her pocket as she left, Bellamy only had one thing left to do—figure out how to propose.

WEEKS LATER WITH A PROPOSAL PLAN IN PLACE, Bellamy woke with a start to Payton shaking her shoulder. Turning onto her side, she blinked her eyes and stared at the clock next to Payton's side of the bed. She was struggling to focus, realizing she'd only been asleep for an hour.

"Maddy's in labor."

"She's like a month early."

Payton sighed. "Six weeks. I know. She was early with Liam, too, but not this early. They tested her, and she came back positive for meth, so they called me to come in."

Bellamy sighed. "It's Christmas Eve."

"No, it's Christmas morning. You're going to have to take Liam to Mom's. I'll get there when I can." Payton leaned over the bed and pressed her mouth heavily to Bellamy's. "Go back to sleep. I set an alarm for six."

"Come here."

Bellamy sighed as she tugged Payton to her mouth and deepened the kiss. Her hand held tight in Payton's hair—once again cut short and styled out of her face. Bellamy wanted to pull her in and lose herself in Payton's warm body, but Payton's hand on her chest reminded her why they were awake in the first place, and it wasn't for a midnight roll in the sheets.

"Text me when you know something."

"Yeah, as soon as I do I'll call." One more kiss, and Payton left the room, shutting the door quietly.

Bellamy rolled onto her back and stared at the crib across the room with Liam sleeping soundly. It had taken her a while to get used to sleeping with him in there, but now she quite enjoyed it, knowing if anything went wrong in the middle of the night that they were right there. However, they both knew he was going to outgrow the crib sooner rather than later. He was already working on trying to climb out of it, and if Payton was bringing home his sister, they were really going to have to figure out a new arrangement for sleeping.

Groaning, Bellamy rubbed her eyes again and stared at the clock. It was going to be a long day if Payton didn't come back from the hospital soon. They were supposed to spend the entire day at Denise's, and she had been planning on proposing sometime in the afternoon when she could steal a minute or two alone with Payton. It probably wasn't going to happen. Giving in, Bellamy went back to sleep, knowing six was going to come very soon.

The second time she woke up that day, Liam was already cooing from his crib. Bellamy shuffled out from under the covers, grabbed him, and made her way back to the small full-sized bed she'd taken to sharing with Payton. Setting him in the center and pulling the covers over his legs and chest, she rested her head down.

"It's too early, baby. Let's snuggle."

"Not," Liam answered, but he had a smile on his face and turned into her chest, breathing heavily.

She must have dozed off, because she woke to the alarm echoing in her ears. Blinking rapidly, Bellamy reached over Liam's sleeping form and slapped the top of the alarm clock. She collapsed into the pillows and grabbed her phone to see if there were any messages from Payton. She smiled when she saw Payton's morning greeting come across the screen as soon as she unlocked the phone. It was rare Payton was awake before her.

Answering back, she turned when Liam moved against her, clearly waking up. She curved a finger over his cheek when his eyes popped open, and he smiled at her. "Good morning, star shine."

"Belly!"

Chuckling, she grinned at him. "You ready to be a big brother? Because I think your sister is just about here."

"Brother?"

"Yup. But first, we have to go see Nana."

"Nana!" He sat straight up in the bed and clapped his hands.

It didn't take her long to get Liam dressed and ready to go. She opted not to shower, still not understanding how Payton managed to shower with a toddler on the loose and wanting to be better safe than sorry. She loaded him into her car with the presents she and Payton had gotten for everyone.

By the time they got to Denise's, it was eight. Denise opened the door with a warm smile, holding her hands out for Liam, but she looked confused when she looked around Bellamy. "Where's Payton?"

"She didn't call you?" Bellamy's head jerked up with a start.

She had figured Payton had made the rounds as soon as she could or when she'd talked to Bellamy that morning.

"No. Where is she?"

"Hospital. Maddy went into labor last night."

Denise's face dropped. "And if Payton is there . . . ?"

"Yes. She tested positive. She hasn't had the baby yet, if you want to go."

"I shouldn't. As much as I want to be there for her, Maddy and I . . . we don't exactly get along. It's better if Payton is there."

"Are you sure? I can handle things here."

"It's fine. Payton will call."

Bellamy followed Denise in with Liam's diaper bag before going back out to get the rest of the gifts. Liam was already playing by the tree with one of the gifts Santa had clearly brought. Zane sat on the couch, engrossed in some video game. Bellamy settled the presents under the tree then went to find Denise.

"Payton did say to just go ahead with everything because she wasn't sure when she would be able to get away."

"She probably won't leave until late tonight, assuming the baby is born today."

"That'd be my guess." Bellamy licked her lips. "Legally, she might not be allowed to leave."

"She's six weeks early. I imagine she'll end up in NICU."

"Hmm. I hadn't thought of that." Bellamy grabbed the coffee mug Denise handed her. "I won't represent her this time around. I already mentioned that to her."

"Conflict of interest," Denise stated.

"Yeah." Bellamy sighed. "Anyway, we won't know anything until she tells us, so let's not avoid Christmas. What are your traditions?"

"I should ask you what yours are so we don't miss anything you might want to do."

Bellamy froze with the coffee mug against her lips. She straightened and shook her head. "I don't have any."

"Surely you have some."

"No, I don't. I haven't celebrated Christmas since I was in high school."

Denise's eyes widened. "Why not?"

"Because Christmas wasn't particularly pleasant at my house growing up and my ex always went to her mom's where I was not invited."

"You weren't invited?" Denise slid something into the oven, the foil wrapped so tightly over the top Bellamy couldn't see what was underneath.

Bellamy sipped at the dark-brewed coffee and hummed at the pleasant flavor. She kept her answer short, trying not to invite any other personal questions. "No. We should probably get out there otherwise Liam's going to have everything unwrapped."

"You're probably right about that."

Before she even got to the living room with her coffee, her phone rang. Bellamy smiled at Payton's name and answered. "Hey! How's everything going there?"

"Well, we have a baby girl."

"Really?" Bellamy's eyes crinkled in a smile. "You'll send a picture, right? I think your mom might kill me if I don't show her a picture."

"Yeah, in a minute. They're trying to get her to sign TPR."

"Wait. What?"

"Termination of Parental Rights."

"I know what TPR is, Payton." Bellamy rolled her eyes. "Who is trying to get her to sign TPR?"

"The hospital social worker."

"Get them out of the room."

"What?"

"Trust me, Payton. Get them out of the room now. Tell them

Maddy needs some time to rest before she signs anything, whatever, just get them out of there."

Bellamy could hear Payton stepping in, demanding that whoever was in there leave. Bellamy could hear someone protest, but then she heard the door shut and Payton came over the line. "Okay, now tell me why I just did that."

"Maddy can't sign TPR right now. There's a forty-eight hour wait, and anyone telling you different is going to get you and them into a lot of hot water with the judge."

"Okay . . . ? So I just have to wait two days?"

"Yes."

"This is all so different from last time."

"I know, but you've got this. Just don't listen to anything they tell you. Maddy needs a lawyer, too. We can pay for it, but if this is her plan and what she really wants, she needs a lawyer and you need a lawyer."

"I've got you for that."

Bellamy bit her lip. "No, I told you, not me. Someone else."

"Okay. I get it." Payton sighed. "They took her back to the NICU already. I got to hold her for a little bit, Maddy too, but she didn't really want to."

"That's okay. Let her do what she wants. This is all about Maddy, remember?"

"I guess. I'll be by sometime later this afternoon if I can. I want to stay with her until she's a bit more with it and we know what's going on with the baby."

"What's her name?"

Payton sighed. "I don't know. Maddy told me to name her."

"You'll pick something great. We're just about to open presents."

"I'll let you go. Send pictures!"

"I promise." Bellamy finally headed into the living room to join the rest of the family. She settled on the couch next to Denise. Zane brought all the presents to everyone as they opened them, and Bellamy was surprised to see some with her name under the tree, ones that weren't from Payton. She took the pictures, dutifully sending them to Payton throughout the day.

It was nearing dark when Payton finally showed up at the house. Bellamy had been helping as much as Denise would let her, but she was largely getting to know Zane a whole lot better. She hadn't really had the time to sit and talk with him. When Payton walked in the front door, she looked exhausted. Bellamy immediately stood up and wrapped her in a hug. Payton fell into her, a tear streaking down her cheek before she wiped it away and put on a brave face.

"How are they, really?"

Payton drew in a deep breath. "Maddy is morose and depressed. Baby is doing as well as expected. She's got some withdrawal to go through and needs to gain some weight before they'll release her. They've got her on some oxygen but not much. They're saying four to six weeks before she can come home."

"Home with you, right?"

"If that's what Maddy wants, yes."

"Well, she's not going to get much of a choice."

"She knows. And I'm pretty sure that's what she wants. Mom!" Payton moved from Bellamy to her mom, wrapping herself in her mother's embrace. Denise kissed the top of Payton's head before sending a look over to Bellamy. "I have pictures."

Payton pulled out her phone and shared more pictures than she had sent Bellamy. They cooed over the pictures before Denise asked the inevitable. "What's her name?"

"Isabella Marie."

Denise took the phone and stared at another picture, tears in her eyes. "I never thought I'd be a grandma twice over before I was fifty."

Bellamy's stomach flopped. She had never thought about how close in age she was to Denise compared to how far in age she was to Payton. Biting her lip, she remained silent as Payton shushed her mom, then begged for food. They ate together before Payton pleaded to take a nap. They loaded up the cars and headed to Payton's apartment, a sense of unease still settling in Bellamy's stomach.

CHAPTER 20

On New Years Eve, Payton was nestled into Bellamy on the couch for the first time all week, her entire body covering the length of Bellamy's as she lay on top, her cheek pressed into Bellamy's chest. She had spent most of her time when she wasn't at work going to and from the hospital to be with Isabella. She was exhausted and had needed a night to just be with Bellamy and Liam and try not to think about the overwhelming amount of crap going on in her life. She let out a deep breath as her eyes fluttered shut. If she wasn't careful, she was going to fall asleep.

Bellamy trailed a hand up and down her back, her nails scraping every once in a while. Payton turned her face into Bellamy's chest and sighed. "I'm going to drop out of school."

"What?" Bellamy tensed under her.

"I'm dropping out of school."

Bellamy turned so they could see each other, forcing Payton to sit up on the couch, much as she didn't want to. "Why would you do that?"

"I can't do it. There's too much going on between work and Liam and Isabella, and now all the hearing stuff that comes with a second adoption, not to mention the cost. I just can't focus on it right now."

"If the birth mother doesn't contest the adoption and there are no issues with the birth father—which there haven't been because they've both signed TPR, then adoption happens very quickly, especially because you're family."

"I know. I know all of that. I'm just . . . stressed I guess."

Bellamy curled a finger over Payton's cheek and ear before gripping her hand and pulling it into Bellamy's lap. "I don't want you to give up your dreams."

"I don't really see any other option right now."

"You have a few more weeks before the new semester starts."

"I do, but that'll be right when Isabella comes home, and I remember what it was like with Liam. There was no sleep for months. I could barely function for a portion of that time. I'm not sure I can do that again especially with a toddler around, not to mention, I really need to find a new place to live."

Payton looked up at Bellamy, hoping the conversation might turn a certain way. She wanted to live with her—they practically did anyway—but at the same time, she didn't feel like she could be the one to make that ask. Bellamy moved like molasses when it came to any big decisions in life, and Payton understood why living with another woman might make her hesitate even more, but she wasn't asking for a ring or a marriage license.

"I really wish you would reconsider. I'll help has much as I can, but school is so important to you. I don't want you to give it up just because you think you can't do it."

Sighing, Payton shook her head, her stomach dropped at Bellamy's words. It hadn't been what she was looking for. The support was nice, and she knew Bellamy would always support her no matter what she decided to do—that had been proven to her over and over again, but she wanted more.

Ever since their talk on Thanksgiving Day, she had wanted

more. She'd told Bellamy it was about a commitment in the moment, but it had been more than that. She hadn't realized it at the time, hadn't thought she wanted more, but as the weeks had worn on and Bellamy had seemed to open up more and she was around more, everything shifted in Payton's understanding of their relationship.

She just had no idea how to tell Bellamy that. She felt like she could ask for anything except that. Lying down onto Bellamy's chest, she snuggled in, lost in her thoughts and in her wants. As much as she wanted to move in with Bellamy, maybe start a life with her beyond what they were already working on, she didn't know if Bellamy was ready for any of that.

Bellamy had been married for ten years before she got divorced. Ten years was a long time to be with someone. Surely it would take a good amount of time for Bellamy to recover from being in that broken relationship and to trust that not every relationship was going to be that way.

"You going to make it to midnight?" Bellamy muttered.

Payton shook her head, then nodded. "I want to, but I don't know. You're so comfortable."

"I want my midnight kiss."

"Can't we just watch the ball drop in real time instead of the replay? Then we can go to bed three hours early."

Bellamy chuckled, her voice ringing through the living room and sending shivers down Payton's spine. "You know, I never used to sleep in, but I have slept in quite a few mornings since we started dating."

With a kiss to the top of Payton's head, Bellamy drew in a deep breath.

"Come to think of it, I also go to bed early."

"It's cause and effect when you hang around a toddler too much. They suck the energy right out of you. I'm convinced of that."

"Maybe." Bellamy dropped another kiss into her hair. "Or it

might just be because I keep finding something other than work to keep me occupied."

"Something better, I hope."

"Much better." With a kiss to Payton's lips, Bellamy's demeanor went from teasing to serious. "Tell me, did you name Isabella or did Maddy?"

Payton sighed and closed her eyes. She hadn't wanted to answer that question. She had let everyone assume what they wanted to assume, but Bellamy liked details, and there was no getting out of it if she tried. "It was mutual. She agreed to the name."

"And where did you come up with it?"

Freezing, Payton bit her lip. She took her time answering. "I wanted something that would connect to her heritage."

"Is that it?"

"I liked that it sounds like your name."

"Hmm." Bellamy pressed her lips together.

When Payton glanced up to look at her, Bellamy closed her eyes and tilted her head back. Payton had no idea what to make of the move. Normally Bellamy was decently easy for her to read but not in that moment. They lapsed into a silence, Payton nearly asleep before she heard Bellamy's voice again.

"I love you, Payton."

Payton wasn't sure she had heard correctly, but her heart was already soaring. Her breathing increased, and it took three triple dog dares to herself to lift up so she hovered over Bellamy and stared down into her beautifully dark eyes.

"What did you say?"

"I love you, Payton. I want you to go to school and finish your degree. I want you to adopt Isabella and make a home for her. I want you to fulfill all of your dreams."

Payton's lips parted in surprise, and she closed them again. Once more, her mouth opened and she shook her head. Leaning down, she pressed their mouths together, her tongue swiping out against Bellamy's as she poured everything she felt over the last few months into that one kiss.

It had taken Bellamy six more weeks to share those words with her, but those six weeks had been well worth it. Payton rested down on top of Bellamy's lithe form and drew in a deep breath as she deepened their embrace.

When she finally broke apart, she grinned down into Bellamy's wary expression. "You have no idea how long I have waited to hear you say that."

"I thought I showed it to you."

"Sometimes, Bellamy, as you may well know, words speak louder than actions."

Bellamy wrinkled her nose, then pulled Payton down for another kiss. Bellamy's leg curled up around her, holding her in place as they continued to make out on the couch. Sure enough, the ball dropped three hours early while they locked lips.

When Payton finally looked up at the cheering on the television, she laughed. "You can stay up until midnight if you want. I'm going to bed, and I'd much prefer if you joined me."

"Okay," Bellamy whispered. "But I do think you might need a bigger apartment."

Payton's heart clenched. It always seemed to be one step forward and two steps back—a confession of love but no offer to move in. Chiding herself, she grabbed Bellamy's hand and dragged her toward the bedroom. They could sort that out another day, she should be happy with all Bellamy had willingly shared that night. The details of what would happen next could wait.

"I still think you need to go to school next semester. Really and truly."

"I'll think about it."

"Please do, Payton. I know how important this is to you."

Payton stopped at the door and kissed Bellamy again. "I will think about it. I promise. But right now, I just want to curl up in bed and crash. I have tomorrow off, and I plan on sleeping before I go to the hospital. Maybe you could join me."

"You want me to go see the baby?"

"I do."

"Am I even allowed in?"

"Sure. We'll drop Liam off at Mom's and head out from there."

"S-sure." Bellamy didn't look too convinced, but Payton ignored her unease and dragged her into the bedroom. They were under the covers and snuggled together before it was fifteen past the hour.

PAYTON HAD BEEN IN AND OUT OF THE HOSPITAL FOR two more weeks, and Bellamy had picked up most of the slack at the apartment. She had taken to picking Liam up from daycare and bringing him back for dinner before Payton would rush home to eat before going to the hospital.

Isabella was close to being released, and the closer it was the more nervous Payton got. Bellamy had barely had a chance to talk to her about something other than Isabella and the apartment and making room for the baby and trying to get another crib in the tiny bedroom somewhere.

The social worker came for the pre-placement visit and mentioned the room issue. Payton took it like a wound to the heart. Bellamy knew the obvious solution—someone had to move. The question of where was what left her in a state of confusion.

While Bellamy did have a two-bedroom apartment, which would certainly afford them room for all four of them, it wasn't going to be ideal. Her apartment was on the opposite side of town and not close to Liam's daycare or to Denise's. It was close to her work, not Payton's or the university. Everything about her apartment screamed her, not them, and she wanted to do this right.

But she had hesitated to bring it up with Payton. She wasn't quite sure where Payton stood on it. They had talked only twice about Payton moving somewhere with more room, but after the smallest mention of Payton moving, the conversation had turned awkward and they had both willingly changed the subject.

However, the ring Bellamy had bought months before still burned a hole in her pocket. She'd stashed it away in the safe she kept in the back of her closet in her apartment, but she hadn't even opened it since she'd bought it. The two times she'd thought about proposing had been all wrong with the timing. First Isabella had been born and second they'd been trying to figure out everything else that came with a new life.

She grabbed Liam from daycare that day like every other day that week, but instead of taking him back to Payton's, she took him to Denise's. Payton had told Bellamy to meet her there for dinner. Feeling comfortable at Denise's, and particularly going there alone had taken time and effort, but in the past months she had gotten more used to it.

Denise treated her like her own child but gave her the credit of not being a teenager and treated her like an adult. She had been worried about that, particularly because they weren't that far apart in age, but Bellamy had come to love her, and she truly appreciated the strength Denise held.

Liam ran from the car to the front door, screaming for Nana the entire way. When Denise opened the door as soon as Bellamy got to the front step, she smiled. "Payton ordered pizza. It should be here soon."

"Is she here?"

"No, something about running late."

Bellamy took Liam's jacket off and hung it by the door before she shed her own. They were all sitting down to eat pizza when Payton called Bellamy's cellphone.

"Hey, where are you?" Bellamy asked, a mouth full of pizza.

"I'm outside. Want to come help me with something?"

"Sure." She hung up and pushed away from the kitchen table. "I'll be right back. Payton needs help with something."

She made her way outside, grabbing her jacket as she passed by the door. When she saw Payton standing by the car, her breath escaped her. Racing faster, Bellamy moved right up to Payton and stared down at the small baby wrapped tightly in warm blankets in her arms.

"You didn't tell me she was getting released today."

"I wanted to surprise everyone, but I wanted to surprise you first."

"Payton." Bellamy glanced up at her then down at Isabella. "She is beautiful."

"She is. She looks so much like Maddy, unlike Liam."

"He's still a cutie."

"Even when he's covered in pizza sauce?" Payton joked.

"Especially then." Bellamy leaned in and kissed Payton's cheek. "Can I hold her?"

"Yes!" Payton shifted Isabella into Bellamy's arms.

Bellamy sighed at the weight settled in the crook of her arm. She was so tiny still. It had been forever since she had held a baby that small. She leaned her head down and pressed her lips gently to Isabella's forehead.

"I can't believe how small she is," Bellamy whispered as she smelled Isabella's hair.

"She's got some growing to do, for sure. Come on. Let's go in. I'm sure Mom's dying trying to figure out what we're doing out here."

Bellamy chuckled but led the way into the house. As soon as she turned the corner in the kitchen, Denise jumped up and ran around the table to see Isabella, and she was gone from Bellamy's arms.

Denise cooed over the baby while Payton and Bellamy ate their dinner and cleaned Liam up. They put him down on the floor to run off some of his energy. Denise turned to Payton and smiled at her. "Why don't you let Liam stay here tonight? I can drop him off at daycare in the morning, but you should have time with Isabella tonight, get used to sleeping with a baby again."

"You sure, Mom?"

"Yeah. I'm sure."

"Okay, but I'm doing bath and bed then. I miss my little guy."

"No arguments here."

Payton left the room and immediately Denise focused her gaze on Bellamy. She put her nose to Isabella's head. Bellamy moved to the kitchen and started to clean up from dinner, wanting to give Denise as much time with her new grand-daughter as possible. When Denise followed her and sat at the dining room table, Bellamy smiled before focusing on cleaning.

"I can do that," Denise said.

"I don't mind. Besides, it's not much to clean anyway."

"Advantage to ordering out."

"Definitely."

They fell into a comfortable silence, but when Denise spoke next, Bellamy's spine straightened.

"I like you for her, you know."

"Pardon?" Bellamy turned around to face Denise, her eyes wide with curiosity.

"I like you for her. You're good together. You bring out a lot in her I don't think she knew existed before you."

Bellamy gave a wan smile and turned her head to the side, not quite sure what to say. She let out a breath, thinking of an excuse or something to go find Payton, but Denise's soft voice stopped her again.

"She can do it all. Payton, I mean. She's capable of doing everything she wants, even if she doesn't trust herself to be able to do it."

"I know. I keep trying to tell her that, but I'm not sure how much she believes me."

Denise smiled lightly before hiding it in Isabella's wave of dark hair. "She's stubborn."

Bellamy chuckled. "Yeah, but so am I. She's a lot more confident about certain things than I am, though."

"She's had less life to live and less failures to experience."

Bellamy sighed. Denise was right. Payton had never been married. She'd never had dreams and hopes dashed quite like Bellamy had, but she had taken to adjusting to new dreams very quickly and without a glance back. Bellamy admired how willing she was to try anything, and how determined she was to stick through whatever came her way. When Payton committed, she gave everything. There was no half-assing it.

"I know you're scared about what she wants, but I think you're ready for it, too."

Bellamy moved her gaze from the baby up to Denise's baby blue eyes, staring straight into a soul that was so much like Payton but so much wiser. "What would make you say that?"

Denise did smile fully at her then. "I see how you look at her. I see how you've changed since she brought you here that first time this fall. You're in love, Bellamy. It's obvious, and Payton loves you just as much, with her whole heart. It's okay to be scared, especially after having been through a divorce. I've seen so many of my friends go through it. I went through it—twice. It's hard no matter what you do next, but it's okay to be scared, to want to take things slowly."

Bellamy pulled her lip between her teeth and leaned against the kitchen counter. She stared out at the living room, listening to figure out where Payton was. When she heard the splashing, she knew she was safe. "I bought a ring, shortly after Thanksgiving."

"Really?" Denise's joy almost went beyond the moment Bellamy had walked in with Isabella in her arms. It was a close second.

"I did. I was going to propose Christmas day, but we had other things going on. It wasn't the right time."

Denise rocked back and forth with the baby in her arms. "I do hope you do it soon. I'm pretty sure I know what her answer will be."

The confidence booster helped, and Bellamy knew she had made the right choice back in November. Actually, she had made the right choice every time it involved Payton since they'd started dating. She wanted a relationship that would last, and for the first time she had hope that Payton would give her that.

"I was thinking of buying a house, actually." Bellamy turned to the sink, not sure she wanted to see Denise's reaction. "There's a smaller three bedroom about a mile from here I went and looked at the other day."

Denise laughed lightly as she came over to Bellamy and put a hand on her arm. "I may be saying it too soon, but I don't care. Welcome to the family, Bellamy. And you know how to make a mother's heart sing."

A flush rose in Bellamy's cheeks. She did something she never expected she would want to do. Leaning down, she wrapped her arms around Denise's shoulders in a hug, making sure to avoid covering Isabella. She whispered, "Thanks."

"Any time."

CHAPTER 21

JANUARY AND FEBRUARY MOVED BY WITH A FLASH, AND Bellamy found herself in court a month after Valentine's day. Only this time, it wasn't for a case that was hers. Payton had made her stand with all of them for the photo with the judge. Bellamy plastered a smile on her face, but her stomach was in knots. Denise had helped her plan everything. Bellamy held Liam against her side as he squirmed and tried to leave her grasp, but she held him fast. Payton grinned as they took another photo.

As soon as they were ushered out of the courtroom, Bellamy's stomach twisted. She leaned in and kissed Payton's lips briefly. "I've got a surprise for you."

"Oh?" Payton turned, Isabella in her arms as her eyes widened.

They both had taken the day off from work, and Bellamy had spent the entire night in a panic about everything going right. She'd even called Denise before Payton was awake to make sure she wasn't going to mess something up.

Isabella's adoption was finalized, far more quickly than Liam's since it was such a different situation. Bellamy had triple-checked the paperwork after the scare with the hospital social worker, whom she'd called to correct on their assumptions. Isabella was officially Payton's for life. She had been through the questions, been through the process, stood before the court, and declared that she wanted to be her parent.

Maddy had made herself scarce, but last they'd heard, she was going through an intensive rehabilitation out of state. Payton tried to get the address to send her some letters with pictures of the kids, but Maddy had refused to give it to her.

"Come on."

They walked out to the car, Denise sending Bellamy a smile of encouragement as they said their goodbyes. They got the kids into the car seats, then Bellamy pulled out the silk scarf from around her neck and held it out for Payton.

"You're blindfolding me?"

"I am." Bellamy bit her lip. "Humor me, would you?"

Payton turned around and waited while Bellamy tied the blindfold. She then took her by the hands, kissed each of her cheeks and led her to the passenger seat of the car, helping her to slide in. As soon as she got behind the driver's seat, she gripped Payton's hand and left the parking garage.

For some reason she was nearly sick to her stomach, and she didn't know why. Denise had told her everything would go perfectly. She'd had the ring for over four months at that point. Denise had gone to the house earlier that morning and set the ring on the kitchen counter, just like Bellamy had asked her to do. If everything worked to plan, she would have her answer soon enough.

"Where are we going?"

"Somewhere special," Bellamy answered as she pulled out onto the interstate for a few brief exits before she got off. She had purchased the house she'd told Denise about. It was a quaint little royal blue house with three bedrooms and a small backyard in a neighborhood full of other kids and families. It would be exactly where she would want to raise a family if she could. They were close to Denise so they could stop by, and Zane could come over after school if he wanted.

It was perfect, or hopefully it would be soon. She parked the car out front of the house and let out a breath. Isabella was no doubt asleep in the car seat as was her norm, but Liam babbled incessantly for the entire drive. Bellamy had tried to pay attention to him but the nerves ran through her belly too much, causing her to have to work hard to focus.

"So . . . where are we?" Payton asked, squeezing Bellamy's fingers.

Bellamy let out a short breath and reached over, undoing the tie at the back of the silk scarf. When it fell away from Payton's eyes she grinned at Bellamy, not looking out of the window of the car.

"What are we doing here?" Payton looked confused.

"Well, we seem to have a space problem."

"We do." Payton's head canted to the side.

Bellamy rubbed her thumb against the fingers of her free hand, not quite sure what she was going to say. She should have planned that out better. For someone who always had a plan, who always went into a situation knowing exactly what she was going to say, this time she hadn't prepared—at least she didn't feel like she had.

"I bought a house," Bellamy whispered, her voice cracking on the last word

Payton's eyes widened. "You didn't."

"I did." Bellamy nodded out the window behind Payton.

Turning, Payton gasped. "You didn't!"

"I did. I promise you."

"Where are we? Like give me a reference for where this house is."

Bellamy gripped Payton's hand. "We're only a mile from your mom's."

"You're kidding!"

"I'm not." Bellamy reached into her pocket and pulled out the keys, dangling them in front of Payton. "Want to go inside?"

"Yes!" Payton gripped the keys and jumped out of the car. She grabbed Isabella's bucket seat, while Bellamy pulled Liam from his seat and held his hand as they walked up to the front steps of the house.

"I can't believe you bought a house," Payton whispered. "It's gorgeous."

There was a small porch out front that boasted some greenery Bellamy had made sure was not going to take a lot of upkeep. She'd already moved everything she owned in, paying the movers to do it the weekend before. She still had to buy furniture for the rest of the house, but she hoped she and Payton could do that together.

As soon as Payton got to the front door, she stopped and turned to Bellamy. "What made you buy a house?"

"You'll see," Bellamy answered as she took the key from Payton, slipped it into the lock and turned it. Liam bounced in his shoes, ready to get inside and out of the chilly late-March air. When the door creaked open, Liam burst inside and ran through the house.

Payton gasped as soon as they walked in. Bellamy's heart thudded harder with each step they took the closer they got to the kitchen. On the counter was a bottle of champagne, the ring and a card. Payton moved over to it, and her jaw dropped. She set Isabella's car seat on the ground and turned to Bellamy.

"What is all of this?"

With a deep breath, Bellamy grabbed the box with the ring in it and bent down on one knee. She was so nervous, the bubbles of anxiety popping in her belly. It wasn't that she thought Payton would say no. It was because she was taking this step to walk into a marriage again, one that she knew would be better, but one that still came with a host of the unknown.

She opened the box and stared up at Payton, praying she didn't ramble. "It may have taken me a year to finally make the step to come find you again, but Payton, you have always been part of my life since the moment I met you. I love you, and I want to be with you. I want to support you through all the ups and downs life throws at us, and I want to be there for everything with the kids. I got us this house with the hope that you would move in with me, and I bought this ring—before Christmas mind you—hoping you would spend the rest of your life with me. So, will you marry me?"

"Yes," Payton whispered. "Hell yes!"

Bending down, she wrapped her arms around Bellamy's neck and pressed their mouths together. Bellamy stood up, and Payton turned her by the hips and pressed her into the kitchen counter. Bellamy cupped Payton's cheek with her free hand, their tongues tangling.

She stopped when she felt Liam at her legs, tugging at her jacket. Pulling away, Bellamy smiled down at him as he stared up at her and pointed to the box in her hand.

"What that?"

Grinning, Bellamy turned to Payton. "This is mama's ring."

Payton grabbed it and slid it onto her finger, marveling and staring at it. Bellamy leaned in to kiss Payton before there was a knock at the door, and they heard it swing open.

"Hope we're not interrupting!" Denise called.

"No, you're not, come in," Bellamy called.

"What? You told her, but you didn't tell me?"

"She helped me set this up." Bellamy wrapped her arm around Payton's waist and pressed her nose into Payton's hair.

Denise grinned as Zane followed her in. "I did, and I have to say, I'm very pleased with the result."

Grabbing her daughter's hand, Denise stared at the ring and nodded her approval. Then she reached around and hugged Bellamy.

"Like I said before, Bellamy, welcome to the family. Now, let's have a party to celebrate all these beauties in my life today."

"Gladly." Bellamy moved into the kitchen and shed her jacket, grabbing the champagne flutes in one of the cabinets. Staring through to the living room at the family she had found by accident, she smiled to herself. Happiness seeped into her stomach and stayed there. The day could not have gone more perfectly.

THANK YOU FOR READING THIS EPIC LOVE STORY. I STILL CAN'T GET *Bellamy and Payton out of my head.*

ABOUT THE AUTHOR

Adrian J. Smith has been writing nearly her entire life but publishing since 2013. With a focus on women loving women fiction, AJ jumps genres from action-packed police procedurals to the seedier life of vampires and witches to sweet romances with a May-December twist. She loves writing and reading about women in the midst of the ordinariness of life.

AJ currently lives in Cheyenne, WY, although she moves often and has lived all over the United States. She loves to travel to different countries and places. She currently plays the roles of author, wife, mother to two rambunctious kids, and occasional handy-woman. Connect with her on Facebook, Twitter, or her blog.

This author is part of iReadIndies, a collective of self-published independent authors of women loving women (WLW) literature. Please visit our website at iReadIndies.com for more information and to find links to the books published by our authors.

DARING TRUTH

Available November 9, 2021

Friends-giving dinner with her ex—what could go wrong?

For the first time in two years, Brook attends the annual dinner. She's avoided group gatherings with her friends since Whisper hinted at love and Brook broke it off. But two years is a long time, and Brook hopes she and Whisper can find a new balance of friendship. Except all those feelings Brook bottled come racing back at the first sight of her hilariously flirtatious ex-girlfriend.

Whisper has kept tabs on Brook for the two years since they last saw each other. When Brook finally shows up, Whisper takes the plunge and dares her to twenty-four hours alone—one day for each of them to take what they need. The only problem is at the end of their day, Brook gives Whisper a dare of her own.

Do it again.

An emotional second chance romance perfect for the Christmas season. With an age gap and soft butch/femme, BDSM relationship, these two women take their relationship to new heights.

LOVE BURNS

Out now!

A chef must learn to open her heart when challenged by her young but wise nanny, who has a knack for turning up the heat.

Kimberly Thompson—or Kim Burns, her stage name—is a celebrity chef whose career is taking off. As a single mom who has a penchant for being a bit of a bitch, she goes through nannies like the flavor of the month until Becca Kline is sent to her by Kiddie Academy.

Becca—known as 'the fixer'—is often sent to homes considered to be troublemakers. In charge of caring for four-year-old Michael, she is determined to make this job her last before student teaching in the fall and finishing up her degree, which she has been working on for the better part of a decade.

Neither Kimberly nor Becca are prepared for the changes headed toward them, and they both have to learn the hard way that love doesn't wait or discriminate.

ABOUT TIME

Available this Fall!

One slip of her tongue, one angry doctor, and her life spiraling into the pits.

Doctor Gisele Vasquez is consumed by bitterness after the messy break up with her ex-husband, and it's not until one smart-mouthed chaplain puts her in her place that she realizes she needs to change. With determination, she sets out to become the doctor and woman she wants, and her first step is to make a friend of the enemy.

Chaplain June Melville loves her job and making a difference in her patients lives. While she looks put-together at work, her home-life is about to all fall apart. When she discovers her girlfriend is cheating, June finds herself homeless, alone, and desperate. With nowhere to turn except one angry doctor turned friend, June takes a step in the direction of her own healing.

Printed in Great Britain
by Amazon